"You don't owe me a thing, Claire."

"I owe you everything."

"You can keep your money," Joshua responded.

"But that would be charity, and I can make my own way."

"I don't doubt that one bit." The center of his chest tightened. He'd make sure she was safe, no matter what it cost him. It was the right thing to do, but this wasn't about responsibility. He wanted good things for her, this woman with a place in his soul.

And then she came up on tiptoes, so close every hair on his body stood up on end, and pressed a silken kiss to his cheek. His heart thumped as she sank her white even teeth into her lush, rosebud-soft bottom lip, as if she were in deep thought. As if she were debating telling him one more time to butt out of her life.

No way, lady. Emotion drove him, a fierce need that had his fingers cradling her delicate chin. He breathed in her sweet rose scent and slanted his mouth over hers.

* * *

Rocky Mountain Widow
Harlequin Historical #765—August 2005

Praise for Jillian Hart

High Plains Wife

"Finely drawn characters and sweet tenderness tinged with poignancy draw readers into a familiar story that beautifully captures the feel of an Americana romance. Readers can enjoy sharp dialogue and adorable child characterizations while shedding a tear or two."
—*Romantic Times*

Montana Man

"Ms. Hart creates a world of tantalizing warmth and tenderness, a toasty haven in which the reader will find pure enjoyment."
—*Romantic Times*

Cooper's Wife

"Ms. Hart's touching story highlights all of the things closest to our hearts; family, children, and the desire for safety. Well-crafted and poignantly funny."
—*Romantic Times*

Jillian Hart

Rocky Mountain Widow

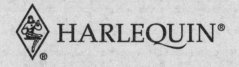

TORONTO • NEW YORK • LONDON
AMSTERDAM • PARIS • SYDNEY • HAMBURG
STOCKHOLM • ATHENS • TOKYO • MILAN • MADRID
PRAGUE • WARSAW • BUDAPEST • AUCKLAND

ISBN 0-373-29365-8

ROCKY MOUNTAIN WIDOW

Copyright © 2005 by Jill Strickler

This edition published by arrangement with Harlequin Books S.A.

www.eHarlequin.com

Printed in U.S.A.

Available from Harlequin Historical and
JILLIAN HART

Last Chance Bride #404
Cooper's Wife #485
Malcolm's Honor #519
Montana Man #538
Night Hawk's Bride #558
Bluebonnet Bride #586
Montana Legend #624
High Plains Wife #670
The Horseman #715
Montana Wife #734
Rocky Mountain Man #752
Rocky Mountain Widow #765

Please address questions and book requests to:
Harlequin Reader Service
U.S.: 3010 Walden Ave., P.O. Box 1325, Buffalo, NY 14269
Canadian: P.O. Box 609, Fort Erie, Ont. L2A 5X3

Prologue

Bluebonnet County, Montana Territory
1884

"You shamed me again, woman." Ham towered on the board wagon seat beside her, nothing more than a shadow in the night. "Again!"

Claire rubbed the bump her gold wedding band made beneath the mitten on her left hand and tried not to give in to the rising resentment. He wasn't through maligning her for the night, not by a long shot. It didn't matter that she hadn't said a word while she'd waited outside in the cold for hours until Ham decided he'd had his fill of whiskey and poker.

Or that during this long wagon ride home across the high country plains, she'd never said a word, either. Not of his drunken state, his careless driving, or the fact that the ground had hardened with ice and no other driver was out on the roads in this frigid night. That anyone else had more sense than that. But not Ham. No, not Ham.

He chucked in his throat, a disgusting sound, and spit with great skill. "You made me look bad in front of the boys."

The boys being a table full of grown men playing poker in the smokiest, seediest saloon in the county. Claire held her tongue, because she'd learned the hard way that when he'd been drinking hard, Ham became mean and was always looking for the chance to get meaner.

He was not a good husband. Was there a chance he could be a decent father? She rested the palm of her hand on the round of her slightly swollen stomach. The doctor today had said she was doing well and the baby's first kicks were strong. That was happy news. But she'd had some spotting.

"You must be careful." The doctor's tone had been grave. "Follow my advice. Go home. Put your feet up. Have Ham get Mrs. Simms to come over and take care of things for a spell."

She hadn't gotten up the courage to tell Ham anything, and he hadn't asked. He never did, especially when he'd been drinking. The alcohol changed him, and when he was like this she had to be careful not to anger him.

Mama had warned her about men. Whenever one comes courting, he's the best man on earth, she'd said. Punctual, attentive and decent. He has manners and treats you right. Once he gets a ring on your finger, then it's a different matter.

You were so right, Mama. Claire glanced sideways at the man who'd wooed her and charmed her and made her believe in the impossible.

As she looked at the bulky man swaying drunkenly at her side, reeking of cheap whiskey and stale tobacco smoke, it was hard to fathom a time when he had been mistaken for wonderful.

Her judgment had been poor and she regretted it greatly.

"What are you lookin' at, woman?" Just like that, Ham had worked himself up into a fury. "You don't got any right to judge me, woman! I'll drink what I want, when I want and with who I want."

"All right, Ham," she said quietly, gently, for it was the wisest way to manage him when he was like this. When he was so irrational, he was like dynamite ready to explode and devastate everything.

"And don't you go givin' me that look."

It was better for her if she kept him calm, so it was desperation that made her set aside her anger. She didn't like the way he treated her. She didn't like how she had to behave to keep him rational. What else was she to do?

She wasn't big and strong like a man. There was no way she could stop or overpower him. No, the best she could do was to keep him from getting more upset while he was so drunk. They were almost home. By the time they reached the little shanty at the top of the hill, he'd be ready to pass out.

And I'll be safe until morning.

She took a shaky breath and purposely tried to appear serene, as if nothing were wrong and he'd never shattered one illusion about love and marriage.

"Oh, so now you think you're better'n me." He spit out another stream of tobacco and swiped his chin with the back of his hand. "Do ya? I'm gettin' tired of you and your attitude, woman."

"I'm sorry, Ham," she soothed, sensing he was near to balling up his fist. "I didn't mean anything. I was just thinking about—" *Home,* she thought as the blow struck.

Pain shattered her left cheekbone where he'd slugged her. Her head snapped to the side and the muscles in her neck tightened with more pain. Her head whirled, she saw dancing white lights in front of her eyes, and she clutched the seat to keep from falling.

"Maybe that'll teach ya to smart-mouth me."

Tears blurred her vision. Her jaw hurt too much to speak, so she only nodded obediently. There was no other way to behave. She knew, because she'd tried everything over time to find peace between them. Or at least, to avoid the pain she was in now. Her skull hammered from the shock and she swiped at her eyes.

Crying only made him angrier. She blinked hard until the blackness subsided and made sure she sat perfectly still. She'd learned a lot from her three years of marriage. Things she never thought anyone should know, but they made a difference now as Ham muttered on angrily about a woman's place and how he worked hard and how costly she was to him.

He could rage on, use his fists and his words like weapons, but he wouldn't break her. Despite the chilly night, for winter had come early to these high Montana plains, and despite the fact that her coat was thin and she wore light mittens, she refused to so much as shiver.

She had every reason to fight, for she could feel the faint fluttery kicks of her child. She'd not been sure this new life was a blessing. A helpless baby would be vulnerable to Ham's drinking and his temper. It was a serious situation, but oh, her heart lit up again, like a lamp left too long unlit, and burned so brightly.

I will love you enough to make up for it, little one, she vowed, willing the promise through her fingertips and into her womb. *I swear I will take such good care of you.* First thing was to figure out how to convince Ham to hire the neighbor lady to come do the heavier housework. And then—

The wagon lurched, and in the dark night it was hard to know why. The horse gave a frightened whinny and the vehicle began to tip. Ham's temper exploded. His swearing boomed as startling as thunder, frightening the horse more as he reached for the whip.

"Stay on the damned road, you worthless nag!" The whip shot into the air, hissing toward the mare's flank. The rasp as the lash cut into flesh was followed by the mare's sharp neigh of pain.

As if time had stretched out, Claire was aware of the wagon tilting to the right, and no matter how hard she tried to brace herself, she was falling. Ham's weight pressed against her as he wrestled with the horse, fighting the mare's panic. There was nothing but darkness—no moonlight or stardust to see by, just the hulking blackness of the high rolling hill and the prairie floor below.

We're going to roll over. Her pulse filled her ears, making the screaming horse and Ham's horrible shouting seem distant. Then came the clack and groan of the wagon wheels skidding.

Breaking.

They were going to die. There was no way she could stop it. This was the way her parents had died, and she could taste the panic on her tongue. Feel it crawl with icy fingertips across the back of her neck.

What about the baby? The seat beneath her seemed to heave and then suddenly, it was gone. She was falling, her arms flinging out. She tried to grab for anything, anything in the dark, but there was only air and gravity and the terrifying scream of the horse.

There was so much noise—the explosion as the wagon broke, the avalanche of earth beneath them, the horse's hooves digging into the bank, and Ham's voice bellowing foul curses. Loudest of all was the cadence of her pulse, eerily slow as time became meaningless. She was thrown backward through the dark and the night. Weightless.

The ground struck her like an ax in the center of her left shoulder blade. Air whooshed out of her lungs and pain slammed through her as the rest of her back crashed against the rocky earth. Her head reeled back and struck granite.

No, not my baby. She curled up to protect her child. She had to stay awake, she had to. But her vision flashed and her consciousness faded piece by piece, like a curtain being drawn against the sky. Wagon fragments and debris rained down on her.

Somewhere far away the mare squealed in pain, an eerily human-sounding scream of agony and then there was Ham rising up over her, miraculously standing, with the whip in his hand. She saw his mouth open and his arm raise, but her vision slid away.

There was nothing but blessed silence.

This was the last time, the very last time he was going to put up with Hamilton's villainy.

Rage beat through Joshua Gable's veins with the power a fueled train barreling down the bottom side of a long steep slope, and he wouldn't be surprised if, like a locomotive, steam whistled out of him. Likely the top of his head was near to blowing off he was so angry.

I'd like to wrap my hands around Ham's throat and squeeze. Pain shot through his molars and he tried to relax his jaw. His teeth had been gnashed enough for one day.

But then the image of what he'd just come away from sent renewed fury through his body and his teeth clacked shut so tight, the audible grind echoed like a whiplash in the silent breadth of the cold winter night.

Wait—that wasn't his teeth making that sound. It only seemed that way. *That's a whip. Striking flesh.* A horse's panicked neigh rang through the vast night, a hair-raising human sound of agony and terror.

Trouble.

His hand fisted around the reins and he was digging in his heels before it was a conscious thought. The pinto cannoned into the dark, hooves striking the frozen earth.

What mad men are out here tonight? Joshua bowed his head into the frigid wind and pressed his mount harder. He was glad he had his .45 strapped to his thigh and loaded. And, in case he needed it, his repeating Winchester strapped in its holster to the saddle.

Faster. Whatever trouble lay ahead, the coyotes began to howl somewhere nearby. The womanlike screams of the horse rose in pitch, shattering the night, tolling across the vast reaches of the prairie like an echo without end, and when the terrified scream ended abruptly, the silence spoke of death.

I'm too late. Remorse ripped like razor-sharp talons through his chest. He hated an animal's suffering. Which was why his rage was fueled tonight. He'd come to stop Ham.

And if that no-good bastard was abusing another animal... Joshua felt the pressure build beneath the top of his skull. *That horse better be all right, or I'll—*

A flash of lightning stabbed from the heavens, and in that brief instant of white, eye-burning illumination, he saw the motionless body of a horse sprawled dark against the crusted white rise. A shattered wagon. A beefy man with his arm uplifted and the sinuous lash snaking back for another strike, but it was not directed at the horse.

Is that a woman?

The skin prickled at the back of Josh's neck with a horrible foreboding. As the flare faded into impenetrable black, he made out another shadow on the ground, but the darkness came too swiftly for him to recognize it.

And then his mind latched onto the image, and rage burned so hot he became like the night. Like the clap of thunder, he struck, uncoiling the lasso at his saddle horn. And as Ham's whip snapped in the indecipherable shadows, Joshua felt destiny begin to unravel like his coiled rope. Fate was set when the noose fell and caught.

Got ya. One jerk was all it took to disarm the low-down varmint who wasn't even fit to be called a man. He vaguely registered the foul cursing of a drunk—yep, it sure sounded as if Ham was liquored up good.

Joshua hauled in his noose, coiled up the lariat for later use and seized the captured whip in his left hand. This left his right free in case he needed to draw.

"Hamilton, you coward. Are you always gonna pick on women and animals? Or are you ready to take on someone who's your own damn size?"

"I could take you down with one hand tied behind my back, you son of a bitch. Get the devil off my land."

"Or what? You're gonna throw me off? I'm a man, not a helpless sheep."

"What the hell does that mean?" Ham growled like a rabid dog ready to fight. His teeth were bared as another bolt of lightning knifed overhead in warning.

"It means I've found one carcass too many. How long have you been killing my sheep now? One month? Almost two? It's not gonna drive me off the grazing land. And since the deputy won't do a damn thing, I'm gonna make my own justice."

The mare that lay like a hump at the side of the road became more visible as the clouds churning in the sky gave off a blue-black glow from the lightning. There was movement—not only the ripple and toss of mane and tail in the rough wind, but her sides rising and falling—short and uneven, but the mare was breathing.

He remembered the animal's tortured screams and

his guts clenched so tight he could taste the bile on his tongue. She was a greater concern, but Joshua knew if he mentioned the helpless woman as equally still on the ground, then Ham's temper would go.

And Ham was much closer in proximity to his wife. He'd hurt her first, the vicious bastard. Joshua gripped the leather until the braid's pattern bit into his palm, scenting the metallic smell of blood in the air and sour fear on the wind. The boiling rage that had first coursed through his veins turned to ice. Not from fear, but determination.

"When you kill my livestock, you're taking from me. From my family," Joshua growled.

"I didn't kill those sheep. Not last week, not a month ago. Not today. Besides—" Ham's voice rose in volume and acidity. "This is cattle county."

Joshua didn't miss the muted rasp, although Ham pitched his voice high enough to try to hide it. Ham was sneaky, but Joshua had learned long ago how to deal with sneaky varmints. And he knew exactly what Ham planned to do next.

As the blackness closed around them, thunder cracked overhead. Joshua let the rolling crash from above hide the snap as he sent the whip snaking through the darkness. It struck with a vengeance before Hamilton could draw.

Victory. Joshua tasted it as Ham cursed in pain and the gun thudded to the earth.

"I need three things from you, Hamilton." He aimed his .45 at the drunk's chest. "Restitution for the sheep you killed—"

"That's what happens when those worthless varmints are too stupid to stay where they belong."

"I leased the grazing lands fair and square. They're mine, and they belong there—" Joshua paused as the woman moaned. He waited. "Ma'am, are you all right?"

"She's about as dumb as one of your lambs. Too stupid to live. I—"

"Shut up, Ham. This is a matter for the law."

I'm not dead. Claire tried to concentrate, but the voices faded and then returned. The pain in her head boomed like a firing cannon inside her skull. She tried to move, but pain paralyzed her and she realized that something warm was trickling down her face.

Blood. She also realized Ham towered over her, jerking and trembling like he did in a rage, right before he became lethally violent.

Her thoughts were fragments. What had happened? Was the baby safe? Who was shouting at Ham? She couldn't recognize the man's voice. Couldn't he understand the danger? Ham had to be talked to quietly, steadily until he calmed. It was the only way. She had to get up and intervene. Groggy, she tried to sit up.

I can't move.

Panic crowded into her throat and she shoved at something hard. Something wooden. A piece of the broken wagon pinned her hips to the ground. Her fingers gripped the broken edge of board and she gritted her teeth, heaving. She felt as if a razor blade sliced through her low abdomen.

The baby. She collapsed onto the ground, dizzy as the heated voices rose in volume and threats. What was going on? She could only see an upward slash from the ground to the sky until lightning blinded her.

Ham's furious bellow. It was going to be even worse for her as soon as Ham got her home. "I ain't takin' this from a sheep man!"

"The deputy is your good buddy, I know, but listen up good—"

Claire caught a glimpse of the intruder as the rolling thunder drowned out their argument. He sat on horseback, a big bold cut of a man as dark as the night, as powerful as the thunder, and as lethal as the fierce lightning that pounded overhead.

Ham's fingers inched to his revolvers, ever present in their holsters, strapped to his thighs within easy reach. How many times had he threatened her with those guns?

Claire closed her eyes, trying to find strength where there was none. Hope when she'd given up. Whatever tiny drop of relative safety she'd been able to forge for herself in her marriage was about to be gone, but she couldn't let Ham hurt this man, she couldn't—

Ham's fingers curved around a beloved revolver. She could smell his glee—he loved to cause harm, or worse. And the mounted man, he didn't see the danger, Claire realized as she tried to shout a warning, but there was no voice. Something was wrong with her throat.

Hell exploded. Thunder merged with bullets, lightning with gunfire, and the pummeling ice that fell like hunks of granite from the vengeful sky beat so loudly she could not hear or see, only feel the danger as violence and murder rose on the heartless wind.

Ham fell to the ground beside her, cursing in pain and clutching his shoulder. It wasn't over, she knew with chilling certainty as Joshua Gable kicked the fallen revolvers out of harm's way and consciousness faded. She heard Ham's threat to kill Gable come from very far away, and then steeled arms lifted her from the ground and carried her away.

She woke up later in her own bed, alone. She heard the echoing sound of a single gunshot, and knew by the silence that followed that someone was dead.

Chapter One

Eight Days later

It was a bad day for a funeral.

Joshua Gable swiped snowflakes from his eyelashes so he could see into the heavy gale, then jammed his gloved fist back into his coat pocket.

It had taken the grave diggers most of the week to cut through the frozen ground. As if the Fates had done everything in their power to hold back this death. There would be no peaceful passing for Halbert Hamilton, Jr. Instead, a fury of cutting north wind and vicious iced snow made it feel as if hell had frozen over, had burst up from the new grave in the ground to welcome a like soul.

For a man few could stand and most despised, a lot of the local folks on this sparse corner of the county had come. Some attended out of relief, Joshua suspected, that the hard man was gone. A few grieved his passing. But most were here out of curiosity, for no one knew what had befallen the rancher—if one could call him that—and what had rendered him dead.

Well, some knew.

Joshua swallowed hard, glad he stood back from the bulk of the crowd. It took all his self-control to fight down the tight grip guilt had on his stomach. If he'd had his way, he wouldn't have come. He had no respects to pay the man who'd been his sworn enemy. He had not an ounce of grief or sorrow to express.

He was damn glad the man was gone—not glad that he was dead, but relieved that Ham was no longer a thorn in his side and a drain on the family's income. He hadn't killed the man—just left him lying in the road with a flesh wound, although he'd have been in his rights to have killed the man in self-defense that night. But knowing the woman would never forget seeing her husband killed before her eyes stopped him.

I shouldn't have left like that. But the woman, half-unconscious, had begged him to go. His conscience had told him not to listen, but she'd been so desperate. He wondered if she remembered that time now. And if she'd been the one to pull the trigger later that night in self-defense.

No, I never should have left her.

Across the crowd spread out on either side of the grave came the curious probe of the deputy's gaze. Coop Logan, his badge obscured by the thick snow covering the front of his fur coat, seemed one of the genuine mourners. He and Ham had been friends as far back as any could remember. And now the lawman studied the crowd as if looking for vengeance.

Yep, it sure would have been good if he'd had his

way, Joshua thought, wishing he'd been able to stay at home and far away from the deputy's measuring stare. Home, where he had fencing to replace and a troublesome cougar to track. The bitter winter weather wouldn't have kept him from it, not on this one day. He'd come only because of his grandmother.

"We have to be there, Blythe would have wanted it," Granny had insisted, and he'd never had the heart to say no to her. He adored the cantankerous old woman, and he knew she'd been close friends with Ham's grandmother. With the dear woman gone from this earth, Granny Adelaide felt it her duty to attend.

He couldn't let her out in these near-blizzard conditions alone, and he'd been unable to convince her to take one of his other brothers—lazy Jordan especially, who had nothing better to do as the youngest and the baby of the family. Gran had thought taking Jordan along with them was a fine idea and made the boy help with the driving.

Not that she needed either of their help. He studied her sideways rather than make eye contact, which would only invite her criticism. His grandmother seemed as fierce as always and attending a funeral did not soften her. The wind blew to him the faint scent of her Irish whiskey. She remained the epitome of a no-nonsense pioneer woman, stoic as the snow began to cloak her in white.

"Stop looking at me, boy, be respectful and mind your manners," she scolded him in a low, commanding voice, as if he were still a small child. "By the grace of God, that could be you dead in a grave. Life is fleeting."

Granny, you have no notion how right you are. Reminded of his fate, and of Ham's, Joshua drew soldier straight and knew that nothing would ever be powerful enough to make him forget this day, this moment.

If he shifted his weight onto his left foot and tilted a bit, he could see past the mourners and over the minister's shoulder to where the new widow stood, shrouded in white so that the ragged black coat she wore was barely discernible. She could have been a snow angel tipped back against the white earth for the way she stood motionless.

No tears stood on her face, so pale the snow clinging to her eyebrows and eyelashes had more color. The crying that came from those who mourned did not come from her.

Ham's mother cried, his brother, Reed, choked back tears, but the young widow, who did not look to be a day over twenty, bowed her face toward the ground, as if watching the snow accumulate on the toes of her Sunday-best shoes. She appeared to be in silent grief.

Joshua knew the truth.

She stood before the opened scar in the earth where Hamilton's casket lay. As the reverend intoned on, his words whipped and battered by the cruel winds, she dipped her head, then covered her face with both slim hands. Rich dark curls tumbled down from beneath her woolen cloak.

"Such a pity," Granny's whisky-rough voice could not be disguised by a whisper but rang as loudly as if she'd bellowed. "So young to bury a husband. How long were they wed?"

"Several years, Granny," he answered in a low whisper while those mourners surrounding them turned to give them scolding, be-quiet looks.

"While none of my grandchildren have yet wed."

"Not here, Granny."

"What will become of the poor thing now?"

A good question. Joshua said nothing more as his youngest brother, Jordan, who had no desire to be here as well, gave Joshua a pained, telling look. *She always embarrasses us when we take her anywhere.*

Jordan was young. He'd had less experience with embarrassment. And since he had his eye on the young Potter girl with whom he'd finished public school last year, his apparent reputation seemed at greater risk. He didn't realize that if he succeeded in wooing, courting and wedding the fair Felicity Potter, Granny's behavior would continue to embarrass him after the wedding.

Any woman who would be so bold as to marry into their family may as well know the hazards beforehand.

Felicity, plump and glowing rosy from the cold, offered a shy wave to Jordan across the cemetery, and it made Joshua feel old. Infinitely, accusingly old. Thirty-six was not so ancient, but as he glanced around, he was the only one of an adult age unmarried.

Except for Claire Hamilton. Her heartbreak echoed in great silence that reached him all the way across the cemetery, carried by the persistent wind. The feel of it left him hollow and cold inside.

What have I done?

The minister's final amen ended the ceremony. *At last.* Aware of Deputy Logan's focus on him, he knew he could not leave yet. It would look suspicious if he did not stand in line, but the hell if he could stomach pretending any amount of sorrow.

"Have you no manners, boy?"

He felt a hard tug on his sleeve. His little grandmother looked sweet, but she was nothing of the sort and he liked her for it. Respected her more for it. In her day, Granny had been one of the first pioneer women in this county. Even now, her skirt hung low on one side, her dark woolen hem skimming the snow from the weight in her pocket.

Good old Granny carried a pistol deep in her skirt pocket, as she had since she was a bride of sixteen. Although the land was no longer untamed and wild.

"Come! Hurry along!" she demanded.

He didn't argue with her and besides, she wouldn't want to stand in the condolence line alone. For with the way Jordan was smitten with Felicity, he was as good as absent.

That's why I'm never falling in love.

He wasn't about to give that much control of his life, his faculties and his freedoms to a woman who, even if kind, would do anything to get exactly what she wanted.

His own dear sister was no exception.

He swore never to hand his life over to a woman, sweet or harsh, pretty or plain, for they were all the same. They wanted utter and complete control over a man.

No, thank you. He'd rather visit the brothel in town and burn in hell. Or, if his mother ever found out she'd likely send him there herself.

"She's such a lovely thing," Granny felt it her duty to add as they took their place in line. "Probably will be looking for a husband. You oughta court her."

"No. And don't talk about that here of all places."

"It was just a suggestion." She leaned around the Potter family to get a better look at the young widow. "She'd make a fine wife. Seems as quiet as a mouse. Not at all like Ham's mother. All drama, that one."

"And you're not?" He couldn't resist pointing out the obvious, even if it earned him a playful cuff on his ear. The woolen earflap from beneath his hat took most of the blow. "Careful, Granny, I'm no longer five and shorter than you."

Her face wreathed up into a crinkled network of laugh lines. For all her hardships and her advancing years, Granny had *lived*. Not merely existed. She'd wrung the most out of her life.

He envied her that. He was likely to spend the rest of his days branding and fencing and tracking and haying and endlessly looking after his family. A man's duty, even if unmarried, came with responsibilities as it was.

The line shuffled forward, giving him a perfect view of the widow Hamilton.

Now I have one more responsibility.

In no time, he was at the head of the line and there was Claire, looking up at him with her melted-chocolate eyes. Guilt washed over him and in an instant scudded away like wind-driven snow, gone forever. She'd tried to cover it, but a faint bruise darkened her left eye. What purple coloring remained could be mistaken for the shadows of sheer exhaustion.

He knew better.

Her small, gloved hands curled around his big one, and she shook casually as she'd probably done with everyone else. But he felt the squeeze of emotion that came with the contact.

"Mr. Gable?" Her voice was as delicate as spring wildflowers and out of place on this harsh winter day. "I'm so glad you came. Thank you."

In her dark eyes shone a glint of genuine gratitude. She wasn't thanking him for attending the burial but for carrying her to her bed while Ham lay bleeding after their fight. Behind him yawned the cruel wound of a grave with the gleaming walnut casket within, becoming lost beneath the accumulating snow, making him remember how furious he'd been that night.

He fought to swallow past a throat dust-dry and past the lump of emotion lodged beneath his Adam's apple. "It was no trouble."

He was not speaking of attending the funeral. But of protecting her from her husband. He hadn't done enough, his conscience scolded him.

The bruise beneath her left eye was not the only mark on her face. No one would notice it if they did not know to look, but she'd arranged her chestnut tresses so that a wedge of hair, twisted down to hide most of her jaw and cheekbone, was pinned carefully to her cloak and collar. Hiding the bruise Hamilton had obviously given her that night.

The clutches of memory gripped him. Faint, dark images of that brutal night crept up like a wraith and took hold. Images of lightning streaking through a merciless sky and of snow falling like rain threatened to take him back in time.

He'd had more than enough of his own problems, but

he'd gotten involved. And, in truth, he'd wanted revenge. When he'd returned from carrying her to the house, Ham was gone, leaving a bloody trail. He'd been forced to fetch the doctor for the woman instead of tracking Ham. And if he had, then he and Haskins wouldn't have returned to find Ham dead behind the barn with a second bullet in his chest. Not the one Joshua had given him.

Guilt choked him. *Don't think about it.*

But the woman before him did not deserve the consequences. It was not grief, he suspected, but fear and deep worry that pushed fine lines into her soft oval face. She hadn't asked for this to happen. She deserved nothing but his kindness.

Maybe even his pity. Life with Ham could not have been easy. Had she been able to sleep at all? he wondered. Her eyes looked puffy and not from crying, he would wager. The thought of her lying awake throughout the night, aching with anxiety and fear, tore at him.

If only he could do something, say something, anything to comfort her. But whatever he tried, he knew he could not make things right.

I'm sorry, Claire. He willed the words into her. Did she sense them?

Tears filled her eyes, the first of the service that he'd been able to notice. It gave him hope.

As if too overcome to speak, she only nodded her thanks.

He released her hand and moved on, and anyone watching would think she was nothing more than a grieving widow. And, in truth, she was too tenderhearted not to be sad. Love, he knew, was a complicated matter. Once spoken, wedding vows were powerful bonds.

He let Granny step forward to offer her terse condolences—she wasn't one to soften blows. "He was the only family you really had, that's a shame. What? Speak up, girl!"

Joshua kept Claire in his peripheral vision—those tears on her soft white cheeks could have been liquid drops of silver—when he felt a blow strike the middle of his chest and knock him back a step—and perilously close to the edge of the grave.

What the devil? Before he could recover, Ham's mother struck him again with all her might. She was a substantial woman, and when the flat of her palm beat against his breastbone, he swore she had the strength to break ribs.

"You!" Her eyes had gone stone-cold. Cold and black and dense with hatred. "You did this! The doc says it was a broken neck, but I saw the gunshot! I saw it with my own eyes."

Panic licked through him like the frigid wind. The doc had sworn he'd keep the woman away from Ham's body. Haskins was a good man, a man of his word, so what had happened—

"The deputy saw, too! And I told him what I know. How you've been threatening to shoot him in the back one night!" The woman was like a rabid dog, frothing and lost from reason.

He had to stop her. "Calm yourself, Mrs. Hamilton. I have threatened him a dozen times before this, as he threatened me in return."

The truth of his confession boomed like thunder and the chatter surrounding him silenced. Joshua felt time stretch between one heartbeat and the next.

"I saw the hole in his chest!"

"You're overwrought, Mrs. Hamilton," he said gently, because she had the right to her grief. He was surprised he felt so much pity for her, in spite of the fact she was reminding everyone of the fact that he and Ham had come to blows before over the grazing lands. And the sheep. A fact he didn't want to remind the deputy of.

"Doc!" Before he could cast around through the crowd for sight of the only doctor in the entire county, Haskins was there, capable and calm, with medical bag in hand.

Without exchanging so much as a look, Joshua knew the sawbones was on his side. On Claire's side. With his quiet courtesy, the doctor took the older Mrs. Hamilton by the elbow and made calming noises.

Just keep her calm, Doc. Joshua knew they would talk later, but for now, there was nothing more to do.

"Excuse me." Joshua touched his hat brim while the woman fell to her knees. He'd help, but he knew it would only aggravate the woman, and that was the last thing he needed or she deserved.

It wasn't her fault that her sons had turned out the way they did. There came a time when a man—or woman—had to own up to their shortcomings or hardships in life and take on the responsibility of them. It wasn't Claire's fault, either. She could not have forced her husband to walk a straighter path, for in the end, Ham's actions were his own choice.

And choices brought consequences.

All too aware of Claire's crumpled face, Joshua turned away from her. He could not offer aid, for the deputy was watching closely. Granny was tending to the young widow, whose knees were giving out, and had ordered someone to fetch a chair from inside the church.

Snow pummeled the world as Joshua looked down at the mantled coffin. It was snowing hard enough, as if heaven were in a hurry to bury Ham's remains.

Goodbye, Ham. I'm sorry, but I think you'll finally get what you deserve.

The sound of thunder crashed through his head as he remembered the gunshot booming in the dark, the lash of Ham's whip and Claire huddling on the ground at her husband's feet. Joshua tipped his cap to the man dead at his feet and felt justice had been served—a rare thing in this world.

He could leave and draw no one's suspicions since most of the attention went to the widow and Ham's mother. Joshua turned his back on the dead and started walking, for he could take no more of it. He did not want to remember that night. Soon, the truth would be buried with Hamilton. It was over.

There was no reason to suspect him, Joshua hoped, despite the feud between him and the Hamilton family. Ham had plenty of enemies and the deputy had no evidence.

"C'mon," he commanded his littlest brother, who was in truth a half inch taller than Joshua. "Stop slathering over a pretty girl and put your mind on business."

"What business?" Jordan gave his girl a shrug, as if to say, Who knows what my brother is angry at now?

The boy gave her a salute while Joshua pulled him away by the collar.

"It's time you learned some family responsibility. When we get home, you and I have tracking to do. Now get the horses and sleigh before I cuff your ears, boy."

"Right away, your majesty." Jordan gave a regal bow before he slouched away in his loose-limbed, carefree manner.

Someone should have swatted that boy on the bottom more when he was young. Joshua pretended it bothered him to no end and he barked out orders for Jordan to hurry up. If the storm got any worse, they'd have a hell of a time getting home, much less getting to work and to the herd needing his protection.

But the livestock weren't the only ones needing him.

Was Claire Hamilton all right? Worry clutched his chest and he glanced over his shoulder. Granny was holding a flask to Claire's lips and speaking to her softly. A swallow of Irish whiskey wasn't likely to cure anything, but she obeyed, choking and gasping. Granny knelt to gather the widow's hands in her own, speaking low and soft to her.

Maybe Granny could look after her.

It was a bracing thought. He felt Logan's gaze boring into his back. The lawman was staring hard. Did he think he would be able to see Joshua's secrets if he looked long enough? Troubled that the deputy continued to observe him, he forced a slow breath through his teeth and kept moving easy and slow.

I've got to act like nothing happened. I came to pay my respects, and now I'm dragging my lazy brother home. Like he always did. Surely that was all the law-man would be able to see. Instead of Joshua's guilt.

"What's your hurry?" Jordan grumbled as Joshua gave him a shove in the direction of the tethered horses. "I had Felicity Potter taking a sparkin' to me. Do you know how long I've had to work for that?"

"You? Work?" That was a laugh. Joshua forced his attention ahead, instead of behind him. "Get the horses ready and don't complain to me about work."

"Golly, what's put you in a bad mood?" He went about his work, sloppy as usual.

The boy was gonna have to grow up sometime. Shaking his head, Joshua swept the snow from the sleigh cover. He didn't mind giving up a life of marriage and restriction for the responsibility of taking over after their father's shocking death.

He'd done what he had to do, making sure the land and animals were managed and the family provided for and protected. But it was more than a one-man job these days.

He sensed the presence behind him a heartbeat before he heard the faint ring of spurs and the pad of a foot-fall.

"Joshua Gable." The words carried on the lethal wind, cold and dark. "You're a dead man."

His blood iced at the sight of Reed Hamilton, a dark presence more shadow than substance in the thick haze of snowfall. He held loaded revolvers in each hand aimed, dead center, at Joshua's heart.

Joshua didn't hesitate. He drew.

Chapter Two

Claire Hamilton couldn't make the nausea go away, nor the way her head kept feeling as if it were swinging to the right and then the left, like a tree branch caught in the clutches of a spring tornado. Not even the burning nastiness of Mrs. Adelaide Gable's whiskey could clear her head.

Of course, if she'd known it was liquor, she never would have taken a swig. She'd thought the elderly widow had handed her water.

"Your color is coming back some, my dear."

Mrs. Gable gave a grandmotherly pat on the side of her face, which was more of a slap. Claire's eyes watered.

The elderly lady grinned. "That's more like it. It's always good to have a bit of fight in you. Now stand up. I've got you."

Mrs. Gable's gruff kindness heartened her. She was in agony from being around so many people. From having to accept condolences that did not come across as sincere. How could they? She'd done her best, but surely her bruises could only be so well disguised.

Anybody who'd met Ham didn't particularly like him. Decent folk, anyway.

She was grateful for the older woman's help. Her quiet assessment was knowing, though she couldn't guess that it wasn't grief that troubled her, but a miscarriage. Mrs. Gable's grip was surprisingly strong for a woman of her advanced years, but then Adelaide Gable was no typical lady. Everyone knew that. She'd raised her sons after the death of her husband and had the respect of nearly everyone in the county. Her bright green eyes had seen a lot in her life and she seemed omniscient.

"Here's the doc, in case you'd rather stay clear of him." Mrs. Gable's rough whisper was loud enough to carry over to Ham's mother.

It was a fine thing that her mother-in-law was preoccupied by her own grief and distracted by her own circle of comforters. She was quieter now, after having tried to hurt Joshua. The doctor had come. He was on the far side of the crowd surrounding Opal and she could not see him directly, but he was essentially only a few steps away.

She was supposed to be resting, and surely that would be the first thing out of the doctor's mouth, well-meaning and all. He could easily come to her and ask how she was feeling. What if he mentioned the miscarriage?

The sorrow was blacker than any she'd known, and while she was not grieving her husband, she was mourning her baby. She felt as if some vital part of her had been cut out and she was empty as a forgotten cup gathering dust.

No, she could not take the doctor's kindness. Memories of his face swam before her eyes, how concerned he'd been. How his was the only kindness she'd known aside from Joshua's that night, and she could not open her heart. It was too raw, and if Opal overheard, then think of the outcry she would make.

Claire knew the only way she would be all right was if she didn't dwell on her loss.

It was better to keep her real grief to herself. And that gave her the strength to pick up her right foot, despite the sharp pain in her lower stomach.

It's only from emotional upset and being up too long, she told herself but feared it was worse. She resisted the urge to lay her hand on her stomach, as if minimizing the movement of her torso would bring less pain.

But such a movement would surely be noticed by one of Ham's brothers. Rick was watching her beneath the brim of his stained hat, his black eyes as inhuman as a rat's. Just like her husband's eyes had been.

It's almost as if he's still watching me. She shivered and slid her hands into her coat pockets and kept them there. She limped through the worsening storm, looking like the grieving widow they all expected her to be.

A sudden shout rang through the snow-thick air. What was going on? She became aware that there was some scuffle. A crowd had gathered around so that she couldn't see. She could barely focus on the ground in front of her, as flakes clung to her lashes and the downpour pounded so hard the snow closed in like a shroud.

Her big toe stubbed what felt like a rock, and she stumbled. Adelaide's grip tightened on her wrist, keeping her upright. Pain sizzled like lightning up her leg, into her groin and into the very center of her belly.

She needed to get home. Everything would be all right if she could reach the sleigh and get the horses headed home. In a storm like this they would hurry there on their own, without a lot of guidance from her.

Alone, she'd be able to close her eyes, rest her head. That's all she needed.

Then the deputy ran past and folks started yelling. Two gunshots fired, popping overhead like thunder-claps. Then she saw the shadows of two men through the snowy mist. One was facedown on the ground, felled by a wide-shouldered man who had his back to her.

She took a step closer and knew it was Joshua Gable. She could make out only his impressive silhouette. Shrouded with white, covered with snow shadow, he was no less awe-inspiring. His over-six-foot height was matched by his strong, working-man's musculature. He held his attacker down with one boot dug into the smaller man's back and cradled a Colt .45 in one hand, cocked and with his finger resting on the trigger.

A truly powerful man.

"Joshua!" Adelaide polarized with fear for her grand-son. "Oh, you must excuse me, dear. That's my boy, and he's in trouble!"

Claire hardly realized the elderly lady was talking. She'd forgotten Mrs. Gable was even holding on to her. Her entire being seemed to focus on the smoking revolv-ers gleaming black in the pure snow, fallen from the downed man's grip. She recognized the elaborate iron-work on the handle. That was Reed's gun.

Reed had thought to attack a Gable? What, was he drunk, too? As if in answer, the powerful scent of the cheapest whiskey wafted up on the cutting wind. Reed was a coward, and even she could glance at the boot tracks already filling with snow to see that Reed had come up on Joshua from behind. Reed could have killed him.

The deputy was there, at Joshua's side, and the men began to argue. Heated words melded together like flames in a growing fire and all she could hear were the hard brutal threats and accusations. Onlookers became involved, and Ham's other brother, Rick, shouldered in, reaching to draw his gun.

In a flash, Joshua reached out and yanked the revolver from Rick's holster. The crowd hushed, but they shouldn't be surprised by Gable's agility. Claire had seen him in action before.

Don't remember, she commanded, taking a wobbling step sideways and leaning heavily against a tree trunk. Her forehead rapped on the thick limb—she didn't notice it. Haze misted her vision and everything went white. Gasping, feeling strangely sick, she rested and counted the thrum of her heartbeats loud in her ears.

No one knew of that night. Only she and Joshua.

As if he could sense that she was thinking about him, his shoulders tensed and he turned toward her enough that he could see her over the impressive ledge of his shoulder. There was no looking around to find her in the murky snowfall. His eyes snapped to hers as if by destiny.

Look away, every instinct within her shouted. But logic told her the whiteout conditions would keep oth-

ers from noticing. She indulged a long moment while
their gazes remained bound.

Was he sorry? she wondered. Was he wishing he'd
never met her and Ham on the road that dark night?
Look at the trouble it had caused him.

The deputy leaned close to speak with him, a somber matter judging by the tight lock of the lawman's jaw.
Coop Logan had come often to her and Ham's high
country ranch, not that she saw him. When he did ride
up to the house, he didn't come to the front door like
decent company but kept to the back door.

Mostly, he waited at the corner where the hill sloped
steeply downward and out of sight to the prairie below.
Ham would make his way from the house or the barn.
What they spoke about or the purpose of the lawman's
calls, she couldn't say. She wondered if he would arrest
Ham's brothers, as he obviously ought to, for drawing
and firing guns on innocent people.

Well, perhaps not so innocent, she remembered with
a painful wince. And she felt the punch of it move
through her and reflect in Joshua Gable's face. A muscle worked in his jaw and he gave a barely noticeable
nudge of his head toward the street, where her horses
and sleigh waited.

He wanted her to go home. First, she had something
to say to the deputy. She grabbed Logan by the forearm
and yanked down the hand holding metal cuffs.

"My brothers-in-law are in the wrong and you know
it." She spoke loudly, scolding him, and she was surprised how her voice carried high above the others', si-
lencing them. "They've been drinking. Everyone here

can smell it. They must have been at it all night. Or worse."

"This is hardly a matter for a woman." The lawman said the last word with contempt. "Gable here is holding a gun on your brothers—"

"*Former* brothers-in-law," she corrected. An important distinction in her mind. "I am no longer part of that family. Let Mr. Gable go."

"I'm afraid I can't do that. I have some questions I need to ask him."

"And not Reed? Look at him. Even I can see he tried to shoot Mr. Gable in the back."

Joshua stepped forward, cutting between her and the deputy. "Mrs. Hamilton, it would be wise if you left this to me. Go home. You must need rest."

His words were not condescending, but they were not kind. Not that he could be in front of these men. She and Joshua were two people who did not know each other—except for the night Ham died.

The last thing she wanted was for anyone to start wondering about how she knew Joshua. Especially the deputy. She could not ever risk putting this man in danger, not the only man who'd ever stood up for her.

She eased back, already forgotten by the lawman and Ham's brothers arguing. Pain spasmed like a fist, opening and closing low in her abdomen and the pain traversed down the front of her thighs.

Time to do as Joshua asked, she figured as she walked carefully through the uneven accumulation of snow. Breathing carefully, she felt only the worst of pain when her shoe slipped or the snow gave beneath her heel.

It looked as if Adelaide Gable had joined the fray and the deputy was forced to deal with the real wrongdoers.

That was a change around here. Not that she was going to get used to it. Claire stopped to swipe the snow from her lashes. The street wasn't far. She could make out the dark humps of horses and vehicles ahead. And a bright flash of red where she'd tied her team.

Trouble. She'd lived with Ham long enough to know the impending feel of it. Easing onto the street, she came close enough to see Ham's mother being helped into the sleigh—Claire's sleigh. And the matched bay horses gave nervous sidesteps beneath their blankets.

Those are my horses now, she thought, feeling rage roll through her. Rage that she'd kept contained during the funeral. Rage she'd held back instead of grabbing the nearby shovel, left by the grave diggers, to beat the casket with all her strength. That man had made her lose her child. He'd tormented her from the moment she'd stepped away from the church, a hopeful and dreamy new bride.

And his family had cheerfully made her miserable days since even more unbearable. And to think that woman, that greedy mother of his, was helping herself to the horses Claire had saved more times than she could count due to Ham's careless treatment of them.

A new woman rose within her like the leading edge of a blizzard. She was no longer a modest and obedient wife but a widow of her own determination. She grabbed Thor's bridle by the bit and held him firm. "Where do you think you are going?"

Opal had the audacity to look insulted. "Home. I'm not well."

"Here you go, Mother." The youngest Hamilton, a sister a few years older than Claire, was quick to slide in beside her mother and seize control of the reins. "Claire, scat. You're in our way."

"You're in my sleigh. And these are my horses."

"My dear brother would not want these fine animals to fall to you." Annabelle lifted her dainty chin. She'd married well and had the attitude to prove it…and the avarice. It seemed to taint her sneer as she narrowed her small black eyes. "You are nothing but a mistake Ham never should have made. Move aside or I'll run you down."

"You will do no such thing." Thor obeyed *her,* and well he should, since they were friends, and she held his bridle hard, pulling downward.

Annabelle gave the thick reins a resounding smack. The big gelding whinnied and shied, as Claire knew he would. She spoke low to him, keeping him in place, and by association, his smaller brother, Loki, who was harnessed to him.

"Release the horse!" Annabelle demanded. "Or I shall get out and be forced to—"

"What? I have shoveled out Ham's horse barn twice daily since I married him." While Opal moaned in her grief, renewed by the sound of Ham's name being spoken, Claire bent, despite difficulty and the pain in her midsection.

She unbuckled the single strap that held the whiffletrees to the traces and forcefully met Annabelle's eyes. "Come and get them if you can."

She wasn't surprised Ham's family turned into vultures, only that they were trying to take what they could so soon.

Claire stepped up onto the sturdy tracing between the horses and, with a snap, yanked the leather straps from Annabelle's kid-gloved hands. Ignoring her fierce, angry shouts and Opal's sobs, she eased onto Thor's back and sent him and Loki into a fast walk.

Pain jolted through her. It was far too much pain. "You need rest," kindly Doc Haskins had said. "Complete bed rest. No stress or strain. No housework and no ranch work. No upset of any kind."

She was only supposed to be up for the funeral. But now she wished she'd never come. She had thought saying goodbye to Ham would give her the chance to cast off the painful memories as well, but it had not worked.

At least she could go home now. The thought of her own bed and the soft flannel sheets made her moan with longing. Exhaustion settled like lead into the marrow of her bones. She had to escape, not only her relatives, but everything.

Sadness overwhelmed her, and to her disappointment, there was no quick escape. Already the swarm of the funeral crowd was buzzing close to the streets, and she drew Thor and Loki to a halt.

Why was everyone stopping? She strained to see over the big covered surrey in front of her. A sled had skidded off the road into the ditch at the crossroads that made up the trading post, the only civilization aside from the church on this remote corner of the county. The vehicle and team had caused a blockage on the only place where the two main roads through the county intersected. They were already receiving help from others nearby, although the traffic wasn't likely to begin moving anytime soon.

Of course. Annabelle was still shouting, and she sounded closer. Claire didn't have the energy to spare to look over her shoulder and in truth, she didn't care. They could have the sleigh, but these were her horses. Hers alone.

And my friends, she thought as she ran her gloved hand along Thor's sleek neck.

The warmth of him permeated the wool, reminding her of what mattered. She had survived. She was still here. Ham had not harmed the deepest part of her. Three years ago on a day more bleak than this, she'd become a bride and naive enough to believe she would be starting a wonderful new life.

Looking back, it was hard to believe she could have been that dreamy girl. She closed her eyes, and she could almost see the young woman who had worked a double shift every day for two months at the boardinghouse, cleaning and doing laundry to scrape enough money together to buy fabric and notions for a beautiful wedding dress.

That dress was the nicest thing she'd ever owned in her life or in her marriage since. She'd loved the delicate sage lawn with the tiniest little embroidered rosebuds of matching sage that looked as fine as anything the wealthier ladies in town wore. And the dainty pearl buttons hadn't been real mother-of-pearl, but they'd looked as if they were. And that had been enough. She'd worn it for Ham, to mark the momentous honor of becoming a bride, *his* bride.

As that young woman spoke the vows in the echoing chill of the sanctuary, she'd meant them with all her heart. She fully intended to love and cherish, honor and obey her very dashing husband.

Obey—she hadn't realized the impact of that one four-letter word until later. In the church holding Ham's hand, her entire being had shone with happiness and hope for a good future.

When the minister had proclaimed them man and wife, she'd nearly floated to the ceiling. She'd been an orphan and little more than a servant in her uncle's home, but now she had a family. A home. A fine man to love.

Claire's heart wrenched with sorrow so deep and dark she could no longer see the present, only the past. The memory of that happy young woman seemed to ride by like a ghost and then became forever lost in the tenacious downpour of snow. If she listened hard enough, she could almost hear the joyful music of that doomed bride's laughter.

"Claire."

She instinctively turned at the sound of the rumbling baritone. Joshua Gable was nothing more than a hint of a shadow in the shroud of snowfall, and then a silhouette of horse and rider, confident and powerful as he rode closer, and then he was beside her, dusted with white, and flesh-and-blood real.

What a man. How he had sneaked up on her, she didn't know. She could feel his nearness like a summer's wind against her skin. And now she could sense him like a whisper in her soul—a whisper she didn't want.

Like that night, he came to her out of a storm, and although she was free from her marriage, she was not free from her fear. Joshua Gable wanted something. He was a man. She'd learned the hard way there were no heroes left to believe in. True love did not exist except in fairy tales.

She was no longer a girl of eighteen. She was a woman who'd learned the truth about life and marriage. She was a widow with experience and hard lessons learned. She would never believe in a man again.

Not even in Joshua Gable, who was hardworking and sincere and had shown her kindness on a night without mercy.

But that was over now, and they could never speak of it again. Before he could say another word, she shook her head, stopping him from saying whatever he'd come to her to say.

With a twist of the reins, she guided the horses down into the fallow field siding the road and nosed them toward home, grateful for the storm that whipped around her in a swirl of white and haze, stealing her from Joshua's sight.

She didn't look back.

Chapter Three

Claire didn't know where she was or if the horses had been able to find the way, for the snow was falling so hard she couldn't see the tips of Thor's ears. She only knew the storm was worsening. And so was the pain knifing from her womb and radiating down her inner thighs. Unbearable ripping pain.

I'm just tired, that's all. She clung stubbornly to that thought as tightly as she gripped the leather top of Thor's shoulder harness. She needed to get home and lie down. Rest, just like the doc said. And then she'd be fine.

She was up too soon after losing the baby, that was all. She willed the pain to stop. Willed it with all of her strength, all of her being. The rock of the giant horse's gait lanced through her midsection. If she could make it home, that's what she needed. But how far?

The prairie stretched out around her, lost in the blinding whiteout. She couldn't tell exactly how far she'd already come. The snow scrubbed like ice at her eyes as the storm worsened. Gradually she could see nothing but endless white, whirling snow. Not even her own mittens in front of her face.

Thor will get me home. The thought sustained her. Time had passed—how much she didn't know, but enough that they had to be nearly home. And that meant rest.

Her bed was waiting, the feather mattress would feel like a cloud after this hard ride, and the flannel sheets and thick goose-down comforter as warm as melted butter. She'd lay her head on her feather pillow and let her heavy eyelids drift shut.

Thor's pace seemed to pick up. Maybe he sensed her need. That would explain why the pain came more quickly. And if the pain changed from hurt to agony, from agony to killing, then it was because she was tired. And if she felt warm instead of cold and then hotter, it was her desperation.

We're almost home, she thought, surprised at how hard it was to breathe. Her pulse drummed in her ears and her head seemed to throb with it. Air rasped into her lungs. She couldn't seem to get enough air.

Maybe it was the storm. Or the cold. She didn't know. Or the shock of seeing Joshua Gable at the funeral. Of having him act as if nothing had gone on between them, as if he hadn't roped Ham like a steer and berated him for his cruel treatment of her. He hadn't deserved Ham pulling a gun on him, and he'd defended himself. He'd defended her.

Joshua Gable's gunshot had been the cause of Ham's death, but she wasn't going to tell that to anyone.

Thor's gait became horribly jarring. It couldn't be the pain was getting worse. No, she couldn't allow that thought. Because she had to hold on. She'd lost her baby, she didn't want to lose her life.

A pain clamped like a vulture's claw and then squeezed. Talons dug deep into her insides, tearing. Ripping. Warmth slid from her body. No, after all she had survived—Ham's treatment and beatings and the wagon accident, her miscarriage and now this, she would not give up now. She buried her face in the horse's ice-caked mane and gritted her teeth, hanging on with all her might.

She tried to hold back the next pain, but it was too strong, an enemy too big to fight or to placate. A sickening wave of nausea washed through her and she fought that down, too. She would not give in. She'd will the contractions to stop, the warm seep of blood to cease. She was going to be okay. She *had* to be.

Agony seized her from the inside, the talons turning into something more monstrous. It was as if her entire abdomen was being vised from the inside out, and the torture blinded her. Seemed to enter every inch of her body until she was screaming helplessly.

She was slipping, her arms and hands clutched Thor's harness but her muscles turned watery. Her strength drained away and she was sliding down the horse's flank, falling like the ruthless snow, tumbling until she hit the unforgiving ground.

Someone help me. The vise within her twisted hard. There was only the bright flash of white sparks before her eyes and then she felt the vising gain strength. She lay helpless on the ground, shrouded by snow. Alone.

The physical pain tearing like a hungry predator at her flesh was nothing, nothing at all. Her heart was shattering, and that pain was why she cried out in the worsening storm, why the icy crust of snow beneath her or the dangerous cold did not hurt her.

Unable to move, lost and alone, feeling the life's blood drain out of her, she listened to the storm rage on, cruel and lethal, as if there was no more hope in this bleak and bitter world.

Joshua cursed the timing of the storm. No, it couldn't blow over, not on this day when responsibility weighed like an anvil around his throat. The blasted storm seemed to be gathering speed for an all-out blizzard.

It was too early in the year. He'd prepared for bad weather early. This was Montana Territory, and unforgiving storms were a possibility every year. He considered himself a top-notch rancher who accounted for every possibility, but not today. He had some things to say to Claire Hamilton and they needed to be said now. Today. Before Logan or Ham's brothers decided to make good on their threats to find the truth.

The truth would stay buried with Ham, and Joshua would make damn sure of it. But nothing had been that simple. Ham's brothers had made it clear they didn't like him, yet how did either of them know he'd been out Ham's way that night? Claire. He had to talk to her. He had to know what she might have said—either intentionally or by mistake.

The widow wasn't his only problem. As Joshua pulled his hands out of his coat pockets to shake the thick layer of iced snow from his muffler and hat, he figured his brother and grandmother ought to have reached the shelter of home by now. His brother—that troubled Joshua, too.

The boy had taken one of the horses, leaving the mare of the matched team to pull Granny's sleigh to the family ranch. But his younger brother knew something was amiss.

"I thought you had a fire beneath your britches to get chores done," Jordan had observed, slouched as usual in the seat. "Now you're headin' off and orderin' me to drive Granny home?"

He had been too irritated, Joshua realized in hindsight as he jammed his fists back into his pockets. "I have things that need seein' to."

"Things." Jordan had sounded doubtful as he'd exerted enough effort to shake the snow from his hat brim. "Why in the hell are you watchin' the road to the mountains? Maybe you could enlighten me, oh lord and master."

"At least you acknowledge my supremacy," Joshua had ground out, his fury rising at his brother's pesky questions. Of course he was in charge. Where would they be if Jordan had taken over the reins of the family? They'd all be starved, homeless and slouching. "Just follow orders and take Granny home. There's something I gotta do."

"What? We're heading into the mountains, eh? Agggh!" Jordan slugged the dashboard in frustration. "I can't believe you're doin' this! I know where you're going."

I should have left the conversation there, Joshua thought as he nudged his left spur gently against General's flank, keeping him on the road that was nearly impossible to see. I should have let him think what he wanted instead of tipping my hand. And now…

A hard gust of wind lashed against him, driving ice through the layers of fur, wool and flannel. Joshua shivered, but it wasn't from the cold. If Jordan guessed any of the truth, then an innocent woman would go to jail, for the simple fact of defending herself. For what other reason could gentle Claire Hamilton have killed her husband?

He remembered the image of that night, when Ham had first come into sight with his arm back holding a whip ready to strike the fallen woman. Why, he should have killed the man himself and saved her the trouble.

Bile filled his throat. Father had always been one to look the other way, not to get involved in other fools' problems, and look where it had gotten him, shot in the back and left to bleed out in the far grazing fields. Playing it safe had not protected Father one bit. And yet, matters could not have been worse if he had taken aim and pulled the trigger instead of Claire. It was a mess.

But like this blizzard, it would soon pass and be forgotten. What he had to do was make sure of it.

General had veered off the road again, fetlock-deep in drifting snow. It wasn't fair to drag the horse out in this. He'd put in a hard day hauling yesterday. Riding into the brunt of the storm was wearing on him. Joshua took his hand out of his pocket to pat the gelding's neck, encouraging him. He'd make sure the horse got warmed mash as soon as they got home.

"We gotta keep going, fella."

When the gelding didn't respond to knee pressure or

a flat edge of the spur, he lifted the reins from the saddle horn, shook off the caked snow, and added pressure to the bit.

General sidestepped to a halt. His opinion was clear. He didn't like the storm any more than Joshua did.

"Sorry, buddy, we gotta—"

Was it his imagination, or did the wind have a strange keel to it? He stopped and cocked his ear. There was something in the wind, a low note to the eerie howling of the wind. A horse? A rider in trouble? "General, you are a fine horse. You take me to 'em."

He gave the gelding his head, and the big animal stumbled in the drifts of snow and hidden clumps of dead buffalo grass. As if the storm were a living thing, determined to hold them back, the wind pummeled them, driving the snow horizontal, closing them off from the world.

While he knew the grand rise of the Rocky Mountains ought to be jutting straight up from the prairie floor directly ahead, he could see only an endless curtain of gray-white that fell around him, draping him from the rest of the world.

It was damn dangerous letting General wander off the road. More good men than he could count had become lost in weather like this. The sounds of the wind and the thickly blowing snow confused a man's sense of direction and isolated him from every visual landmark. A man would wander off course and freeze to death, sometimes having come within a few feet of his own house or barn.

But one thing was certain—if he didn't help, then

whoever or whatever was in trouble was facing a death sentence.

He did his best to fix in his mind the position of the road. If he could find the road and keep to it, then eventually it would lead him to shelter. If he could survive the below-zero winds.

General was a well-trained horse, a pure Morgan, strong, sturdy and smart as a whip. He had good horse instincts, and they served both of them well as he pricked his ears, listening. The wind seemed to be teasing them with its sound. It had become a living thing, a lethal force, allowing them a hint of sound and then blowing it away.

But General was true—he halted abruptly and stood. Whatever he found was at his feet.

"Good boy." Joshua dismounted, stiff from the cold, and without a saddle beneath him, slid easily to the ground. He sank into snow well over his ankles. He couldn't see a thing. "What did you find, boy?"

Then he heard it—a faint nicker. Not a nicker exactly, but it was some animal in trouble. Joshua trudged forward, keeping a hand on General to guide him along. A shadow moved in the endless swirl of snow. A big Clydesdale with his head hung low lumbered out of the shadows and bumped confused into Joshua.

The impact nearly knocked him off his feet. Joshua realized the animal was panicked and suffocating. How long he'd been standing in this was anyone's guess. And he was not alone. Another draft horse huddled behind him, looking even more frightened.

All it took was a hand to the animal's frozen muzzle

and most of the snow that had iced to his warm nostrils broke away. The workhorse shook his head, his sides heaving in strong currents of air.

I hate to think what would have happened to you, fella. Joshua prided himself on his no-nonsense toughness, but he couldn't abide the thought of any animal suffering. He caught the Clydesdale's thick reins and realized they were driving reins. He'd been harnessed to something but was loose now.

With the shadows of the storm and the thick mantle of white on the animal's coat, he couldn't make out the color of the big boy's coat, but there was something familiar. Neck-pricking familiar.

"You're not out here alone, are you, boy?" In the instant it took for Joshua to puzzle out the possibilities— a sleigh accident, a runaway animal, vandals—none of them felt right. The big horse sank his teeth in Joshua's jacket hem and pulled.

"Hey!" He lifted his arm to try to pry away, but then he realized the horse was deliberately pulling him along. What a loyal friend this horse was. Instead of running off to find shelter and survive, the big fella had stuck with his master. That meant someone was hurt—

And then realization hit him like the full-force wind, and he stumbled. The horse—that was a star on his forehead, wasn't it? The horse Claire had ridden off on had the same markings. Claire. What had happened to her? If those brothers of Ham's had slipped away and followed her…

Fury roared through him until he felt ten feet tall and powerful enough that no storm could hamper him. He followed the horse a few more feet and there, sprawled in the snow, looking as if part of the rumpled prairie, was a form.

Claire.

Frigid shock washed through him and he dropped to his knees. Expecting the worst, already seeing her dead frozen face in his mind's eye, he gently laid his gloved hand on her snow-covered shoulder.

Was she breathing? Was she alive? Agony twisted through him as he wrestled with his glove. Ice crackled, and he finally sank his teeth into the loose wool around his fingertips and yanked. The instant his warmed skin was exposed, the vicious cold sank into it. He ignored the pain as he slipped his fingers beneath the layers of her wraps and felt along the cool satin of her neck for her pulse.

Nothing.

Hell. He didn't know if his fingers were too numb to feel her pulse, or if there wasn't one to feel. He suspected it was the latter, and sorrow cleaved through him. He had to cover his face, had to take a breath before he could try to figure out what to do. What had happened here? She'd been pale and weak, he'd remembered that from the funeral. But Granny never would have let her go if she'd been truly ill.

Had it been the Hamiltons? Had they done something to her? *Did they suspect the truth?* Is that why they'd followed her? But how could the boys have gotten ahead of him on the road, when he'd left them behind arguing things out with the deputy? Well, they could know a shortcut.

The road was the long way around—there was no telling how fast they could have caught up with her had they disregarded property lines and ridden their horses through pastures and grazing land? What had those ruffians done? And to a helpless woman? Agony was torn from his chest as he swept the snow from her motionless form. She lay facedown, with her hands clutched beneath her as if she'd died in agony, her legs akimbo, her face turned away, her soft woolen outer wrapping iced stiff.

It took him a moment to realize the sheen of dark crimson staining the skirt and seeping upward through the snow was blood. A whole lot of it.

I'm so sorry, Claire.

She didn't deserve this. No woman did. To be struck down and left alone to die. Misery coursed through him. *I should have been with you. I should have protected you.* He'd played a hand in the course of events. And he knew what the Hamilton brothers would do if they figured out the truth.

That made him responsible for her death, too. Sickened, he let the storm's fury batter him. He'd failed. It had been a long time since he'd failed someone. He put his face in his hands and closed his eyes. *I didn't want this.* Grief left him as cold as the blizzard. As the vicious winds rocked him, he vowed to take care of her now. The past couldn't be changed.

Life once lost could not be brought back. And he couldn't think of how he'd go on, knowing he'd failed to protect her. Knowing that his suspicions had been right.

The big Clydesdale nickered, nudging his mistress

with his nose, an affectionate gesture. His head hung low and stayed there, his sadness palpable.

I can't leave her here. Joshua gathered his strength. He'd take care of her from here on out. Too late, his conscience mocked him, as he leaned over her and caught sight of her face in profile, her skin nearly translucent, lying as still as an angel. With her dark lashes long and curled and the ethereal cut of her fine cheekbones and chin, she could have been a snow angel taken form. She'd been such a sweet thing, he thought, though he'd hardly known her.

Maybe it was just his wishful thinking that somewhere in this world there could be a kind and gentle woman, instead of one out for her own gain. Maybe it was how vulnerable she'd been that night he'd come to her aid and how small she seemed now as he gathered her into his arms.

Her lifeless body was still supple and as he adjusted her against his chest, he swore he felt a soft exhale of breath against the underside of his jaw, where his muffler had fallen away. But no, that had to be the feathery snow, for the sensation was cold, not warm.

He just couldn't believe she was gone, that he was clinging to false hope. The Clydesdale lumbered at his side, his nostrils wide and sniffing over his mistress. An eerie trumpet of a neigh sounded from the big boy's throat—one of pure sorrow.

General stood at attention, the good horse he was, and he did not balk or sidestep at the scent of blood and death. Joshua supposed some men would think it prudent to strap her body to the back of her horse, but he couldn't bear it.

She'd died alone. She felt as cold as the wind against him, and seemed to seep a deeper cold into him, but he didn't care. He wasn't going to leave her alone. Hell, he was sick with regrets and grief. He hefted her onto General's back—she didn't weigh more than a hundred-pound grain sack, and it saddened him as he climbed up behind her.

He gathered her into his arms, her weight falling softly against his chest. He fought a powerful thrust of emotion. His heart felt as desolate as the frozen plains as he turned General and struggled to find their tracks in the wild haze of falling snow.

General's hoofprints were nearly swept clean. After a few yards, they were gone completely. He was alone with a dead woman and three horses, and no idea which way to safety or the open prairie.

He wasn't a praying man. He'd lost faith in most things long ago. But a little help wouldn't be unappreciated, he thought, as he tried to gauge if the wind had a direction—if it was coming from the mountains, west, then he could keep the wind straight at his back and he'd eventually come upon homesteads and, finally, town.

But no, fate wasn't about to lend him a hand. The wind was twisting and swirling as the blizzard hit its momentum. A clap of thunder echoed overhead—a sure sign the storm was worsening. Even if he could find the road, the temperature was dropping. Well below zero, Joshua figured. He couldn't sustain his body temperature long enough to reach town.

As for a homestead, there weren't many on this desolate part of the Montana plains for this very reason. The winters were so brutal few could stick it out.

The only hope he had was to keep going. He'd climb off and walk if he had to. This would keep his blood pumping for a while. But it would only delay the inevitable. If he was as far from town as he figured he was, then he was a doomed man.

Maybe it was justice, he figured, as he brushed snow from Claire's face, an eye for an eye. One life for another.

She relaxed against his throat and he felt it then, the faintest tickle.

Claire Hamilton was as still as the dead, but one thing was sure. It was impossible. He didn't believe it even as he ripped off his glove and felt her pulse again— nothing. His fingers were too frozen, that's what he told himself, even as he figured she had to be gone.

Then he felt it: a weak feathering against his wrist. She was breathing. *She was alive.*

Chapter Four

Alive. Barely. Joshua cursed the Hamiltons. Who else would have done this to her? The fierce weather would reveal no clue of where they were.

What was the good in finding her if they were lost? Already, he knew she was too cold. She might very well die before General could take two more steps. And the realization forced fear into his veins, then a calmer determination.

He'd not failed her yet. Strong with purpose, he gave General his head. The gelding had good horse sense. "Shelter," he told the animal, although he knew the wind snatched the words away so that the horse could not hear them.

Cold coiled tight in Josh's guts as he cradled the widow against his chest. He'd will warmth into her cold body if he could. He'd will life. If they could find a place to weather the storm, perhaps he could save her. Warm her up and tend her wounds and… Who was he kidding?

he thought bitterly as General came to a dead halt. They were lost on the open prairie.

Now what? Joshua looked to his right and then his left. Saw only a gray-white shroud. Ahead he could not make out the General's head—his dark neck rose up into the swirling whiteness and disappeared.

Behind them, he knew Claire's Clydesdales were there, obediently following their mistress, but he could see nothing of the great animals. If the wind stopped, then they'd have a fighting chance. But as the blizzard raged, there was no change. No way to be sure of a direction.

Their survival was up to him. The horse was confused, and that had been Josh's last hope. Now, he had to pick—right or left, not knowing if it was north or if it was any other bearing. It won't matter, he thought sadly, as he lifted one hand from Claire's limp body to break away at the ice massed over his muffler.

As he rewrapped his muffler, he was intensely aware of the woman in his arms, her weight almost as nonexistent as her life. He brushed the accumulating snow from her head, shoulders and face, and turned the horses right. These efforts might be in vain, Joshua figured as he urged General to a faster pace, but he would not be like some who curled up into the snow to let the blizzard win. He would not go without a fight.

His will was iron strong as he bowed his head into the wind.

Awareness came to her in small pieces.

Claire heard the wind first, the eerie, alive sound of a winter wind at full force. This was the vicious wind that came from the far north and rode the glaciers of the rugged Rocky Mountain Range and swooped down gaining speed on the prairie below.

She recognized, too, the wild shriek of the blizzard as it drove snow in an impenetrable shield. Snow pellets hammered into the ground. The sounds confused her, because she could not remember where she was as she struggled toward consciousness.

But it was too far a length to reach, caught as if in a dreamlike place she feared Ham would find her. The wagon had broken apart, she remembered that clearly enough. The falling. The ruthless pain as she struck the earth. The lash of a whip against her flesh.

That must be why I hurt. She felt it suddenly as if she was slipping into a hot bath—although it was not water that rushed up from her toes and through her legs. Burrowed into her abdomen and raked upward until the backs of her eyes burned. Fiery sensation that was more than pain. Beyond pain.

Images returned. Of Ham drunk, towering over her, cursing and blaming her. She could smell the alcohol and his rage. Memory gripped her and it was good, because she at least knew what had happened. A wagon wreck. She'd fallen and was trapped, unable to move, because there was no way she could make her limbs or fingers stir. And the pain from his steel-toed boots hitting her ribs.

The baby. I must protect my child. She had to regain consciousness before the next blow struck. Her eyes could not see. Her lungs seemed unable to draw in enough air to speak with. She could not seem to make her mouth or tongue form a single word. Ice pellets struck her face as she clawed her way through the darkness of unconsciousness, struggling with all of her strength so that she had a chance. So her babe had a chance.

Fight, Claire. Fight. With all the strength in her soul, she struggled toward a single spot of grayness so far away in the darkness it was like the head of a pin.

But her will was strong and she focused on that single speck until it grew closer and larger still. Until it was the size of a tea saucer and she could see the hail of iced snow shooting from the gray heavens, feel the sharp, cold pricks on her face.

Then a shadow moved over her, shaped like the curving brim of a man's hat. *Ham? Was it Ham?*

Panic pummeled her heart and it flapped in her chest. She was not yet strong enough to move. She was groggy, her body unresponsive, heavy and floppy like a rag doll's. Terror rushed into her blood and she could feel it turn her veins to ice. Feel it drain the strength and the light. Her vision dimmed, and her entire being shouted at the injustice of it. The unfairness.

No! She had to fight. But the darkness was taking her, leaving her helpless as she awaited Ham's next blow— by whip or fist or boot.

And then a man's face moved into the fading circle of her sight. It wasn't Ham's face. This man had a strong square jaw, unshaved and rough with a few days' growth. Brackets etched into the corners of his tight, almost harsh-looking mouth. High cheekbones and eyes the color of steel.

Joshua Gable. Realization lifted her up and she was floating away into the void again. Awareness faded even as she dared to hope that he'd come to save her.

I can't take this anymore. Joshua gritted his teeth, although he couldn't actually feel them. He was quaking all the way to the core of his bones.

He'd been this cold once—when he'd been hauling hay to the livestock and got caught in a blizzard with Pa. They'd made it home by luck and by good old common sense. He was using his best judgment, but that was no reassurance.

He could have been riding for ten minutes or two hours. He couldn't tell. Time meant nothing. Distance meant nothing.

If the storm didn't let up soon, the horse was going to freeze out from beneath him. General's gait had slowed. There was no sense in even hoping the woman in his arms would live. The pale skin above the scarf he'd covered her face with was a deathly gray.

This was not the way he wanted it, either, he thought, unable to feel even her weight against his chest, her soft presence, her wool scarf. He couldn't feel the horse beneath him. Or his feet—and to keep the blood flowing, he'd have to start walking soon. But no man had the strength to carry a woman through the foot-high drifts and against the pounding wind. He'd have to leave her on the horse—unprotected from the brunt of the storm.

He needed just a little help, a moment of intuition. An unmistakable landmark that he could make out through the thick curtain of ice. Anything, because chances were he'd missed the road. He'd missed any chance of finding shelter and was heading to the Canadian border, largely unsettled and uncharted.

Death. He'd never figured it would come for him this way. He'd been knocked upside the head by an angry bull a few times. That ought to have sent him into the afterlife, but he'd come out of it with nothing more troubling than a headache.

He'd been pinned against a barn wall by an irate stallion and kicked in the guts by an ornery mare. He had slipped on an ice patch trying to put out a chimney fire one winter years back. Those close calls had taught him he'd likely meet the same end doing his daily work.

He'd lived his life for his family. He did not regret it now, he thought as he brushed snow from Claire's hood—she felt diminished more than she had earlier, as if something essential within her drained away with every minute that passed.

I'm sorry I couldn't do better, he said silently to her, his thoughts weighed down by a passel of regrets. *You deserved better.* He leaned his cheek against her head, a gentle pressure, but the contact somehow tugged at his empty heart.

General stumbled, pitching forward. Joshua's reactions were slow. He saw the horse going down and he knew what to do—he was kicking his foot out of the stirrup and swinging down, hauling Claire's body against his chest, but not fast enough. His legs held no strength. His sluggish leg barely cleared the saddle. His knee wobbled as he tried to stand in the remaining stirrup and he couldn't kick clear.

He went down with his horse, holding Claire up even as his ankle wrenched, caught in the stirrup, and snapped. His knees hit next, and the impact jarred through him like a body blow. He sank into his left hip, Claire unharmed but his body silent with shock.

He was too numb to feel the pain of whatever had happened to his ankle, but his body somehow knew and was reeling. A sick feeling built in his gut.

With the way his luck was going, he'd broken the damn thing. He couldn't move it, and it was twisted nearly all the way around and stuck in the stirrup. He grabbed hold of his trousers at the knee and wrestled his foot free—and considering it came away at an odd angle only confirmed what he'd already guessed. He'd broken it—and good.

Hell. What else could go wrong? Couldn't a man freeze to death in peace? Was it too much to ask for a moment of peace in this life, damn it!

Not that he planned to sit here and freeze to death, but a second without misery or disaster would be appreciated. He felt his temper lifting him up and he gave thanks for the tight laces on his boots. It served as enough of a splint to let him move forward one dragging step at a time.

A smart man would accept that he was licked and give in to it. But no, not Joshua Gable, he thought as he settled the woman's weight against his shoulder.

Not that he'd ever been a smart man. He'd lived with his mother and his sister long enough to have endured numerous insults about his intelligence. You are simply a man, Betsy's soft alto voice rang in his mind along with the huff of frustration.

You think just like your father, may he not rest in peace! Mother's shrill drill-sergeant manner actually brought a smile to his hard and decidedly frozen face. He'd miss them the most, he decided as the storm swirled around him, breaking apart to give him a glimpse of the mighty snow-shrouded Rockies towering to his left—before the downfall curtained him again. As for Granny—

Was it his imagination, or was that her red plaid scarf he saw? There was a spot of color hovering in midair, but he couldn't figure out why he could only see the corner of what looked to be a scarf.

The storm thinned, and he saw it more clearly. A red flannel saddle blanket on a gray horse. A man in a gray wool coat perched atop the saddle.

"Gable? Is that you?" Doc Haskins called out as the snow shrank back and a blinding light seared his eyes. The storm had broken.

Joshua's knees hit the earth in disbelief, because it wasn't from weakness or pain. See? He was one tough son of a bitch. Not even a blizzard could best him.

Even if it was a near thing, he admitted more truthfully to himself as he breathed deeply, battled off a wave of dizziness and took time to feel the sunlight wan on his face before he handed over the woman in his arms.

He knew by the look on the doc's face that it was too little, too late.

She'd hovered like this before in the dreamworld of darkness. The only sense left to her was her hearing; all else had faded. She heard voices. Two men, talking low. Not Ham. She tried to remember what had happened to him, how drunk he'd been, how violent. She couldn't recall. Only that she'd feared for her baby's life and then someone had come—Joshua Gable—and driven him away. Shot the gun out of his hand, disarmed him and knocked him to the ground.

She remembered in a distant way how Mr. Gable had knelt at her side, his tentative touch to her shoulder meant to comfort her, to let her know she needn't be afraid of him.

He'd protected her when she'd needed it the most. And while she'd witnessed the violence he was capable of, she saw too the kindness as he moved the broken piece of wood from the wagon that was pinning her down. Noticed the round of her stomach no longer disguised by the thick fall of her skirts, for the fabric was in disarray, and saw his pity.

Pity she did not need but knew this babe in her womb deserved. Consciousness had bled away as he'd gathered her into his arms and carried her. She'd remembered the last sounds of his boots crunching on the thick ice before silence reigned. And then awakening to an awareness of men's voices.

Yes, that was what had happened, she figured out now. Mr. Joshua Gable had returned with the doc in tow.

The voices faded and returned and warmth came with it. Like a fire hotly burning. She could hear the crackling of the seasoned cedar popping in the stove. And water, hot, sweet, seeping into her bones, lighting a river of pain in her midsection that made her afraid for her babe.

She would endure any pain, any hardship, any loss. As long as her little one remained safe beneath her heart.

Fierce love filled her and she held on when the clawing pain returned. Then the doctor laid something bitter on her tongue and the blackness reached out to imprison her.

But nothing—nothing—could diminish this love for her baby.

Just when he thought the chilblains couldn't get worse, they did. Joshua growled like a hungry bear fresh out of hibernation and he knew he was about as surly as one. He gulped down the bitter concoction Haskins had steeped for him. Nasty. The chalky, acrid taste clung to his tongue like ice to a roof and didn't let go.

That didn't improve his mood. The traveling pain in his feet and both hands could have been spikes being driven into his flesh over and over without end. Hardly pleasant. If it had been any other circumstance, he'd have roared in fury at the unrelenting pain, but the truth was, watching Claire Hamilton's life fade had silenced him.

"She lost too much blood. Some women do after a miscarriage," Doc said, his examination through as he washed up in the Hamiltons' tiny kitchen. "I can't imagine what she went through out there all alone. It's lucky you found her when you did."

"Luckier that you found us both when you did."

He poured two fingers of Ham's Jack Daniel's into a cup and tossed it back. The fire in his stomach took some of his attention away from the pain in the rest of his battered body. If he kept working and living at this pace, it would be time to put him out to pasture before General, who he'd best go out and check on.

Better than trying to imagine what Claire Hamilton

had suffered alone in the storm before he'd found her. Since it was all he could think about, a change of scenery might help. Because as bad as this pain was, it wasn't enough to keep his gaze from wandering toward the front room, where a fire blazed in the big stone hearth and, on the other side of the brushed-velvet sofa, he knew Claire lay motionless.

An odd feeling burrowed into his chest. Figuring it for pity, he jumped off the chair with a groan, the chilblain pain spiking new and his ankle tormenting him enough to chase away the hollow of feeling deep in his chest. He wasn't a man with feelings. He had one feeling—anger. And it drove him now as he lifted his jacket from the back of a chair.

But he hadn't taken two limping steps before he swung northward to where he could see the widow on her back with her knees elevated, draped in heated blankets. The blood stilled in his veins. "My grandmother will come sit with her, if you think there's time for that."

"It's hard to say why she's lasted this long." Haskins dried his hands on an embroidered towel and hung it back up on the dowel over the basin. "Are you gonna let me take a look at that ankle?"

"Maybe. When I get back from the barn."

"You just keep walkin' on it. That's sure to make it better." The doc rolled his eyes, as if he knew better.

Joshua had no time for a broken ankle. He had the last of the work to get done before the midwinter storms hit in earnest. Until Thanksgiving, a man could expect a lot of sunny days—not warm, mind you, but bright enough the snow would melt and give him plenty of time to finish up with leaky roofs and surprise chimney problems. Livestock moving and hauling in enough grain for the barn and supplies for the house. All of that required hard physical work. None of it would get done if he was favoring his ankle.

Why he didn't head straight to the door between the front room and the kitchen, Joshua couldn't explain. He found his boots heading north when they ought to turn east and the roaring heat from the hearth burned against his outer leg as he stared down at Claire.

He'd seen her unconscious and wounded too many times. He'd first thought the Hamilton brothers had found her, then he realized, when the doc explained, something equally sad had happened.

Losing the promise of a baby was no small thing. He was old enough to remember the brother that was still-born before Jordan—the last of the family—was born. And James's wife had miscarried twice.

The sorrow had been palpable the last time he'd seen that woman, even if she was a dreadful moneygrubbing leech—well, he'd promised his mother he would try not to dislike the woman so much, but it was like pushing a boulder uphill with his nose. He believed his sister-in-law embodied everything essentially female that he despised. Greed, manipulative behavior and selfishness.

But Claire looked so innocent and guileless lying beneath thick buffalo robes, she hardly made a shape beneath the blankets. He couldn't stop the roll of emotion—it had to be pity—that tumbled out of him. It was a surprise that he could feel even that. His heart had become too hard over the years. Ma said that it was a sorry result of not marrying, that a woman would have kept him from hardening up and spoiling like forgotten milk in the cellar.

He'd always figured it had more to do with his father's death. He'd been the one to find him, twisted in agony, dead and stiff with rigor mortis, and Joshua had lost his faith in any member of the human race the moment he'd spotted his father's body and pulled him into his arms.

So, why did he feel anything at all when he was near Claire? She was a lovely woman, but he'd been around plenty of lovely women. They were everywhere in town, in the stores, serving meals at the diners, and yet he'd never felt this spark before.

Obviously, it wasn't simply that Claire was a sight to behold, her skin like porcelain, her hair thick and lustrous and a beauty of its own. Maybe it was her vulnerability that appealed to him, since he'd witnessed Ham's brutality to her. Joshua wouldn't treat a rabid dog the way Hamilton had taken a whip to his wife. Maybe that was why he ached as he turned his back on her motionless form. Why he closed down his heart like a fire's damper and left the sparks to smolder out.

He pushed open the door, welcoming the biting sting of winter. The cold gave him something to think about besides the beautiful widow. He had enough troubles—his cracked ankle was killing him. And General had been pushed beyond his own strength. Once that happened, sometimes a horse was never the same.

Yes, he cared about his horse. They'd been buddies for a long time. And General had given his all to save them. What a great animal. Warmth edged into Joshua's heart as he climbed into the stall. His equine friend didn't acknowledge his presence, too exhausted to do more than blink.

"You did good, boy." Joshua eased down beside him and ran his hand along General's firm neck.

Maybe it wasn't right that a man's best friend was a horse, but they'd been through a lot together. He trusted no one like he did General. "I was gonna come back for you, buddy."

The gelding nickered low in his throat, as if he understood both the English language and the situation, the choice Joshua had had to make. "I couldn't believe my eyes when I saw you coming up behind us."

General nickered again and, with a painful-sounding sigh, closed his eyes. Drifted off to sleep.

A good horse. A better friend. Joshua creaked to his knees, limped through the cramped, dirty-smelling barn, and found a few horse blankets that hadn't been cleaned or aired, but left to gather dust in a corner. Ham had been a lazy rancher. God knows how he managed to have enough animals survive to keep this place.

Joshua shook the blankets out and covered General with them. Time would tell if he'd make it. Or have to be retired to pasture.

Loss. It clung to him like the ferocious air; it speared at him like the pain from his thawing flesh.

He'd take the Clydesdale back to the homestead. He had his conscience to ease and his family to protect.

And if he added a prayer for Claire's unlikely recovery, then it wasn't an actual, real prayer. Just more of a hope, for Joshua Gable was not a praying man. Life was a gamble, and he felt as if he were holding the lowest cards in the deck next to a dealer's king and an ace.

Not good betting odds, but life was far from a sure thing. A wager everyone lost in the end.

Chapter Five

The sound of a gunshot brought her to awareness again. The single shot had seemed to come from far away, too. She knew instinctively that she was home safe, that the single, distinctive pop had come from behind the barn. It was Ham.

Ham being shot. Her mind spun forward, as if it were a nightmare, bringing her to the edge of the grave where her husband's casket gleamed in the failing daylight. Where snowflakes began to fall one by one as if to bury the image from her sight. The confrontation with her mother-in-law, Ham's brother's confronting Joshua, the horror of collapsing in the snow as contractions seized control of her midsection—

No. That had been a nightmare. None of it was true. She couldn't let it be. Because if the baby was gone, then she'd lost everything that could ever matter. She would be alone without anyone to love. She had so much love in her heart. So much she'd planned on giving to her child. And now…

It was gone. She was empty, hollow. Her mind had been playing tricks on her. Letting her hold on to what had been long gone. What should have been a terrible wave of grief seemed to be at a distance, too. She'd learned sometimes the greatest of pain was that way. A sudden shock that kept a person from feeling the initial blast of agony.

But eventually the shock would break away and then there would be no escape.

The sounds came again. The door, she realized. Someone was approaching the door. It wasn't Ham; he wasn't here anymore. The funeral, the ride home, all of it had been real. Her mind kept trying to reject what was only fact. The shock faded away and the grief came in a hot, strangled wave. She was suddenly alive, the darkness was gone and tears rolled up from her soul.

Alive, she opened her eyes to stare at the stone wall hearth in the cabin. At Ham's six-point elk head hanging above the mantel. His collections of knives and revolvers and his tin of tobacco. The fire roared in colors of orange, yellow and red. Flames writhed and twisted in on themselves, and she thought hell would have fires like that.

She shivered, although she was not cold, but her heart was freezing, as if buried six feet under snow. Wetness rolled down her face, warm rivulets that trailed over her cheeks and ran along her jaw and along her neck to drip onto the pillow. Someone had brought one from the bedroom—the pillow slip had her favorite pattern she'd embroidered. A spray of honeysuckle, their trumpetlike flowers delicate, their vines curlicued, framing the mated pair of hummingbirds.

The two birds had seemed so happy together, that was why she'd chosen the pattern when she'd made the pillow slips for her hope chest, naive girl that she'd been. She rubbed the tip of her finger along the hue of tawny thread she'd used to stitch the outline of the female bird's chest. The design was easier to concentrate on than the man whose boots knelled in slow, steady steps closer.

Joshua Gable. She didn't need to rip her gaze away from the embroidered design to know it was him. She could feel his presence as if it were the radiant heat from the fire.

The image of how he'd come to her rescue that first night, protecting her from Ham's drunken violence, telegraphed into her mind. The image of him towering above her at the funeral, genuine concern etched into his strong face, swept into her mind's eye. Followed by the feel of his iron-solid arms around her, carrying her through the blizzard.

Maybe it was this almost dreamlike place she was in, maybe that was why she could sense a strange connection to him. Why her very being seemed to turn toward him, like a sunflower to the dawn.

He stood over her now, and she could feel the shape of him, thrown like a shadow on her skin where his body blocked the stifling heat from the fire. She'd never felt such a thing before. Surely never with Ham, even before they'd married when she'd thought herself so much in love with him.

Maybe it was simply because she felt so alone. Isolated and drifting and he was a man made of granite, anchored and unyielding. Seemingly good and decent and strong, when she was used to being around Ham, who was not one of those things.

And she admired the good qualities in a man, for they had once seemed rare. And now that she knew the truth about men, they were even rarer still. Or maybe it was because he'd helped her when no one else had or would. When her neighbors and acquaintances and family all looked the other way over the years, ignoring the bruises marking her face or the way she shielded her sore ribs or forearm or leg. She'd craved help when there was none.

When others, including her own aunt, would see her situation and turn away. *It ain't no one's concern,* she could hear her aunt's voice in her head, the one time Claire had outright asked for help early in her marriage. *The reverend said, what God joined together let no man put asunder. You lay in this bed of marriage you made, jus' like the rest a us.*

And Joshua had not stood aside. He'd not looked the other way. Back when she'd been young and dreamy and believed in the fairy tales and the novels of romance she used to read, before she'd ever heard Ham's name, she would have thought him her champion. A hero. A man to admire. But she'd learned that no man was that. No man was that great, that strong, that good. Men didn't need to be kind to get what they want. Men didn't love. Men made the laws and the rules, and as far as she could tell, men cared only about themselves.

And if she saw something admirable in Joshua Gable, then it was only illusion. Or her own wishful thinking, nothing more.

So, why did her entire being prickle with awareness of him? She was foolish, that's why, because deep down, beyond the pain and the weakness and the miscarriage, when it would have been easier to give in to the darkness, she'd chosen life. Because beyond all of her experience, she could not let go of the tiny thread of hope she clung to with both hands.

That even when the logical, undeniable fact was that she'd lost everything and there was no reason to hope, she did hope.

Tears burned in the corners of her eyes and tapped onto the pillow. The roar and crackle of the fire filled her ears. The spikes of pain lancing her entire body came to full awareness and she could smell the wood smoke, the soft down of the buffalo blanket covering her, the scorching heat from the warming irons tucked alongside her and the gnawing agony of her unfreezing feet as if a bear were feasting on her bare toes.

"Claire?"

His baritone rumbled low and resonant and whiskey-rough, and the vibration of it seemed to sink inside her like a sensual stroke.

No. It was instinct to protect herself, to stop the flood of sensation into her drained heart. She was vulnerable and weak, and that was the reason she was responding to him so stridently.

Don't turn to him. She knew it would only make her more defenseless to the caress of his voice, the fiction of his presence, and only stroke the sparks of hope fighting for life within her. Fighting to keep that undefeatable hope from rising up.

She heard the rustle of his denim trousers and the creak of boot leather as Joshua Gable knelt. The cool shadow his big body had tossed over her was gone—the heat radiated across her entire being. She did not know where he knelt, only that he was close, that he was watching her in a way that felt as tangible as a physical touch. She knew he could hardly miss the tears gleaming on her cheek and trickling sideways down her face.

Why did this man, this stranger, know the most intimate piece of her life? Her family did not know it, Ham's family did not know she'd miscarried, let alone that she'd been pregnant. Ham was not a proud father-to-be. He had no love for mewling brats, he'd told her. He hadn't wanted to hear more about the pregnancy, and she'd watched the exciting early changes her body went through alone.

Eleven weeks later, it was as if there had never been a new life started within her, at least to those looking in from the outside on her life.

And Joshua Gable's knowledge and pity lapped over her like a shallow lake's warm waters in mid-August. Lulling and comforting and sweet enough to sink into, and it was tempting to give in when his baritone rolled through her again.

"I have to ask you a few questions." Joshua Gable cleared his throat, and that rough sound moved through her, too.

She squeezed her eyes more tightly shut. *Don't give in to the impulse, Claire. Don't believe in him.*

"I need you to answer honestly, no matter what." He paused, as if to let his words sink in. "Did the Hamilton brothers have anything to do with you lying in the snow? Did they pressure you? Did they hurt you? Did they follow you?"

Another man's voice, placid and warning, came from the other side of the hearth. "This wasn't from direct physical trauma, Joshua. She'd been having problems right from the start."

The doctor. He'd been so quiet that she'd forgotten he was here. She'd assumed he'd left after Joshua did some time ago. It was hazy, but if the doc had stayed, she couldn't imagine how much time had passed. And how much she might owe him, a bill she could not pay.

Worry about that later, she told herself, opening her eyes, wondering if there was any money at all. She did not know where Ham kept the earnings he made on the ranch. She did not know what bills were still owed, or even if the land was mortgaged. It was too much to think about right now, not when Joshua answered, and the impact of his words rocked her hard.

"Doc, if those boys get it in their harebrained heads that she was somehow responsible for Ham being shot, they'll come after her. They won't care if they're right or wrong, they'll come just the same."

"I've got to get to my rounds." A chair creaked in the direction of the kitchen, and Doc Haskins sighed, as if he were bone weary. "Thanks to your grandmother, Claire will have the nursing care she requires. But she needs protection. At least until those boys settle down. You didn't say, Joshua. Are you hurt? They roughed you up a bit."

"I can handle them." Joshua's answer rang with the

confidence of a man used to taking care of things. Used to prevailing. "Claire, answer me. Have those boys threatened you or approached you? It doesn't matter if they've warned you to stay quiet. I intend to keep you safe."

That made her look at him. "Why? I don't even know you."

"You do. You know everything that matters."

"You're right, Mr. Gable. I know that you're a man." The effort of turning her head brought a sick dizziness that gripped her hard. Her skull felt hollow. She didn't think any emotion could penetrate the fog of bleakness and resignation that melded together, but anger seemed strong enough to lift her off the pillow and to make her forget the pain.

She met his eyes, strength for strength, and held them. "You're a man, and that means you want something."

Joshua Gable, kneeling at the foot of the sofa, paled. Whether in guilt or surprise, she could not tell. Only that his steel irises darkened to the flint of a thundercloud and his nostrils flared like a bull's, ready to charge.

Whatever initial response he'd had to her honest statement had changed to rage quickly. She'd been a wife long enough to know the signs of it. The quick rise and fall of his chest, the fisting of his hands, the way he seemed to swell up from hips to shoulders, all male, all fight.

She did not flinch. She was no longer afraid of anything. Her gaze remained on his, an unspoken challenge. She did not blink or look away as he cleared his throat again, inhaled long and slow.

Interesting. Perhaps this man would only rage at a woman who was his wife, his to dominate and subjugate. With his mask of composure in place, he seemed to struggle until he found the right words. "I only want to help you."

"I don't believe you." Her eyes felt dry and gritty, but still she did not blink. "You asked me to be honest with you, and so I will. No, the Hamilton brothers did not approach me, although I expect they will. Now, you be truthful. What do you want? The livestock? The land?"

Joshua's eyes darkened from thundercloud ominous to unreadable black as his pupils expanded. A bad sign. She waited, wondering what he would do as he unfolded his big frame and rose straight up, his handsome, rugged face tightening into pure granite. Like the mountain peaks outside her window, he was immense, immovable, dominating.

"My grandmother is in the kitchen. She stopped by to check on you, saw that you weren't well and made up her mind to stay. I had intended to apologize for her belligerent ways, but I misjudged you. You'll get along with her just fine."

He gave a curt, single nod, dismissing her, and strode away, giving the door a solid clap as he shut it behind him. Gone, he was gone from her presence, from the room and from her house.

Then why did she still feel the shadow of him falling over her? Why did her focus remain on the door as if she could sense him on the other side of the thick oak panels, standing with his hands on his hips?

Why did a sense of guilt haunt her? She'd been right to be blunt. He was not her husband. He was not family. Perhaps he wasn't used to outspoken women, but then his grandmother was the most outspoken female Claire had ever met. So, perhaps he simply hadn't expected her to see through his ruse so easily.

He wanted something. All men did. She wanted to believe otherwise, but she'd learned a hard lesson about the other gender. She would not make the mistake of thinking there was any good in them. She'd lost her baby, the only thing that had mattered to her, but she had survived. She was still here. She would rest, regain her strength and go on with her life. She would never trust another man again.

"That boy always has a temper." Adelaide Gable limped into the room, balancing a tray as if she'd done it all her life. "Always has had, I'm afraid. Comes from bein' the oldest. He didn't have an older brother to put him in his place. Lord knows I've done my best and failed miserably."

With a wink, Adelaide cracked a smile, belying the severity of her words. "He's grown on me, what can I say? He looks too much like his grandfather, my dear husband. Here's a spot of tea. Can you hold the cup?"

"Yes." Claire's hand trembled when she tried to lift it.

"Never you mind. Let me take care of you. I've had the same sadness, my dear. Wasn't able to carry four babies. Then I had Joshua's father. So it doesn't mean you'll be childless for sure." The older woman's brusque tone softened as she stirred a generous dollop of honey into the tea with great effort before holding the cup to Claire's lips.

Four miscarriages? She couldn't imagine, but she saw the weight of it on Adelaide's wreathed face, the sorrow that remained after decades. Claire managed to swallow the sweet tea that ran across her dry, swollen-feeling tongue before collapsing back into the pillows.

"You did nothing wrong." There was a clink of the ironware cup into its saucer and the brush of Adelaide's surprisingly gentle hand on Claire's brow. "A doctor told me once that whether a new life takes firm root or not, it is out of our hands. Sleep, dear girl, and put your conscience to rest. One day there will be a next time. Another baby to wish on."

Scalding tears burned in her throat, keeping her from answering. Claire forced her tight muscles to relax. Let the sorrow lift upward and out of her. She held on to Adelaide's unprecedented kindness with both hands.

The older woman was wrong, there would be no more babies, no more wishes. The only comfort Claire could take from that knowledge was that she would never again have a husband, a man in her life to drain the joy out of it.

Comforted by that thought, and that thought alone, she sank downward, welcoming the numbing darkness of sleep's warm embrace.

Chapter Six

When Joshua had thought the day couldn't get much worse, he'd been wrong. With Claire Hamilton's razor-sharp words embedded deep, he headed out into the bitter cold, taking advantage of the break between one storm and the next one gathering swiftly on the northwest horizon.

Not even the frigid temperatures could numb the widow's remarks, which stuck with him like a handful of needle burrs. She'd accused him of helping her for some ulterior motive.

Did she really think he was after more livestock to take care of? More land to tend and protect? No, he had more than enough to keep him busy. The last thing he needed was to try to pressure a new widow out of her rightful property or to be unjustly accused of being that kind of low-down scoundrel.

Well, the pretty little widow could insult him all she wanted. That didn't change his obligations—self-imposed obligations, it was true, but if he didn't make sure she was protected, who would?

Troubled, Joshua turned away from the fading rays of sundown and circled around back of the stable. Haystacks with their rounded tops crowded together, on the east side of the barn and not the northwest, which would have better insulated the animals from the harsh winds.

Ham sure wasn't much of a rancher. As far as Joshua could tell, his work was halfhearted at best. There was a visible hole in the barn roof, not more than a few bushels of grain—barely enough to get through the rest of the month. And not an animal in sight. He hadn't even bothered to bring in the stock for the winter. Ham probably figured he would leave the animals to graze as long as snowdrifts weren't burying the cattle alive. Less work to do, but tougher on the livestock, and the risk of loss was pretty great.

Not that he expected Ham to have been a model cattleman. Not if the slaughtered bodies of sheep, which he'd been responsible for, was an indication. No, Joshua thought Ham was about as low a varmint as they came, but here he was, probably standing on the spot where the man had died. Where he'd been shot point-blank.

I should have stayed longer that night. Joshua rubbed the back of his neck, where his scarf had grown itchy. It wasn't the first time he'd thought that. It wasn't the first time guilt had hung heavy about his neck. He'd thought Claire a victim in all this, and her harshness toward him a few moments ago didn't erase the fact that she'd lived a sad life. She didn't need to say a single word for him to know the truth.

The cabin where she and Ham had lived, the home she'd made with her husband, the house she kept, had not one feminine article in it. Nothing that obviously belonged to a woman. No tatted lace doilies sat on the tabletop. No crocheted afghan was thrown over the back of the sofa. And no scraps of ribbon or delicate porcelain knickknacks picked up dust on shelves.

It was as if a woman didn't live there at all. What kind of life was that?

"Hey, big brother." It was Jordan lumbering out from the back barn door, batting hay off his coat, as if he'd been lying down on the job. "I got the horses ready for the night. General got up to eat. That's a good sign, eh?"

"Yeah. Thanks." Whatever his faults, Jordan had a special way with the horses. "I appreciate that you sacrificed a long nap to help out."

"Hey, I do what I can. As long as I don't break a sweat." Thinking himself so funny, Jordan winked. "Do you want me to stay here for the night? You'd have another gun in case the Hamiltons come callin'."

Joshua tried to imagine how Jordan would act in a gunfight. How did he tell his youngest brother, who thought himself so fine and manly at nineteen, that their grandmother would be all the gun power Joshua would need at his side? If Jordan knew that, it would take some of the crow out of the rooster. As much as he wanted Jordan to grow up, Joshua knew how frail a man's self-opinion was at that age.

"What I need is to have someone keep watch back home in case the Hamiltons bring any trouble there." Joshua didn't think the brothers would be foolish enough to show up at his family's house, not when two more of the Gable brothers still lived there. They were a bunch of bachelors who knew how to use a gun and to defend what was theirs. "If you head out now, you'll beat the storm home."

"What do you want me to tell Ma?"

"That I'm staying to protect Granny."

"Right. She's the best shot in the entire county." Jordan rolled his eyes, pulled his hat down closer to his head as the wind gusted and brought tiny snowflakes. They shifted through the air like powdered sugar. "Need me to bring anything back come morning?"

"Yeah. Stop by the mercantile and have Shannon charge up some groceries for Mrs. Hamilton, here. And bill it to me."

"To you?" Jordan's brow shot up an inch. "But why? You're not a neighbor. We live on the other side of the county."

"I lease the public grazing lands not far from here. You know that. That makes us neighbors enough. Besides, Granny is the best one to be helping Claire out when she's so infirm. Do you want to leave Granny out here with few staples and angry Hamiltons threatening to strike?"

"Okay, okay!" Jordan held up his mittened hands as if he were a guilty man caught shoplifting. "Golly, you don't have to get all het up about it. I'll drop by sometime in the mornin', if it's not blizzarding."

"Make it early. It's about time you got your lazy ass up before nine o'clock."

Jordan seemed unaffected by the insult, just as Joshua

knew he would be. Jordan took life easy, one day at a time, without a worry about what tomorrow would bring.

Must be nice, he thought, heading toward the back of the cabin. There had been some split wood, scrap wood mostly, stacked in the lean-to. Surely there had to be a seasoned pile split and stacked somewhere. Or a supply of coal laid in for the long winter. But there was only a covered coal bin mostly empty of coal. Enough to see them through a three-day blizzard, no more.

Figures. Joshua added coal to the mental list in his head. One thing was for sure—Claire Hamilton wasn't likely to be making a weekly trip into town for supplies, not for a long while. The doc said she wasn't out of danger yet. And remembering how pale the woman had been—more of an ashen gray—and how she'd struggled to lift her head from the pillow, he knew she was lucky to be alive at all.

Fate had put her into his path more than once. He should have stayed that night to make sure she was good and safe although she had needed the doctor. Then she wouldn't have had to shoot her husband in self-defense and pay the price for that action.

The plod of horses on hard-packed snow echoed in the hush. It must be Jordan on his way out, he thought as he hopped up the back steps. When he heard the rattle of harnesses and the distinctive squeak squee-eak of a buggy wheel, he scrubbed his hand over his face and hoped he was imagining the sound. It couldn't be his sister. What would she be doing way out here? She didn't know Claire Hamilton, did she?

He peered around the side of the cabin and sure

enough, there she was, Betsy, his only sister, in the seat of her little buggy, guiding her gelding up to the Hamiltons' front door. The boot of the buggy was overflowing from the bags of laundry she'd picked up, presumably on her route, and she drew the horse to a halt and set the brake, unaware that he was watching her.

His little sister. He'd protected and looked after her all his life, and he thought he knew her better than anyone else. They were the closest in age among their siblings. They were the oldest and so when their father died, she had pitched in to help, too. To keep the family together and their father's land and legacy intact.

And now she'd turned into an independent woman living in town with her own laundry business and her upcoming wedding to plan. It was the wedding that stuck in his craw like a foul worm. No man on this earth was good enough for his Betsy. He was the first to admit his feelings on the subject, but she'd chosen an inappropriate man. An ex-convict and an outcast. How could someone like that ever be close to being good enough for her?

Hold your tongue and your temper, man. He could feel his anger rising, and it was enough to melt the airy snowflakes sifting weightlessly in the air. Enough to send the blizzard speeding in the other direction.

He had problems, all right, and they weren't only with the land, the livestock and taking care of the family. Keeping his sister out of trouble was an impossible job, one he'd failed at so far.

"Joshua! Is that you spying on me on the other side of the door?" Betsy breezed toward him, despite her thick layers of wool coverings. Her eyes were as bright as sapphires and her cheeks were rosy and, he feared, not only from the cold. "What on earth are you doing here?"

"Ham's funeral was today. Granny and I are assisting the widow."

"There's trouble?" Genuine distress chased the brightness from her features. "Mrs. Hamilton is such a nice lady. Has grief disabled her?"

"If you'd attended the funeral, you would know."

"I had my delivery route." She shrugged one slim shoulder easily, as if it couldn't be helped. As if a woman in his family had to work!

It grated on him, that was for sure, but he bit back his opinion on that. They'd already argued over it enough. "Hamilton's brothers seem to think he was murdered."

"I thought he fell from a horse, or something like that."

Joshua decided not to mention the bullet hole he'd put in Ham's shoulder, since the doc hadn't mentioned it and he'd been the one reporting to the sheriff on the body. "The Hamiltons aren't the most logical of folks. What are you doing here?"

"Mrs. Hamilton hired me to do her laundry, because of her condition. Do you think it would be imposing to disturb her at a time like this? I already separated out her husband's things, so she wouldn't find them when she went to put her clothing away."

That was his sister, thoughtful and sweet. How had she wound up engaged to the wrong sort of man? She claimed it was true love, but he didn't buy it. He feared she was throwing her life away, to wind up as sad and miserable as Claire Hamilton was. Except for one small difference—no man would dare raise a hand to his little sister. Not while he drew breath. "Granny's in with her."

Betsy's eyes widened. Her mouth drew into an *O*. That could only mean one thing. They both knew it. Granny looked after those who needed it from time to time. She had a way with herbs and a healing touch, for all her outlandish behavior. She liked to say she could shoot you and patch you up and cook you a hearty supper, all in the space of an hour.

"This is no time to be bothering Mrs. Hamilton. I hate to see this happen to any woman, but she's all alone except for an aunt or something. She would have sure wanted a child." Betsy ambled right up to him, unaware that his earlier anger still boiled beneath the surface, and laid her hand on his arm. "I'm glad you're here, helping out. She's such a kind lady."

"Some might say so, but I've seen her real side." The side he was convinced was the true nature of woman. It disappointed him, he realized, that Claire was no different from other women. Not even from his own dear sister. The more she wanted something, the more ruthless and blind she became to all else. "I'll take her clothes in. You hurry home before the storm breaks."

"I don't want to disturb Mrs. Hamilton. If you'll set the laundry to be done out on the back porch, I'll come by and fetch it. Or, you can bring it into town with you."

"You're determined to turn me into an accomplice. I don't approve of your business. I'm not going to start making deliveries for you."

"Then do it for Mrs. Hamilton. Since you've seen the real her, then you know she's the nicest person. I hate to say it, but her husband's death may be a blessing in disguise for her."

"You wouldn't be the first to think so."

"I'll get her things. It's really starting to snow."

As Betsy hurried away, snow danced around her, tiny dry flakes that spoke of a long snowfall to come. And he'd be stuck here, standing guard, making sure the woman inside the modest plank-and-board cabin remained safe.

Whether she wanted him to or not. Whether she believed he had an ulterior motive or not.

Betsy left the clean clothes, gave him a quick hug and hurried away. She had a long way to go before reaching town. He tried not to think of where she might have been, visiting her fiancé who lived alone in those mountains, now lost in the storm's veil.

Hours later, after he'd fed the fire in the front room and gratefully gulped down a huge bowl of his grandmother's Irish stew, he had plenty of time alone with no woman to trouble him. Just the long cold night, where a full white moon peeked between the traveling wisps of torn clouds and brushed silver on the sleeping prairie. No danger could lurk unseen on this night.

With his Winchester at his side, he watched and he waited. Trouble was coming. He could sense it like the flakes on the wind. He'd be ready.

She woke to the final chime of the mantel clock. Not knowing which hour it was—perhaps midnight? Or one?—she sensed it was not the quiet musical ring of the clock that had awoken her.

The fire glowed, burned down to heavy chunks of gleaming coals snapping in the grate, and cast a menacing dark orange shine upon the hearthstones.

A snoring sound came from the wing chair, which stood alongside the hearth where the shadows seemed darkest. Claire tried to remember if the doc had left. She remembered overhearing him say he couldn't stay. Joshua Gable had stormed out the door. She clearly remembered that.

Then whose leather boots were those on the ottoman pulled before the chair? The size of the man's riding boots was small—certainly not Joshua Gable's. And she doubted that either of Ham's brothers, who surely had bigger feet than that, would have broken in to fall placidly asleep in the chair.

Before fear could take hold, she realized Adelaide Gable had promised to stay and a shadow moved through the far edge of her vision. She snapped her head in that direction, causing a horrible hollow pain and sickening dizziness. She saw only a faint, barely noticeable lightness at the big square of the window. Snowfall.

Had she imagined it? Her heart began thudding wildly in her chest, as panicked as a trapped bird, and that was how she felt. Caught, unable to escape or fight. She was so weak she squeezed her eyes closed and locked her jaw against the nausea rising from her stomach. Leaning back into the pillow helped. Forcing her breathing to slow helped. But now her pulse was thundering in her aching head.

What if she hadn't imagined a moving shadow? What if it was the Hamiltons come to take what they felt was theirs? Law didn't matter much to those people. They put no stock in rules and justice. If they came in the dead of night to put her out of her house, how could she stop them in her weak condition? She couldn't even crawl off the sofa to fetch Ham's gun to defend herself.

I intend to keep you safe. Joshua's promise came back to her now. Or, was it more like an offer? One she'd turned down. She remembered how indomitable he'd seemed with those wide logger's shoulders of his and the dark crop of hair framing his rugged face.

He'd walked so tall, in her view, when he'd stood up to Ham. When he'd met Ham's brothers' violence stone for stone. He was a man who looked as if he could have made good on that promise easily.

I shouldn't have been so blunt with Joshua Gable. Then she wouldn't be alone with this problem now. Not that she would ever use anyone, but she didn't have to drive him away. She could have accepted his help. She could have found a way to compensate him. Her words came back to her, hard and shameful. *You're a man, and that means you want something.*

What a terrible way to treat a man who'd done nothing but help her. She knew there was a reason behind his offer, but she wouldn't have minded paying what he wanted. She'd just…looked at him and seen a man, any man. She'd been wrong to malign Joshua so easily. He may have his own reasons for helping her.

Well, as it was, she was now alone with an old

woman to protect. Somehow, she had to figure out if trouble was outside her door and, if so, to stop it.

If only she knew how to use a gun. Ham's revolvers, if she could reach them, were hung across the nail next to the front door. Two of his many rifles were below the elk head. Another—his older, single-loading pistol—sat on the edge of the mantel. She'd be more effective throwing them at Ham's brothers than trying to shoot them.

Reed and Rick were excellent marksmen. Unless she got in a lucky surprise shot, she'd be far too outgunned to risk it. No, she'd have to defeat them another way. This was her home and her land.

Hers alone now. She had nowhere else to go. She'd been homeless before, cast out with her mother after her father's death. She'd lived in the back of an abandoned store off of Second Street in a little town in the Dakotas until the fever that had taken Pa had drained the life from Ma as well.

Yes, she knew what it meant to be without a roof over her head. She was no longer a child. She was a capable woman, and she was not about to be bullied around by anyone. Not ever again.

If only she could lift her head farther off the pillow. *Come on, Claire. Try harder. You have to do this.* The hollow pounding in her head increased until it felt as if someone was standing behind her with an ax and swinging.

Her temples squeezed with agony and she collapsed back into the pillows. Okay, she wasn't going to be able to stand upright. But she couldn't lie here. What options did that leave? Staying here helplessly while the Hamiltons seized her house and put her out into the wintry night?

No, not while she drew breath. All the steel she'd developed from living beneath Ham's boot had not made her a victim, nor had it made her weak. She hadn't realized how strong her will had become. Like iron shaped in a forge, she pushed the pillows and thick furs onto the floor and rolled.

More pain, but she refused to give in to the jagged claws of it. She took a moment to catch her breath, but it wouldn't come. *Move anyway, Claire. You have to do this.*

She had no choice. Since she couldn't stand, and her knees were like water, there was only one way to move forward. Her body screamed in protest as she pushed her right arm forward, her forearm scraping against the rough floorboards. With all of her steely will, she dragged her body forward.

One inch. Two inches. Then there was no more strength. She collapsed, her chin resting against the wood. Dizziness tormented her. Nausea overwhelmed her. The hammer inside her skull was breaking through the bone. A cold sweat popped out on her skin and her vision wavered.

I will not lose consciousness. She clawed ahead, hardly moving an inch, but it was progress. She slid her left arm along the cracked grain of a floorboard.

A nail head had popped up and scraped her skin, but she didn't feel it. Her muscles were trembling. Her heartbeat came so fast, too fast, and the air rushing into her lungs seemed to stall.

Keeping fighting, Claire. But her body became fluid,

watery without substance. Her fingernails dug into the edge of the braided rug and she pulled with all her might.

But she didn't move.

Chapter Seven

He knew they would come.

Joshua peeled off his extra layer of woolen gloves meant to keep his hands somewhat warm. He gave his fingers a good stretch. He'd trusted his instincts and that had put him and Claire at an advantage.

The pair of brothers had some skill. It hurt to admit it, since he thought so little of the Hamiltons. Whatever those men were, they knew how to sneak up on a man in the dead of night. Too bad for them he was waiting for them and he knew just how to keep watch. He'd been protecting his animals from rustlers, predators and everything else for more years than he could count.

He drew his rifle into position, supporting the barrel, careful not to make a sound. The brothers were ignorant of his position on the hill just behind the house, elevated enough that he had a bird's-eye view of the landscape and could clearly see both cabin doors.

He was more than ready. The chambers were loaded, and he had more bullets tucked into place on his .45 holster, strapped to his thigh. Jammed in his left coat pocket, he had extra bullets he'd made to carry a special punch.

That's right, boys. Come a little closer.

He dusted the snow on the site's metal rim and slowly swept the barrel's scope down the hillside until he had both brothers sited in the crosshairs.

They were moving fast. No horses, no packs, just a lot of gun power. They must have left their horses down below, out of sight—no, they would have also brought a wagon mounted on snow skids, he realized, although he hadn't heard a harness in the resounding silence of the night. Probably used rope instead of proper harnessing. It's what he would have done.

But keeping to the fence line, using the split rails for cover, was just plain lazy. The brothers assumed they only needed to be quiet enough not to warn Claire of their approach, and to keep out of sight of the windows. They were heading to the back door.

It didn't take a genius to see what they intended. They probably even knew where the key was hidden, so their trespassing would be quiet. With any luck, they planned to surprise Claire in her bedroom, which was just inside the back door and off the kitchen.

They'd never get that far. Whatever their plans were, it was his job to stop them.

Remembering how quick one of them had been to try to shoot him in the back, Joshua was glad his back was solidly against a fifteen-foot-tall granite bolder that jutted out of the concave hillside. The boys made no sound as they kept low, rapidly moving and using hand signals as the taller one—Reed—took the lead.

The fools weren't even looking for trouble. Joshua shook his head in disdain. Those men deserved what they got. It would be best if he could just pull the trigger and take care of the situation from here.

But best wasn't always right, although he thought of the woman inside the cabin, weak and in pain, and how those men's brother had treated her. He knew that they would not be kind to Claire. Rage built behind his eyes, remembering the tone of her hurtful words.

How badly she must have been treated to hold such an opinion. Not even a woman with a sharp tongue ought to be treated badly by a man. He didn't much like the gender—thought they were hardly the fairer and weaker sex—but they were smaller against a man's greater size.

And so he would shed no tear if tonight he sent one or two more Hamiltons to hell where they belonged.

Snow whispered from the dark heavens, making not so much as a hush as it fell on the white iridescent earth. The snowflakes seemed to give off their own light. He knew it was the faint glow from the clouds where the moon hid, and the ice of the flakes reflecting what light there was, making the midnight world shine like a black pearl and giving him enough illumination to see well.

The brothers had reached the fence line closest to the house. The dark silhouette of the leader disappeared as he hunched down behind a thick post, studying the lay of the backyard. The cabin was dark and silent, so why did he hesitate?

Joshua's heart gave a thump of realization. Maybe Reed could sense his presence. The bastard just couldn't tell where the danger was lurking. Joshua fought down a grin. Now it was going to get interesting. He didn't mind the challenge. He was ready, and he wanted a little justice. The gun in his hands remained steady and sure, camouflaged well in the shadows.

Come on. Just try to take her. His finger leaned against the trigger, ready as Reed lifted up like a gopher out of its hole to get a better peek at his surroundings.

One wrong move and you're mine, boys. He willed them to move, but they stayed low and looked to the road, as if they were expecting someone else. This would be a hitch to his plan, but he was prepared for that, too. He lowered his rifle a notch so he could scan the landscape freely.

No sign of anyone. That didn't mean they weren't there. He waited, neck prickling, straining his senses to hear, see, scent approaching danger.

It came in the form of the shadow moving in from the north, crossing the driveway and ducking between the rails. The deputy. Reed raised a hand in a show of welcome and the pair hunkered down, heads together, repeating rifles held handy and ready.

Three to one. Not the best odds, but Joshua would take them. He waited, determined and focused. Watching to see how the men intended to proceed. Waiting to see how he could use that to his advantage.

They broke up and moved in three different directions. The deputy headed back to the road—maybe to the barn, Joshua figured.

Now, wasn't that interesting? He hadn't noticed anything of interest or value in that unkempt place. Maybe he ought to have looked a little harder. Surely there was something that had brought the lawman out tonight—and it was important enough to trespass for.

The brothers broke up. The tallest headed to the front, the other came up the draw between the house and the hillside, moving as if he didn't expect anyone to be pulling a gun on him. Rick wasn't the smartest brother, but he was the meanest. *At least I get to take him out of the bet first.*

Joshua waited, knowing his steps before he made them. Moving like lightning, fast and silent, he drove the barrel of the Winchester into the back hollow of Rick's neck. "Move. Go on. Give me a reason to pull this trigger."

Rick froze. "Gable. Might have known it was you."

"Might have. Should have done some scouting first and you might have noticed the extra horses in the barn." An owl's hoot broke the silence, sounding on the other side of the roofline, and Joshua cocked his head, listening. The signal that the other Hamilton brother was in place, maybe?

Rick remained silent, perhaps his signal in return that something had gone wrong. He continued to clutch his rifle, his tension palpable. He didn't so much as blink.

"You're disappointin' me, Rick. I was sure hopin' to send you to your just reward. Drop the gun. *Do it.*" He drilled the Winchester's nose harder into vertebrae. The gun thudded to the ground, the sound low but distinctive enough to bring the other brother running.

"On the ground. Hands behind your back. *Now.*" He caught Rick's upper arm and helped him along, kneeing him to the snow and snapping the fencing wire into place around one wrist, then the other. With his free hand, he wound the man's hands tight.

Joshua dug his boot heel into the man's upper spine. "Make a sound, and I'm coming back to quiet you for good."

Satisfied he'd stopped the man from entering Claire's house, he raised his rifle and sensed the danger before his eyes could discern it from the thick shadows near the corner of the cabin. The hairs on the back of his neck prickled and he raised his gun, ready to fire, meeting trouble head-on.

Stretched out on the floor, Claire struggled to make her quaking limbs move. Her fingertips were curled into the edge of the carpet, but no matter how much she commanded her arms to pull, they disobeyed. Her muscles remained slack.

No matter how she tried, she couldn't move any part of her. It was as if her bones had lost their substance. Her head cracked with a strange, bone-splitting pain and her vision dimmed at the edges, so that it was as if she were looking through a glass at the hearth.

Not a promising turn. The glowing coals writhed and brightened as if mocking her, for they were so infinitely far away.

Don't give up now.

But her vision dimmed at the edges. Just four more feet. A distance she'd crossed easily this morning. The iron poker hung from its metal hook too far away to do her any good. It may as well have been on the opposite side of the earth for the chance she had of reaching it.

You can't give up. She thought of what she had left to lose. It wasn't nearly equal to what she'd lost, not by a long shot, but she had to keep trying. She rested a moment, gathered the shards of her strength and pulled with all her might. The rug stretched beneath her grip, and a hot sweat broke out across her face.

She'd given it every bit of will and might she had, but her chin was still resting solidly on the plank floor. Her fingers were caught in the edge of the rug and she hadn't moved an inch.

I can't do it. Pain telegraphed through her like electricity, snapping and searing. She'd lost so much blood that she could feel the strange galloping drum of her heart, fast and shallow.

As much as it shamed her, she had to admit she needed help. All she could see of Adelaide was her boots on the ottoman. She hadn't moved at all, slumbering in the corner. The tough woman's kindness had been unexpected but appreciated and she hated now to disturb the older woman's sleep.

What if she'd imagined the sound? Then how would she explain this to the elderly lady who'd done so much? *Then again, what if I didn't imagine it?* That realization sank like a stone to the bottom of her stomach. How was she going to defend herself, an older lady and the home, from men every bit as ruthless as Ham had been?

That's when she heard it. The blast of gunfire on the other side of the kitchen wall. She hadn't imagined it.

The Hamiltons. They'd come. To take her land and her animals, her home and everything inside it. That only left one question. What did they intend to do to her?

They were men in their prime, and even before her pregnancy, she could never have fought one Hamilton brother and won, let alone both of them.

And now, she was helpless. Her mouth opened to shout, to scream, but no sound came out. Her voice was gone. Adelaide lay undisturbed and silent.

That's when she felt the faint vibration of a man's step on the other side of the door. Then she heard a muffled thud of what could only be a man's boot on wooden planks, a sound she barely could make out above the loud rush of blood in her ears.

I can't stop them. She rolled her focus toward the door. It was too late. The doorknob began turning. There was nothing to do but face her enemies.

The door swung open, revealing a slice of the black night and the snow falling like slivers of opal. She felt the gust of icy wind roll through the opening and across the floor to freeze the sweat beading on her face. She tasted the grit of dread on her tongue and felt a bottomless fear as she fastened her gaze on the threshold. The door swung wide to reveal a bulky man, wide shouldered and tall.

Much taller than Ham's brothers. The snow dusting the wide brim of his hat, the fall of his storm-dark hair and the impressive line of his shoulders shone in the faint light. He held a drawn rifle in one hand and a revolver in the other with the ease of a gunslinger.

This was no stranger. This was no renegade come to bring harm. The air rushed out of her chest. *What a man.*

He lifted the .45 to push his Stetson a few inches higher and the faint shadows from the dying fire brushed over his square-cut jaw and unyielding mouth. An uncompromising blade of a nose and high, granite-hard cheekbones. Eyes as fathomless as a midnight sky met hers.

And she felt the impact unspool through her. *Joshua Gable.*

What was he doing here? She'd made him angry and he'd gone home, hadn't he? But judging by the slight crackle of his outer garments as he took a step into the room, he'd been outside for a long spell. And not riding, judging by the snow clinging to him.

Had he been outside all this time? Had he been responsible for the gunshot? Had there been trouble after all?

His eyes stroked over her like a flame's hot reach. "Do you need any help?"

"Uh-uh." It was a sound low in her throat that kept her from actually having to try to speak. She had her pride.

"I don't think you're telling the truth." A wry twist of his hard mouth softened his fierce eyes. "Granny, you awake?"

The silence in the corner became significant. Adelaide had stopped snoring a while back, Claire realized, as the older woman answered from the shadows. "I am. You got those two troublemakers?"

"Trussed up like ornery cattle. One's bleeding, but don't hurry out to tend him. Let him suffer a little." Joshua backed into the night. "I've got one more to secure. You'll keep an eye out?"

The horsehair cushion creaked as Adelaide moved, placed her feet on the floor and stood. "I will. Fire two quick shots if you get yerself into trouble, boy. I'll come rescue ya."

"Not every man I know would consider his grandma coming to rescue him a boon." He tipped his hat, studied her one long last time and backed away into the darkness and storm, his shadow merging with the night.

But his presence lingered, as substantial as the man and as impossible to explain. Why had he stayed to protect her land when she'd insulted him like that?

"What are you doin' down there, missy?" Adelaide stepped over her to close the door. The air had turned frigid and her breath rose in clouds as she set a polished Colt revolver on the lamp table. "Not to worry. I like a girl with spunk. Not many've got it these days. Life's gotten too easy. You can buy soap in town or order it from that newfangled catalogue."

She crouched down next to Claire and took her by the arm. One surprisingly strong tug and Claire was on her feet, wobbling and dizzy. The blood in her veins rushed downward, and her vision circled to blackness. Before she could gasp her next breath, she was on the couch. Adelaide gave her a push backward onto the pillows and grabbed hold of her ankles and plopped them on the high armrest.

"Now in my day," the older woman continued as she retrieved the blankets and furs from the floor, "the frontier made a woman out of ya, no doubt about that. You learned to make your own soap, spin your own thread, protect your livestock and shoot rustlers alongside your man. Those were the days."

She shook the blankets over Claire with a no-nonsense efficiency and turned her attention to the fire.

Breathless, Claire struggled to keep the darkness at bay. The room spun in a sickly swirl and she squeezed her eyes shut. I will not get sick, she chanted to herself, not sure if her will alone would keep her stomach from revolting.

Slowly, the nausea and dizziness eased a notch. Breathing came easier and the tinny pulse in her ears slowed to the sounds of Adelaide stirring the hot coals with the poker, laying on kindling and retrieving wood from the lean-to at the back door. The comforting scent of wood smoke filled the air and heat radiated from the hearth once more.

"You stay put." Adelaide returned to tower over her. "If you need something, you holler. Don't try and get it yerself. I like you, Claire Hamilton. And I don't like a whole lotta people. You let me know if you need somethin'."

At the surprisingly comforting brush of Adelaide's hand at her brow, smoothing away her stray, sweaty hair, Claire's eyes filled. Kindness. It was such a rare thing. "Thank you."

"Just sleep, my girl. I've got to check on those no-good Hamilton boys. Give 'em a kick or two if they deserve it. Don't you worry. I've got my gun. I'll keep you safe."

I'm not worried about me, she thought as the slim, fragile-looking lady moved with feminine grace and retrieved her gun from the lamp table.

"You close your eyes and rest now." Adelaide pulled her wool coat from the peg by the door, lit a lantern and disappeared into the night.

The rapid pop of gunfire, muffled by the falling snow, came from the barn. Joshua. Unable to so much as lift her head, all Claire could do was hope with all her being that he was safe. That whatever danger he'd gone out to stalk in the night hadn't found him first.

More gunfire followed, and she hated being stuck unable to move. She wanted to be out there, defending what was hers. She hoped it would not cost her more than she could pay.

Somehow Joshua's presence remained in this room—or maybe it was with her. Indomitable. Capable. Heroic. If he was harmed or killed this night, the cost of his life would not be worth her keeping the land, no matter how much she wanted it.

What in the hell is that bastard doing? Joshua had spent long, cold minutes stalking Logan. Creeping on his hands and knees sometimes to keep to the shadows, to stay out of the sharp-eyed man's sight.

And for what? So the fool could perch on the rise behind the barn and fire off enough shots to send livestock into a stampede?

Pressed against the iced boards of the barn, Joshua hated the crunch of snow beneath the ball of his foot. He froze, waiting, but the son of a bitch kept firing off shots like it was the Fourth of July.

What on earth is wrong with that man? Joshua would have liked nothing more than to storm up to the fool and wrestle him to the ground, but he was standing out in the middle of a rise with no cover, no shadows, nothing. Joshua wasn't so fond of getting shot, so he pressed against the frigid corner boards and peered cautiously around the edge.

He saw it all in a flash—the cattle leaping up from their sleep on the prairie floor below, the bull in charge of the herd pacing to the rear to challenge the danger. Logan on horseback charging down the slope, the flash of his revolver like a lightning burst over his brutal, determined face.

The idiot was stampeding the livestock on purpose? Joshua wondered if there were more men on the valley floor, disguised from his sight by the storm. As if in answer to his thoughts, distant gunfire popped below. The herd's panicked bellows drowned out the sound and Joshua found himself standing on the rise, watching the fading darkness of Claire's cattle disappearing.

A bullet whizzed past his left shoulder and he dropped to the ground. *Hell!* Another shot zipped overhead and plowed into the barn wall. He waited, breathing hard, rage rising until the night around him shone red.

I should have seen that one coming.

Furious at himself, he crawled on his elbows until he was able to see over the ridge. Too late. There was nothing but night snow and the dark smudge of the herd racing away on the dark sheen of the open prairie.

At least one mystery was solved. Joshua debated riding after them—but he'd be outnumbered and outgunned. He'd be easy to spot on the plains, with the way the snow gave a soft purplish glow to the landscape. He'd be easy to pick off with a single shot.

Plus, the only lawman on this side of the county was one of those gunmen. Not odds Joshua was interested in. But that didn't mean he was done fighting.

He ducked into the barn and hitched up Granny's team. The family's surrey, mounted on runners for winter, was just what he'd need to haul the Hamiltons all the way back to town. He'd let the town sheriff deal with the Hamiltons. At least the last time he looked, trespassing, horse thieving and cattle stealing was a damn serious offense.

It was snowing harder when he drove the team out from the barn. Great, it was going to be a cold, miserable drive. Just what he needed to top off his day. He'd been cold since the moment he crawled out of bed at four this morning. And there was no end in sight.

So, he wasn't in the best mood when he found the Hamiltons tied up like pigs for a roast and left alongside the cabin like yesterday's garbage. Frostbite was setting in, but he didn't care so much. Not when the square of light of the front room window caught his eye, and he saw, between the hemmed halves of the brown curtain a tiny slice of the sofa where Claire rested. Her hair was fanned out in a soft cloud on the pillows, hardly more than a small bump beneath the thick blankets.

He remembered finding her in the snow, thinking she was dead, and the feel of her weight in his arms. He thought of the iron will he'd seen in her eyes when she'd been facedown on the floor, all fight when she couldn't even move.

Her terse words, her suspicion, all of that paled next to the unexplained thump of emotion in his chest, emotion he didn't want to think about or analyze. Because if he did, it would do neither of them any good. He didn't want a woman. He didn't want complications. His life was demanding enough.

He turned away from the window, but not before his grandmother caught him looking. He tossed the furious Hamiltons, bound and gagged, into the back of the surrey, keeping far away from the reach of the window.

But even as he drove away into the night and the storm, he welcomed the bitter cold. Because half-frozen, he couldn't feel anything. Not his fingers, not his feet.

And not his heart.

Chapter Eight

Gunfire ripped Claire awake.

As the sunlight cut into her eyes, the echoing thunder of bullets faded with the wisps of sleep. Night was over, and the morning sounds of a crackling fire and the clink of the ironware cup against its saucer reminded her. *It was only a dream.*

As the brightness of sunshine stung her eyes, she realized it wasn't early morning. It had to be at least ten o'clock with the way the light burnished the window.

How long had she slept? She came fully awake and was sitting up before the pain slammed her back against the pillows. *Oh, I hurt.* She squeezed her eyes shut, realizing the night had passed, but what of Joshua? Was he all right?

"Good morning, missy." Adelaide rose from a chair at the table. "Been keepin' some vittles warm for ya. You feelin' any better?"

"Some better." Last night had seemed unreal. "Let me try to get up. You needn't trouble yourself anymore for me."

Adelaide glared in disapproval before she disappeared farther into the kitchen. "You stay where you are. You got up more than you shoulda last night."

The gunshots echoed in dream and memory as she struggled to sit. Those gunshots had been real, strange on this peaceful, quiet morning. The curtains at the table were pulled open to the sun, letting in the south light, and what she could see of the house looked perfectly tidy, as if there had been no trouble last night.

As if Joshua hadn't stood in the doorway with snow falling in all around him, drawn rifle and revolver in hand. How inestimable Joshua had seemed, midnight-dangerous and heroic. Her whole being still tingled and last night, after she'd collapsed, was hazy. A galloping panic rushed through her veins. "What happened to your grandson?"

"Oh, he's around here somewhere." Adelaide ambled into sight, carrying a breakfast tray. "He was in for a cup of coffee not too long ago."

For some reason the image of Joshua Gable, his big body dominating her tiny kitchen, a cup cradled in his rough hands made that tingling feeling intensify within her.

"There he is. Joshua, Claire's awake." Adelaide's affection was as warm as the radiant fire as she smiled into the kitchen.

Joshua. She could hear the steady knell of his gait, coming closer through the kitchen and then rounding the corner. He had on a blue flannel shirt that turned his eyes into a striking gray-blue. Ironed denims hugged the long lean muscles of his legs.

"That's good news." He kissed his grandmother's forehead and lifted the tray from her solid grip. "Give this to me. I'll serve Claire. You go back to your dime novel."

"Not *my* dime novel. I just found that old thing layin' around. Get away with you." While she feigned annoyance, there was no mistaking the bond between them. The kitchen chair scraped as Adelaide settled back down to her coffee cup and her book.

"Apparently you and my granny have similar reading preferences." He came closer, and he was all she could see. A hero of a man she didn't want to believe in, but he came to her anyway and knelt on the floor at her side. "You are looking better. You gave us a pretty bad scare."

"I'm fine." She might not be so sure she ought to be sitting, for her body strained with the effort and she felt as weak as an infant. Pride held her up.

He slipped the tray onto her lap as competently as he'd handled his guns last night. A simple act, bringing him so close she could smell the wood smoke clinging to his shirt and the woolly, woodsy scent of a man's clean skin.

This close, she could see the individual stubs of his whiskers shading his jaw. And the fall of his thick hair, which fell past his collar and had a wave to it. It wasn't black, as she'd first thought, but a bold shade of brown.

Why was she noticing? There wasn't a man she'd looked this closely at since she was a naive girl who believed herself in love. And never a man who made her *feel*. His presence roared through her like a fire's heat, making the numb, iced-over places in her heart crack painfully.

"Granny's the best cook in Bluebonnet County, when she has a mind to do it." He winked, not exactly friendly, but as if he were trying hard to be. "Is there anything else you need? Butter? Sugar for your coffee?"

She shook her head, unable to look away. Whatever was on the tray was fine. She didn't want to disturb Adelaide, who'd done so much for her already.

"Someone's coming." He shot up with a male predator's grace, pure strength as he crossed the room. He kept to the side of the window and peered through the slit in the curtains. He seemed to take in the lay of the land and wait for the approaching traveler to crest the rise of the hill.

I'm lucky he was here last night. She couldn't bear to think where she would be and what terrible consequences would have befallen her without him. The suspicious part of her wanted to ask why. But in truth, it didn't matter. He'd saved her, and he was still protecting her. For his own reasons, and that was all right. She was here, she was safe, and she had a fighting chance, because of him.

It was simply gratitude that she felt. The overwhelming flood of feeling filled her up like rainwater in a barrel. Heat flushed her face when she realized she was staring at him like a schoolgirl in the throes of her first crush. It took all her dignity to tear her attention away from the rugged cut of his face. But that didn't stop her mind from holding his image or halt her from shivering when she heard the sound of his intimate, rough-velvet voice.

"It's only Jordan." He pushed the curtains apart to let in light. Brilliant rays danced over him and into her eyes, blinding her to him as he moved away. His gait rocked faintly on the wood floor until he was in the kitchen. She turned her head and this time the light could not steal him from her sight.

"I can't believe the lazy bum is here before noon." Joshua didn't sound all that harsh, but rather fond of his brother. "And I wasn't there to kick his arse out of bed."

"Will wonders never cease? Now move, boy, you're in my reading light."

"I thought you said that was some old thing laying around." A twist of his mouth almost made it look as if he could smile.

Claire tried to imagine that severe mouth of his breaking into a tantalizing grin. Would his eyes sparkle, too? Did he have dimples? She couldn't see anything that soft in him, so why did she hope? A man who'd defeated both Hamilton brothers single-handedly was no soft and tender man, but one to be wary of.

And yet, how he teased his grandmother, kindly, by stepping between her chair and the window again until she swatted his arm and told him to stop it or she'd take a belt to him.

"Go ahead," he said and didn't budge.

It was apparently an old joke between them, because Adelaide's chuckle was warm and lenient. There was no arguing, no orders given and received, no telling looks of anger between them.

What a rare gift, she thought, remembering how close she'd been with her own grandmother when she was just a little girl. One couldn't help what family one was born into, and she'd found that real bonds and real ties of affection among family were rare and all the more precious.

It was what she'd been hoping to find since she was nine years old.

While Joshua grabbed his coat from a wall peg and jammed one arm into it, she stared at the breakfast he'd set before her. She'd never had a man do such a thing. Not her father. Certainly not her husband.

Even when she looked away from him and studied the plate before her, she didn't see the food. She saw how his big calloused hands had set the tray on her lap. Serving her.

A cool puff of air rolled into the toasty room as Joshua opened the door and shut it quickly behind him. The cheerful sun was deceptive; it hid dangerously cold air. Through the window she could see the spread of clean snow frosting the trees and hillsides and the endless span of prairie butting into the gleaming mountains. The mantle of snow sparkled like fallen stars for miles, giving the land a haunting beauty.

"Eat up, girl!" Adelaide called from the table. "I don't wanna have to beat Jordan away from you. That boy'll eat everything including what's on your plate."

The older woman seemed cantankerous, but Claire recognized that it was only an act. She couldn't help liking Adelaide a little bit more. "I'd hate for you to have to hurt him. I'll eat."

"Good girl." Adelaide's sparkling green eyes beamed approval.

Not that she was the least bit hungry. Claire did appreciate the generous plateful of scrambled eggs, buttery biscuits, hashed browns and crisped bacon. The steaming cup of sweetened coffee was at least a place to start. She cradled the mug in her hands and let the heat warm through.

When she sipped deep, the bold taste was simply heaven. She'd made coffee every day since she was nine years old, at her aunt and uncle's house. Every morning she ground and measured the beans and put a pot on to boil. And every morning of her marriage had been the same.

No one, ever, had made coffee for her. Somehow it tasted ten times better, although it was the same beans from the crock in her cupboard. Perhaps it was Adelaide's kindness that made the difference.

She could see Joshua through the window. A large, expensive sleigh sat in the driveway, just outside the front door. The man who wasn't quite grown into his frame yet must be the lazy Jordan. He didn't look so bad with his smiling face and relaxed manner. She remembered the young man from the funeral. Joshua clapped him on the shoulder, as if in approval, and then pointed toward the sleigh.

As she munched on a strip of bacon, crispy and done just right, she watched him join his brother in lifting things from the sleigh. What were they doing? She couldn't make out what they were lifting, probably because she kept watching the man who'd saved her.

The wind tangled through his shaggy hair, but it didn't diminish the granite might of the man as he disappeared from her sight. The door sprang open. It wasn't Joshua's dark woolen sleeve she spotted, but a light brown one. The younger brother's.

"Gran, you want this anyplace in particular?" Jordan Gable had his brother's velvet-rough baritone, but it wasn't as deep and rumbling. He ambled into sight with a heavy sack on his shoulder.

A sack that read Flour on the side in bright red lettering.

Claire's mouth dropped open. What was going on?

"Try the pantry, smarty." Adelaide looked up from her book. "Did you remember my tobacco?"

"How could I forget?" Jordan paced out of sight. There was a bump as the sack met the floor. "It's gonna cost ya."

"What are you up to, boy, trying to skin an old woman?"

"Yep." The young man bounded into sight, tipped his hat in Claire's direction and held a red packet high above his head, the promised tobacco. "There's the trouble of getting up before sunlight. That's gotta cost somethin'. And then the delivery charges for me comin' all the way out here."

"I'll give you delivery charges." Adelaide grinned, as if she enjoyed the arguing. "Cascara bark in your mornin' cup of coffee oughta be payment enough."

Claire bit her lip. Bark from the mountain tree was an excellent laxative.

"Yikes! I say, what delivery charges? A package of the best tobacco at the mercantile for you. I'll just finish up bringing in the stuff. And don't trouble yourself, Gran. I'll get my own cup of coffee."

Jordan slammed the door behind him good-naturedly.

"You gotta know how to motivate a man." Adelaide chuckled as she opened her package. "It never hurts to have a wicked knowledge of local medicinal herbs to use as punishment. With men, you gotta be ruthless and keep 'em in line. Cascara bark is the secret to a good marriage."

"Not for the regularity?"

Adelaide laughed heartily. "The threat of it works wonders. There was a few times my dear husband suspected I'd doctored his coffee, and it kept him respecting me. Think I'll leave a few pieces of bark in your cupboard. Just in case you decide to get yerself another man right away. You can't let 'em get the best of ya. If he makes you mad, then make him pay."

She was kidding, right? Claire couldn't imagine such a thing. "I'm not marrying. Ever again. One husband was enough for me."

Jordan clambered back in, carrying smaller sacks, one on each shoulder.

"That's exactly how I felt." Adelaide pulled a cigarette paper from her skirt pocket. "After I buried my dear love, I didn't want to bother with training another husband. They're like mules. They're stubborn, but they can learn. You just have to be disciplined with their training."

The faraway look that gentled Adelaide's face made Claire wonder how long she'd been a widow, and if the marriage had truly been good enough to justify that amazing look. Or more likely, time had softened the truth, making Adelaide's memory better than the reality.

The back door banged open. Claire was used to the sound, for Ham liked to slam doors. But already she knew the rolling, confident rhythm of Joshua's gait. She felt his approach like spring on a February wind even before he turned the corner.

"Got the coal bin stocked full." He slipped off his hat, respectful and polite. "Claire, the doc said you're gonna be taking it easy for a while. I hope you don't mind we took it upon ourselves to stock up your pantry, since you won't be up for a long ride to town and back."

It was charity, she could see that in his eyes, not hard or demanding or calculating. This made it harder somehow to accept his kindness. "I am obliged to you. It will be a while before I can get to the bank, but I know Ham always left a little cash under the tablecloth. Perhaps you can take that as part payment."

"Why don't you hold on to that money? Finish up your breakfast and then you and I have to talk."

Here it comes, she thought, her stomach too weak still to hold much more than the coffee. "You may as well tell me now."

Jordan slipped outside and Adelaide stood to disappear into the kitchen. Whatever Joshua had to say wasn't good news. Or, perhaps what he wanted wouldn't be beneficial for her. Still, she set her chin, determined to face whatever needed to be dealt with, regardless of her ringing head and weakness.

She'd survived Ham, she'd survived the night, and nothing at this point could break her. There was nothing left to break.

He approached slowly, like a stalking cougar. "Ham's brothers spent what was left of the night in the Bluebonnet jail, but I figure they won't stay there long."

"Then you did find them outside last night?"

"Yes. And there's more. They weren't alone." A muscle ticked in his jaw and his big hands fisted. He lowered himself onto the ottoman, his big frame tensed and his forearms dug into his knees. Although he was perfectly still, he seemed like motion leashed. "A band of rustlers took off with your livestock."

"Rustlers?" She closed her eyes. She hadn't even considered the question of what to do with the cattle.

She knew there were rustlers in the county, but she had been lucky so far. Their ranch had never been hit. She always figured it was because the rustlers knew Ham at least by reputation, and no one in their right mind would want to anger him. But Ham was gone, and that left her herd undefended.

"Is the whole herd gone?"

"They tried to wipe you out, but the storm made it hard for them, as far as I could tell." Deep frowns bracketed the corners of his mouth as if he were angry. As if maybe he'd been thinking to strike a deal with her over the animals. "After I came back from leaving your brothers-in-law with the sheriff—"

"Not my brothers-in-law," she corrected, stopping him.

A dark brow arched, whether in a question or disapproval of her outspokenness, she couldn't tell.

"I rousted a few of my brothers out of their beds and got them to come with me," he went on to explain.

"What? In that bitter cold? That late at night?"

"I'm a rancher, I'm used to it. I did what needed to be done. I do it every day and night on my own place. We've rounded up about twenty head of strays and penned them up in your horse corral. It's close quarters, but they'll be easier to watch and harder to stampede."

"Twenty? The rustlers ended up with most of the herd."

"Between five hundred to seven-fifty in market value, depending. I didn't get a real good look at what you've got. But that's not the worse part of all this."

"The Hamiltons. They're the rustlers, aren't they?"

"I figure they're part of the gang. The trouble is, I think this means Ham was, too. With the law for sale in this county, I don't think you'll get far pursuing it."

"You mean to let them have the cattle? That's not right."

"I did take a look at the brands. They've been doctored, and you know what that means?"

She nodded. They weren't her cattle at all. They were stolen. And that was a hanging offense in Bluebonnet County. It explained a lot, in terms of how Ham had such good luck with his herds. "What do I do?"

"I'd normally say bring in the law and explain everything, but from what I saw last night, that would be asking Logan to throw you in jail. Sell 'em. I'm going to the auction down in Great Falls next week. I can take them for you. We'll hope I don't end up in the clink over it."

"There's no way to return them to their rightful owners?"

"If there was, I'd have done it by now." Joshua stood, the only stability in her view as the room began to spin. "I'll handle it, Claire. It's the least I can do, considering what went on that night."

His rough, rich tone came with an apology. As if he mistook her sadness for losing her husband. He couldn't know what she'd lived with. He was a man, what did he know about marriage and sacrifice? "You made Ham stop hurting me. There's no need to be sorry about that."

"I see." He studied her a long while, and she wondered what he thought.

It was her weakened physical state, that surely had to be it, for her head had stopped ringing and her heart began to open, as if seeking warmth and affection, as if believing there was hope in men after all. When she knew there wasn't.

Joshua Gable was a decent man. There was no getting around that fact. He had a good relationship with his family, he worked hard, and he had a respected reputation. He was a fair man and that was rare in this selfish, self-gratifying world. And made more attractive because of it.

And, she'd learned the hard way, the heart sees what it wants to, is blind to all else. So she'd do well not to put too much weight on his good qualities. "There's something I've done and I feel horrible about it. What I said when you offered to stay the night and help. I was ungracious and I'm sorry. I never expected you to stay without compensation."

"You expect the worst from me."

"I was wrong. I am very grateful for what you did. It was cold last night. You must have had only a few hours of sleep. And then all the supplies you brought…" She fell silent, unable to find words powerful enough to thank him without sounding as if she were worshipping him.

"I can see what your life was like here. Don't worry

about thanking me." He fidgeted, betraying the only hint of discomfort she'd ever noticed.

So, was the respected Joshua Gable humble at heart? Or uncomfortable with the attention? She couldn't help liking him as a person, because maybe beneath that mask he wore there was genuine goodness. And that, too, was rare.

Then his capable calm was back and firmly in place. "The thing is, the Hamiltons seemed to know I was out here that night. Considering they want me dead." He radiated cool sensible logic, not blazing anger.

"They said that?" It surprised her only because there was no reason to target Joshua. "They couldn't know about that night."

"If you said nothing to them, then I've got some questions to ask. There's no doubt about their threats. And I'm bettin' that my hauling them to jail the way I did, didn't improve their opinions of me."

"You're in harm's way because of me." She'd been numb from her miscarriage and ill from it, that she hadn't taken time to consider his end of things. "What will you do? The Hamiltons know how to hold a grudge. And how to get even."

"I figure I can handle them. But what I need to know is what side of the fence you come down on." There was that tick in his strong granite jaw, a ripple of emotion that betrayed a hint of anger.

He was a man very much in control of his impulses. She couldn't help wondering how deep that anger went. It was a good thing she was smart enough not to trust any man again, especially one who came across so temptingly, not that she was tempted. "Mr. Gable, I think I've made it clear. My husband's death has severed any ties between the Hamiltons and me. Those people never made me feel like family, and they are now no family of mine whatsoever."

"They know how to put pressure on a person. They'll try to take your house and your land."

"Let them try." Her chin shot up. "What's troubling you?"

"I figure if your enemy is my enemy, then we'd be smart being friends." Joshua stood, as if something important had been decided, but what, she couldn't tell. "Granny insists on staying here for a spell, until you're stronger. One of my brothers and I will rotate keeping an eye on things for you."

"Thank you. I know it's not enough. I don't think there's a way to pay you back enough for what you've done."

"Pay me? I'm not doing this for money, Claire. Sometimes you have to do what is right, whether it's in your best interest or not." He turned at the door. "Someone's comin'. I best go see who it is."

Before leaving her, he gave one curt nod, but there was kindness in the hint of a smile that broke the hard line of his mouth. The impact of it almost cracked her heart open even wider, but she managed to hold on to her common sense just in time.

Chapter Nine

"Missy, what are you doin' up?"

Claire ignored Adelaide's question. She knew she shouldn't have crawled off the couch, not after she'd lost so much blood.

But it wasn't simply curiosity that had gotten the best of her. It was the hard, coiled knot of dread in her stomach. She had to know what trouble was coming down her road and to her front door. No matter the doctor's orders or Adelaide's wise care, she had to face the Hamiltons and whatever disaster they'd come to rain down upon her.

The pair of dark bays drawing a medium-size sleigh were miniature figures too far away to recognize. That it was only one vehicle was hopeful. As least the Hamiltons wouldn't be showing up as a group with their guns drawn and their threats. One vehicle. It was too much to hope that perhaps the coming visitor had nothing to do with the Hamiltons at all.

"I need wash water." She limped into the kitchen,

careful not to move her left leg overmuch. Pain still lingered in her groin and thighs, and she winced when she reached too fast for the kettle.

"Put that down!" Adelaide jammed her chair back with a squeak of wood and tossed down her book. "There's no way you should be up."

"The doctor said I could get up some if I'm better this morning. I'm better." She plucked a folded towel from the upper shelf and tried to hide the way her arm trembled.

Adelaide stormed around the table, spry as a twenty-year-old. "You are as weak as a kitten. Look at you! You're ready to fall over. You are not well enough for whatever it is you've got a mind to do."

"Sometimes a woman has to fight when she's down. There's no other choice."

"What's got into you? Whatever needs to be done, Joshua can do it. And if he can't handle it, I can." Adelaide winked, taking Claire by the forearm. "Look at you, ready to go tumblin' down at a sign of a strong wind. You need rest, missy. You fight the world when you're stronger."

"I don't need to fight the world. Just the Hamiltons."

"Joshua already did that." Adelaide tugged surprisingly hard in the direction of the necessary room. "Tell you what. You come wash up. We'll get your hair brushed and plaited. Once your hair's up and you're in some fresh clothes, you'll feel better and see reason. Come."

See reason? Claire bit her lip. Adelaide might mean well, but she didn't understand. She had strong grandsons who would stand up for her in a heartbeat. Men like Joshua who would wait in the below-zero weather for hours on end to defend a stranger's property. What more would he do for his own grandmother? Adelaide had known hardship, but she'd never been alone. And never would be. How lucky.

But Joshua Gable was not her husband or relation. He was more stranger than friend. And whatever sense of doing what was right fueled him, it would soon be gone.

A storm of hardship was coming, and she would not have the Hamiltons thinking that she could not stand against them on her own. Because she could stand on her own two feet just fine. She didn't need Joshua Gable's charity.

She didn't need any man.

Joshua didn't recognize the pair of fine-stepping bays. Two figures were tucked beneath blankets on the front seat, but he couldn't make out who they were. Not until they pulled to a stop behind his vehicle and he recognized one of the town's most prominent lawyers and his wife. Annabelle Hamilton Clise.

Trouble. The feel of it brewed like a blizzard in his gut as he strolled out into the road. The horses drew to a stop in front of him, and there was no missing the irritated look on Clise's doughy face. That told Joshua everything he wanted to know. The fancy lawyer was expecting him. And was already dismissing him.

Good luck, Clise. I'm not so easy to beat. Joshua pulled his unbuttoned jacket open enough so that the lawyer could see the double Colts holstered, one to each thigh. Silent, he stood blocking the road. Actions spoke louder than words.

"Gable." The attorney gave a brief nod, but his handlebar mustache couldn't hide his sneer of contempt. Just as his fancy wool jacket and tailored clothes could not disguise the lesser quality of the man.

Joshua despised men like Clise. "I expected the vultures to start circling. And that you'd be leading them."

"I oughtn't to be surprised to find you here. I suppose there's a whole crop of you ignorant country boys who think in order to come to own this land, all you must do is marry for it."

"No worse than you city boys thinking they can get hold of this place by strong-arming a woman."

"This is my place now."

Joshua cocked a brow, his fingers itching for the smooth walnut handle of the .45s. Clise's place? "Claire Hamilton doesn't seem to think so. I agree with her."

"Go herd your sheep, Gable, and leave the legal matters to those educated enough to understand them."

"I understand plenty, Clise. And I know a thief when I see one." Some folks just thought themselves so fine, when they were anything but. What kind of man would steal land from a widow? "Ham is barely cold in his grave and you people are already flocking like vultures. First the brothers and now you."

"Get out of my way, or I will run you down."

"Go ahead and try."

Dark anger narrowed the lawyer's features, making him look like the crook he was. This only fueled Joshua's certainty more. His right hand covered the cool grips of his revolvers, ready to draw. One thing Joshua had learned a long time ago. Fancy city boys were no match for a hardworking country boy.

Clise snapped the thick reins on his bays' rumps with an audible whack, but the horses did not leap forward. They stayed in place, sidestepping in their traces.

"Be a good boy, Clise, and turn around. Save yourself some trouble and head back to town."

Joshua watched the effect of his words. They hit like a snowball's icy punch right in the middle of Clise's face. Bull's-eye.

Clise puffed up inside his expensive clothes and reached for the whip sitting primly in its socket. "This is no game. I'll come back with the sheriff if I have to. Toss the lot of you in the county jail. Would serve you right for trying to swindle a grieving widow."

"It takes one to know one," Joshua said.

He heard the soft whisper of footsteps on the snow behind him a few seconds before Annabelle Clise's eyes hardened beneath her black hat. Her chin shot up, and Joshua knew the woman wasn't reacting to his brother coming to add his weight to the argument. Jordan's bold, careless gait could never be mistaken for the featherlight pad coming closer.

It was a woman, but not Granny. She wasn't one to tread softly. But could it be Claire? It had to be. He could feel her approach like a winter's dawn, and it troubled him that she pulled at his concentration. He'd never had that problem before, and it was as if all his senses were straining to pick up a hint of her—the rustle of her skirts, the rose scent of her hair and her skin.

He forced his attention to Clise, refusing to let his

focus stray from the man who held a whip and probably hid a firearm, although it was as if Joshua's eyes ached for the sight of her.

Probably because he was worried about her health, he told himself, because that was the only reason he wanted to get a look at her. Because she wasn't well and he was used to taking care of everyone around him. It was what he did. It seemed like all he would ever do. It wasn't a personal thing. It wasn't *attraction*.

Now you're lying to yourself, Gable.

"Thad Clise, put down your whip." She rewarded him with the sound of her voice in no way he'd ever heard before. A formidable alto came, not sharp or shrill, but muted and certain.

This was Claire Hamilton? Sure enough, there she was, at the edge of his vision, wrapped in a huge wool shawl over a flannel calico dress. Her hair was brushed and lustrous as it tumbled down her back, stirred by the wind.

His hand nearly slid off the Colt's grip. He'd seen the quiet, mousy wife in town in the company of her husband, but she'd been background, for Joshua wasn't in the habit of noticing other men's wives. He remembered her battered and in pain. The pale widow at a snowy graveside.

But not *this* woman.

This woman met Clise's eyes with a challenge. "Thad, you heard me. Put down that whip, turn your horses around and get off my property."

"All right!" Clise slid the whip back into its socket and held up his hands, the reins having fallen to the dashboard, as if to prove he meant no harm. "This is family business, Claire. Send Gable on his way, this is none of his concern. You and I need to go over Ham's paperwork. There are documents you must sign."

What paperwork did Ham have with him? The question troubled her as she fought to keep her knees from wobbling with weakness. She knew with a woman's instinct, along with the gleam of greed in Annabelle's hard black eyes, that Thad wasn't here for her best interests. "As far as I know, Ham hated you. He would not have had legal dealings with you."

"No, but he did trust me to make sure you were taken care of in the event of his death." Thad projected concern now, his voice dipping down like that of a tender patriarch. "We all want what's best for you now, when you must be ill with grief. Look at you, my dear. Trembling and ashen. Should I send a rider for the doctor?"

"No, a doctor won't be needed." She disliked his pretense. Thad Clise had never been concerned about her in the three years he'd looked down his regal nose at her.

He's a wolf in sheep's clothing, come for his own gain, but what? Whatever it was, she knew he was sly enough to get what he wanted if she wasn't careful. Perhaps he thought himself so fine with his education and expensive horses and sleigh and clothes. Next to Joshua, he seemed even more false. A shallow imitation of what a man should be.

She couldn't help the way she naturally turned toward Joshua. He stood warrior-strong at her side, his gaze unbroken as he stared hard at Thad, as if waiting for his next move. How could she not be grateful for Joshua, who not only stood up for her, but also at her side.

He could have been a legend, like the heroes inked on the front of her beloved dime novels, and the breadth of his shoulders and the way he stood like justice personified, why, it tempted a woman to believe, beyond common sense and experience and hard lessons learned.

She was fortified to know that a man like Joshua was on her side. At least that's the way she explained the rush of warmth building in her chest.

Appreciation, and nothing more.

There was no sense letting Thad have the upper hand, so she made sure her voice was condescending and she looked him dead in the eye. "Give me the papers."

"These are legal documents, honey." Thad's soothing tone rang false. "You're a simple country girl. That's why I'm here. To explain everything to you, so you can understand."

Did Thad really think she would be that easily misled? Or fooled by the fact that this was only the second attempt by the Hamiltons to get what they thought was theirs. This land. "Get off my property."

"Technically, it's not your property."

"It's not yours."

Joshua stepped forward, a towering figure of granite. Formidable. "Clise. Hand over the papers."

"But I—"

"Or go." Joshua drew one of his revolvers. "It's your choice."

Thad's grimace was more like a warning. "I wouldn't start moving my livestock over yet, Gable. She's not worth what you think."

"She's worth more than a quarter section of rocky, high-country foothills. *Where are the papers?*"

The controlled boom of command startled her. In that moment, his handsome rugged face turned dark and threatening, like a storm cloud churning in the sky. Clise blanched and, although he looked down on both her and Joshua with derision, he reached into his breast pocket and withdrew a thick fold of long, legal-looking papers.

What business could Ham have had with Thad? Claire shivered as the blood chilled in her veins. Was it possible the house and land wouldn't go to her? What if Clise was right, that this was his property after all?

"Claire?" Joshua was calling her. "Here."

He thrust the folded papers her way, not turning from the lawyer who, she now realized, had a repeating rifle tucked beside him on the seat. Between him and his wife. Joshua did not seem intimidated, no, not in the slightest. He seemed to swell up with more fearless power.

She'd never known a finer man. She took the paperwork, freeing up his hand in case he needed his other gun.

"Time to go, Clise." Joshua caught hold of the lead mare's bridle and steadily pulled her in a tight circle, drawing the second horse who was harnessed to her and the sleigh along with him.

An amazingly efficient way to get rid of unwanted company. Claire heard the sharp buzz of Thad's words, low and muffled, and then only silence. She felt the change in the air and looked over her shoulder. There on the hillside above, stood a tall, powerful man with his hands on the handles of his holstered revolvers, shoulders wide, feet braced, his silence an undeniable warning.

Thad must have decided not to tangle with the Gable brothers because the mares took off at a gallop and the sleigh disappeared down the slope of the hill. Thad was leaving without getting his way. Without threats or a scene or worse.

He'll be back. That single thought shot like ice down her spine.

"I'll make sure he leaves." Joshua stayed where he was, gun ready to fire, as alert as a soldier on point. "You might want to head on back to the house. Unless you want me to carry you back."

The thought of his arms around her one more time, to have her cheek resting against the hard plane of his chest…why, the memory lingered with her and she could not purge it from her mind. She knew exactly how unyielding his upper chest would feel and how safe she'd been in his arms.

A tinkle of desire fluttered low and deep within her abdomen. Desire that she'd thought her wedding night had destroyed, so why did it seem to remain, a slow liquid beat?

If she were to lay her cheek on his chest again and hear the intimate rhythm of his heartbeat, then this physical response to him would intensify. And her lonely heart would begin to make foolish wishes that could never be found.

Just walk away, Claire. It was the sensible thing to do, and heaven knows she was a sensible woman. Or at least, it was her intention to be from now on. She was not a young girl. She was a woman widowed and wise to the truths of men.

You're better off alone, she reminded herself firmly and turned away from the flesh-and-blood man. He was not a hero out of her dime novels where right always conquered evil, where heroes were always heroic and true love prevailed.

Fiction, only.

She had to make decisions for her life based on what was real. What was and not what could never be. "I'll head inside under my own steam, thanks."

"Well, you're starting to look gray again. You go inside, warm up and rest. Take good care of yourself, Claire. Something tells me this isn't the end of it. Only the beginning."

You have no idea how right you are. She could feel the truth of it in the meat of her bones.

Winter blew callously on dark clouds that whisked over the sun. In the shadows, on snow dull like ice, she ambled up the graceful slope of her driveway and into the house where Adelaide waited and watched at the window, her gun in hand.

She was grateful for this family that had come into her life, for however brief and for however kind. Maybe she would take Joshua's advice. She'd rest up. She had today and tomorrow to regain some of her strength so that come Monday morning she'd be able to endure the trip to town and whatever fate awaited her.

As she shut the door behind her and leaned on the wall for support, she couldn't say why her gaze skimmed the slope of the hillside down to where Joshua kept guard. If her heart winced with want, she ignored it. There would be no more dreams of romance. Of love. Of believing a man so strong and fierce with his enemies could be tender to a woman, or have the heart to do so.

She shut the door firmly and did not look upon Joshua Gable again.

"What did Clise want?" Jordan said, his revolvers back in their holsters.

Joshua was proud of his little brother. He might make a good man yet. "He brought some papers for Claire to sign."

"Makes you wonder why he'd drive out all this way on a Saturday, doesn't it?"

"Yep."

Joshua was wondering about a lot of things. What the Hamiltons wanted with this rocky, hard-to-till earth. What was on this property that mattered so much? Nothing that he could see. But then, some people just wanted anything they could get their hands on. "He's gone for now. You fed the cattle?"

"Made sure their haymow was full and pumped some water. Should keep them until nightfall." Jordan knelt to scoop his hand through the snow. He came away with a loose palmful and began to pack it. "What's the deal with you and the widow?"

"What deal? I found her in a storm and helped her."

"You're helpin' her still. Not that I mind getting my toes frostbit for the sake of a pretty lady, but I'd like to know the reason."

"Some things aren't for you to know, little brother."

"I noticed a change about the time you shook the little widow's hand at the funeral. Next thing I know, you were in a brawl with the Hamilton boys."

"They threatened me."

"No, they threatened her."

"Don't speculate on what you don't understand."

"Whatever you say, big brother. I'll be headin' over to the ridge, to keep a good sharp lookout in case Clise decides to double back. Or those Hamilton boys come callin' again. They could be outta jail by now."

"Anything's possible. Thanks, Jordan. You did good."

"Hey, I'm just lookin' to protect my future sister-in-law." With a wink he was gone, loping quick to get out of earshot.

"You've got that wrong, too, dumb ass!" he called, but he couldn't summon up enough ire for a good hot anger.

It probably looked that way to everybody. A helpless widow on her own, against the law and her vicious in-laws. Of course a man might step up to help a woman he cared about. Except for two things. He didn't care about her, and Claire Hamilton was no helpless widow. She might be down, but that was only temporary. The way she'd lit up like a prairie wildfire, all tough and bright and fearless, had surprised him, but only initially.

He'd never bought the image of a helpless woman, subservient and demure. If the women in his family were anything to go by, men were far more likely to be henpecked and browbeat. A woman was like a donkey. Not as big as a horse, but tougher, more stubborn and long lasting. And packed one hell of a kick.

If he felt attracted to the pretty widow, then it was only a physical thing. And passing. He'd been attracted to women before and it had gone as quick as it had sparked to life.

Attraction was a physical need, quickly relieved by a trip to the seedier parts of town. He was too smart to get involved and tied up and tied down by a woman looking for a man to henpeck, browbeat and provide for her.

Not that Claire Hamilton seemed to have a mean bone in her body. No, but she was strong. She was tenacious. And she'd put a bit of fear in the lawyer. Women just got their claws into a man, they couldn't help it.

It was up to the man to be smart enough not to be caught.

And if that meant turning his back and walking away, then that's what he'd do—as soon as he'd done what he was here to do. It was his overdeveloped sense of responsibility, as tough as a wild plains mustang.

He hadn't put the fatal bullet in Ham's chest, but he'd left Claire to do it in self-defense, something no woman should have to be forced to do. He'd set things to right for her and she'd be fine.

She'd probably have a husband by the end of the month, and rightfully so—a woman needed a man to provide for her. Then his conscience would be clear.

His conscience was the only reason he was here.

Or that's what he told himself as he paced the hillside, keeping watch. When at last he heard the faint squeak of runners and the dulled clomp of horseshoes on the iced-over snow, he began to pack up. His brother Liam was here. He'd keep watch on things for a spell.

Joshua saddled up General. When he rode away, he didn't look back. He refused to acknowledge the tug in his cold heart or the heat building in his loins as he remembered Claire, with her hair loose and tousled, standing against the wind and ready to fight.

It was an image that did not fade, not during the long cold journey home or throughout the exhausting day of hauling hay, feeding animals and mending fences.

It lingered into the night while he lay awake staring at the ceiling in his room and followed him into his dreams where it was not cold, but warm as fire and Claire's long hair tumbling everywhere, in his hands, over her shoulders, against her creamy bare skin.

He awoke, hot and shaking and in need, but cold water would not slake the thirst he felt. Thirst not for the water, and not for a woman.

But for her.

Chapter Ten

⟡

It was her first night alone, for Adelaide had returned to her home Sunday night. Claire couldn't sleep. She'd spent most of the hours after midnight watching the pattern the moonlight made on the wood floor. And the cold, silent hours before dawn feeding the fire, wandering around the kitchen and the front room. Seeing for the first time all that the Gables had done for her.

Her pantry was stocked, her coal hod brimming, her laundry folded and put away. The house had been cleaned, meals prepared and left down in the cellar, and outside the corral was silent and empty. The middle Gable brothers had taken her stock along with theirs to the cattle auction down Great Falls way.

As she pulled back the hem of the curtain to stare out the kitchen window, she knew Joshua was there in the night, keeping watch, keeping her safe.

Joshua. How much had he sacrificed for her sake? Surely his comfort in the night. And his conscience. He'd shot Ham—she'd seen it with her own two eyes.

The taking of a life had to weigh heavily on Joshua's conscience. Yet here he was, indistinguishable with the night, keeping watch when there were those who would do him—and her—harm.

I hope the Hamiltons never discover the truth.

Vigilante justice was the swiftest kind in Montana Territory, the fast snap to judgment that she worried about now. While Joshua was out there keeping her safe, who was protecting him? Watching his back?

Dawn came not with brightness but with a sullen shift of light. The clouds were an angry lavender-gray behind which the sun remained hidden. The Montana high country was unforgiving, and Claire thought of Joshua as she watched airy snowflakes crystallize in the air, weightless, floating and swirling like minuscule feathers.

The coldest morning of the winter so far, she'd guess. And if Joshua had stayed outside, he must be nearly frozen solid. She scraped her thumbnail against the thick sheet of ice coating the windowpanes. She shivered in the frigid draft through the walls. The stove blasting heat at full damper could not seem to melt away the ice.

If he was out there somewhere, was he watching her now? She slipped a candle onto the windowsill and drew the curtain away from the flame in hopes that he might come to the door on his way into town. She set potatoes to warm in the stove, in case he did stop by.

She broke the ice on the bucket and set wash water on to heat. While she waited for it to steam, she milled a handful of coffee beans from the ten-pound burlap sack the Gables had brought her. She would need to tally up every purchase. The Gables meant well, but she was no charity case. She would never allow that!

A rap on the back door brought her out of her bedroom, where she'd retreated after her wash water had warmed. Joshua. She knew before she opened the door. Mainly because he had a brash distinctive knock—five quick raps like a hammer's blow. But also because she knew.

"I saw the light," he explained, tugging his muffler down to reveal his face made white from being too long in the cold. "You need anything?"

"You're the one who's frozen solid. Come in and warm up before you head home." She closed the door after him, not at all surprised to feel the cold rise off him in waves. "I have hot coffee."

"Words I'd kill for. It's got to be twenty below out there. An early cold snap." He walked in a little stiff, raining down ice shavings from his clothes onto the wood floor. He knelt in front of the cookstove and sighed. "You sure you ought to be up?"

"I'm better. Your grandmother gave me the okay, since she thinks she's a better doctor than the doctor is." She spoke the words with affection.

Okay, he had to like her for that. His grandmother was a harsh woman, but he'd always known the hardest exterior protected the sweetest heart. "Let me get my own coffee, Claire. You shouldn't be waiting on anyone. Sit down. I'll pour you a cup."

"No, Joshua. I want to do this." She reached past him to the coffeepot boiling on the stovetop, using a thick hot pad to grab the metal handle. She felt the steady press of his attention like a touch she could not escape, even when she moved away to the table to fill two cups.

"You've done so much for me," she explained as she carried a steaming cup to press into his hands. "It's time I did something for you."

She wants something. Why else would she be so accommodating? If there was one thing Joshua knew, it was women. Maybe not in the wife sense, since he'd never even courted a woman—he was too smart for that—but he lived his life around his grandmother, his mother and his sister. And as the head of the household, he'd clashed with the female powers on a constant basis.

Women did what it took to get what they wanted. It wasn't the nicest opinion but it was the honest one. That's what Claire seemed to be, sincere as church bells tolling on a Sunday morning.

She moved with careful grace as she brought the sugar bowl to him. He glanced down at the sugary white crystals in the plain gray ironware bowl and tried to imagine a woman in his family doing the same.

Yep, she sure must want something pretty bad, that cynical voice within him commented. And he saw it all at once, a woman alone and not physically strong, vultures for in-laws out to get hold of what they hadn't outright stolen.

She was trying to butter him up by being so accommodating; maybe she was on the hunt for a husband. Who could blame her? It was a tough life on these sparc, rugged foothills. She probably thought he'd do fine protecting her and providing for her.

He surprised himself by taking the spoon she'd

plunged into the bowl and scooping sugar into his cup. This near, it was easy to see how the single lamplight caressed across the bridge of her nose, and hers was a dainty beauty. Fine bones beneath her silken skin made a face that was heart-shaped sweet with gentle doe eyes beneath thick lashes and a mouth as soft-looking as a rose petal. The curve of her face from cheekbone to her fine jaw would fit perfectly against the palm of his hand.

Tenderness nudged to life in his chest, liquid slow and dangerous. He was no weak-willed man, but what of his reaction to this woman? He was frozen to the bone, but hot in his veins, and he had to know what it would be like to claim her lush mouth with his. Would her kiss taste as sweet as the fine sugar she stirred into her coffee? Would the soft warm satin of her kiss be merely nice? Or light a wildfire of need he wouldn't want to control?

This is how men fell, he realized. Desire blinded a man. It overwhelmed his logic and led to bad decisions. His blood roared in his ears as he tried not to listen to her. She was talking, telling him something, but what? He had no notion. Her gentle alto caressed over him and his mind couldn't make sense of the words, but he tingled like one raw nerve.

He managed to slurp the scalding coffee that scorched his tongue and the roof of his mouth. He swallowed swift and hard anyway. Her hair was down, thick and glinting like temptation and tumbling over her small shoulders to hide her breasts. Before he could start imagining those, he gulped down more coffee, his eyes stinging, his throat burning. When he finished, he plopped the empty cup on the edge of the worktable.

"Th-thanks," he choked out and headed for the door.

"Joshua?"

What was it about her voice? Soft as a hymn, as peaceful as sunrise. He turned at the doorway, his fingers clutching the wooden jamb, holding back, holding on. Because he didn't trust himself to speak, he hooked an eyebrow in a question.

"The papers Clise brought? I looked over them yesterday after your grandmother left." She stared down into the cup she cradled in her slender hands, her long hair falling forward to hide her face.

Through the sensual locks of silk, he could see the half moon of her lashes against her porcelain complexion. He didn't know how but he could *feel* her, heart to heart, for lack of a better way to describe it. A mix of outrage and determination that fisted in his gut.

"He tried to get you to sign over the property to him." Joshua knew it with a certainty.

"He had all sorts of things I needed to sign. Not just the deed, but bank papers and family papers. I don't know all what Ham had, but it didn't feel right. I don't believe they were legitimate."

"I doubt it." He didn't have the breath or the patience to explain to her what each horse was worth or each head of cattle. The land might not be worth much, but certainly a whole lot more than nothing. And instinct had him thinking there was something more here. Something the brothers had come to fetch that night, and not only the cattle. He would put Liam to work on that problem.

"What I mean to say…" She set her cup down and

crossed toward him, coming fully into the light so there was no way to miss seeing her loveliness. And the honesty that he could feel. "I am grateful for all you've done, but this is my battle, Joshua. I will manage it from here."

"The Hamilton brothers are probably out of jail by now."

"You need to distance yourself from me." *I'll miss you.* Claire hadn't realized it until that moment. Until the instant the palm of her hand covered the middle of his chest, where the hard bone and muscle covering his heart felt like steel against her hand.

The rise of his breathing, the pump of his pulse seemed to course through her skin and up her arm. Connected, when she didn't want to be. Bound, when she needed to be alone.

Anger dug harsh lines around his mouth as his fingers caught her wrist, keeping her from pulling away, from breaking the invisible tie between them. His fingertips seared like blue flame.

The power of his touch thundered in her soul. He seemed to swell up, as if ready for a fight, but she remained frozen in his grip, watching as his eyes turned flinty.

His voice pealed like winter thunder. "What is this? You're telling me to abandon you now? When the danger to you still exists?"

"There is a greater danger to you. I'll not have the Hamiltons coming after you or the sheriff asking questions about Ham's death. As grateful as I am—you've made an enormous difference, you saved my life—" Her voice broke, betraying her. Maybe she was betraying herself. She pulled away from his touch. "You need to stay as far away from me as possible. So there are no questions. So you and your loved ones are safe."

"And what will you do, Claire?"

"I can take care of myself."

God save him from independent-minded women. With the way she was standing with her arms folded over her breasts like a shield and her chin tilted upward, she reminded him of a picture of a siren he'd seen in one of his father's old books. There wasn't one pure thought in his head as his focus lingered on her lips, full and made for a man to kiss.

See? He was losing sight of his judgment and every ounce of the sound mind he always prided himself on. He didn't doubt her sincerity or her determination. The truth was that the world treated women alone with cruelty, at times. His chest ached with a strange tug of emotion, for hadn't Claire Hamilton shouldered enough unkindness?

The thought of her facing more ripped him savagely and he wrestled down a long string of curses and enough anger to melt a few dozen acres of snow outside the cabin walls. "I'm the kind of man to finish what I start. I said I'd help you, and I will."

"No one, not even my own family when I was girl, has been this kind to me. But the sheriff is going to start wondering why you are here. The Hamiltons already have. I don't want them taking the law into their own hands. They are lawless enough as it is."

"I told you. I can handle those boys."

"I don't want you to, Joshua. Not anymore..."

Couldn't he understand she was trying to do the right thing the same way he was? It wasn't as if he planned on keeping his brothers watching over her forever. "I owe you more than I can repay you as it is."

"I'm not here for your money, what little you have."

"And I'm not comfortable accepting help that borders on charity." His eyes flared and a muscle ticked in his jaw as he broke away from her, and she wondered just how much she'd offended him.

She was no match for the Hamiltons when it came to a gunfight. And yet she could not bring more trouble onto this good man's name. "You keep staying here, other than to help me when I…was infirm, but now Opal knows her son was shot, not killed from a fall from his horse. The doctor made that up, I know, to fool the sheriff."

"To protect an innocent. Self-defense is a hard thing, to be forced to kill, and to be forced to live with it after." Joshua's hands fisted. "I can't leave you alone, Claire."

"There's no other choice. You are not my brother or my friend or my husband. You have your own life far from here."

"Not so far." His throat was aching again, making it impossible to swallow. And nearly impossible to speak the words lining up in his head. "And you're wrong. Dead wrong."

She blanched at his harshness. He watched what little color she had drain from her lovely features. "I'm wrong about what?"

"That I'm not your friend." He headed straight out the door, keeping his back to her, refusing to look around as he slammed it shut behind him.

He stood in the bitter chill, drawing in cold air, as if that could freeze over the aching edge of emotions he didn't want to feel, didn't want to admit. He watched dawn paint the eastern rim of prairie lavender and the bellies of snow clouds a cool dull magenta.

He waited until reason returned, but it was a long time coming.

Almost an hour later, Claire couldn't help noticing her words to Joshua hadn't encouraged him to leave. As she wrapped her thickest muffler around her throat, she had a perfect view through the window.

There he was, as somber as the meager snowflakes falling dutifully to the ground. He was hitching up a sleek pinto to the small cart box, which he'd put on runners to make a boxy sleigh. He worked earnestly with his head down, as if impervious to the temperature.

Self-defense is a hard thing, to be forced to kill and to be forced to live with it after. I can't leave you alone, Claire. His words from earlier this morning haunted her as she watched him straighten and pat the mustang on her flank. The horse trusted him and turned to nuzzle her soft white nose against his gloved hand.

He was not a bad man, not bad at all. And that made it so much more difficult. Because if he was a horrible man, cruel or violent or inappropriate, then she wouldn't get this warm rush of emotion when she didn't think she could feel anything through the dark gray fog in her heart.

Then she wouldn't have this sting of attraction and admiration and bittersweet sadness because she already knew what she felt couldn't be realized.

True love didn't exist, not in this world. Perhaps men did not have the heart for it. Heaven knows she was worn through and too weary to love a man again. The trouble was, Joshua Gable made her want to believe.

Oh, yes he did. He's like a dream, the image of what a man ought to be. The kind of man she had wished for when she was growing up, taking what spare time and pennies she had to embroider pillowcases for her hope chest and wondering what exciting turn her life might take. What man she would end up falling in love with and marrying.

Life had once seemed packed with promises and possibilities. And now…

Now those possibilities were different, she realized as she double-checked the stove's damper and locked the door carefully behind her. Life was once again hers to make. What became of her future was her choice. Hers to make and hers alone.

Joshua spotted her and gave the mare one last nose rub. "I thought you might want to borrow a horse."

"What's wrong with Thor or Loki?" Alarm tickled through her and she knew before he said it. "They were taken along with the cattle, weren't they?"

"I've got my brothers keepin' an eye out. We think we know who has them."

Was it her imagination or was Joshua smiling? Actually grinning, showing his dimples and all. "Does that mean you can get them back for me?"

"Fine workhorses like that, a matched team, could sell for as much as five, six hundred dollars. And the thieves can't take them to the local auctions because someone is bound to recognize them."

"That was part of the paperwork of Thad's. I didn't read it because there's no way I would sell my horses. They're family to me."

"I know how that is." Joshua's smile faded as he stroked the mare's neck. "I'm fairly confident I can liberate them eventually. In the meantime, this is Stormy and she's gentle as can be. Tender-mouthed, though, so keep a loose rein on her and you won't have a problem."

"She's valuable, Joshua." This is why she couldn't help liking the man. On one hand, he was domineering, just providing her with a fine driving mare and assuming that it would be no problem. As if he had every right to solve her problems.

And then, on the other hand, he'd been thoughtful enough to care. "I can't accept anything so valuable, whether you're a friend or not."

"And just how are you getting to town this morning? You don't have wings to fly."

It ought to be against the law for a man to have dimples like that. Dimples that framed his spare grin and softened the hard, craggy features of his face. How was a woman to stand strong against such a man? "I can walk easily enough."

"What would the doc have to say about that?"

"He doesn't have bills to see to and a lawyer to hire, does he?" She peeled off one glove and let the mare scent her hand. She was a nice little thing, compact and sleek, with a white-and-brown painted coat that looked like expensive velvet. "I really can't walk all the way to town, although I'd like to."

"Not so soon after…" Joshua didn't finish his thought.

After complications from a miscarriage. She fought back a terrible sorrow. One so big it could drown her if she let it. Holding on tight to her emotions, she shoved the thought from her mind. "I meant what I said earlier. I can't accept this. Your help, your involvement. I won't have the Hamiltons wondering why you're here."

"They already are." He could see it wasn't just that independent will making her turn down a perfectly sensible solution to her situation. It was pride, too. And conscience. However low his opinion of most women, Claire just kept surprising him. She was a decent woman. "Tell you what. You rent her from me."

"She's still out of my budget."

"Then we'll settle up after your cattle sell and we get your Clydesdales back. How about that?"

"It's tolerable."

"Hell, now I'm relieved. Are you gonna get in the sled, or do I have to watch you ice over?" Annoyed, that's what he was. Not captivated. Because it was impossible. He'd never let a woman get under his skin like that. And yet, he couldn't help liking her, and not just a little.

"This is the end of it," she said, taking the reins and refusing his offer of a hand as she stepped into the sled. "You ride to town with me and you and your brothers go back to your lives. Don't misunderstand. I'll never forget what you've done, but I'm getting stronger. And I can do this just fine on my own."

Respect her? Yep, he did that. He saw the steel in her and that willowy strength. Not one complaint, and not one manipulative ploy since he'd come into her life. He'd see her to town first, and then he'd see.

"I guess I'll ride shotgun this one last time. Did I mention I have a cousin who's a lawyer in town? You might want to look him up."

"Somehow I knew you were going to say that." She settled her skirts on the board seat with one hand, keeping her gaze there, although he could see the hint of a smile on those soft lips so temptingly sweet. "How do you stay in such complete charge of everything? Of solving every foreseeable problem?"

"It's a talent." He shrugged, not at all humble, because he was good at being in charge. He didn't mind that she saw it, too.

All the way to town, he kept a few paces behind her sled. But there was no danger he sensed. No gut instinct that trouble was lurking.

Maybe she was right. The Hamiltons were managed. The danger to her was past. It was a legal matter from here, and his cousin could handle that for her. His part in her life was done. If it made him a little sad to leave her in town, outside Callan's law office, then he ignored the tug in his chest.

Or the sense of something lost, something he couldn't name, as he tipped his hat to her and left her standing in the sugary snow, an image of loveliness and strength that stayed with him.

Chapter Eleven

Claire's eyes popped open to utter darkness. The night thrummed with tension.

The threads of dreams were gone. There had been no nightmare, and the silence felt heavy in the bedroom as she sat up, letting the warm covers rustle as they fell from her upper body.

What had awakened her? A noise? Some danger in the night? Or simply her own unease at being alone, all alone, on a quarter section of land on the edge of civilization. Then she heard the eerie howl of a wolf right outside the cabin wall. So close she could hear the gasp of breath the creature took as he howled again.

Far away in the distance, another of its kind answered.

There were no cattle to worry over. No horses in the fields. Only Stormy, who was locked up tight in the stable. Alone.

Damn the Hamiltons and whoever had stolen her horses and milk cow. She'd lost her deal with the town's mercantile. She couldn't very well sell butter if she had no milk to make it from.

And then came her meeting with the banker, where she realized that Annabelle and Thad had emptied and closed Ham's accounts. There had been signed documents from Ham to prove it, although she wasn't sure if Ham's signature was real or forged.

The wolf howled again so close to the house the boards seemed to vibrate with the eerie, hair-raising sound.

That's it. They were way too close. She sat up in bed and fumbled for the match tin. A single strike had a weak flame tossing enough light for her to find the lantern's wick and light it. Illumination chased back the dark shadows, and the pad of the wolf's gait didn't seem as frightening. She'd heard wolves before, but not when she'd been alone.

Her movements echoed in the silent cabin, the darkness a strange living entity, growing thicker and more menacing in the corners as she made her way through the cabin. Tiptoeing, she moved carefully on the wood floor, careful to avoid the planks and joints she knew would creak.

It was important that she make no sound, because Ham hated it when she woke him. He'd go from snoring to frothing rage in a breath's span, and—

Claire, Ham is gone.

The realization lit her mind with clarity. What was she doing, how could she have forgotten Ham was no longer ruling her life? That he never would again. That she'd never have to worry about making noise and waking him up. Or what kind of mood he'd wake up to every morning. Or when he came home from riding the property, if he'd be violent or if he'd really been out drinking with his buddies.

It's over. It was as if her heart realized it for the first time. She was free. Really, truly free. She'd never need to tiptoe or work so hard to keep a man from finding an excuse to lose his temper. Never again.

Tears burned in her eyes. Emotion ached in her throat. Her thighs felt shivery with relief so she hauled out a chair from the nearby kitchen table and sank into it, reveling in the squeak the wood legs made against the wood floor. The sound reverberated faintly against the bare plank walls before fading into silence.

Of course, she'd known she was free, but she hadn't realized how deep her habits had become and all the ways she'd changed her behavior because of Ham so as not to upset him.

She was no victim; she'd never crumpled. She would never let a man break her spirit the way her mother's had been broken, but marriage was forever. Once done, the vows spoken, there was no going back. And she never would have married Ham if she'd known the real man beneath the charming manner he'd pretended to have. She'd been tricked, and she'd done her best.

It's over. Really and truly over. The silence around her answered by echoing back her own stifled sob. Just as it had taken her heart a while to understand what her head had already figured out after her marriage—Ham didn't love her, not at all. Married life was not going to be the way she'd dreamed of it.

And now she saw the truth of her life. She had peace,

she had her life back. Hers alone. No man could ever have the right to rule her again.

The wolf outside had followed her through the cabin. She could sense his presence on the other side of the wall. The cabin wasn't well sealed, and the icy cold had frosted on the table and the floor at her feet, turning the nail heads an icy white that glistened whenever the lantern light touched. She could hear a second padding gait through the tiny cracks between the boards. They were pacing, still they weren't stalking yet.

But they would be.

She swiped the dampness from her lashes. This was her property to defend. Hers and hers alone. Leaving the lantern on the table, she waded through the shadows to the mantel, the hearth beneath it dark, the embers well banked, and let her fingers wander among the handguns.

There were several different kinds, but she knew next to nothing about guns. One revolver slung in a hook on the wall caught her interest. It was like the one Joshua used. A deadly iron nose and a smooth wooden handle that felt oddly powerful against her palm.

She spun open the chamber as she'd seen Ham do a thousand times. The lead of the bullets gleamed dully back at her. Good, she wouldn't have to worry about loading the thing or which bullets to use. She'd rather not waste any more time.

The window was iced and the sill groaned and crackled when she gave it a push. Too much noise, more than she'd been hoping for. But one glance through the frost-glazed glass told her that the wolves hadn't moved. Not two, but three giant creatures, too wild and dangerous to ever be thought of as doglike, had backed up to get a good look at her.

The faint starlight trickling between the heavy banks of clouds above was enough to dust the snow like silver, making the wolves nothing but black shadows and gleaming feral eyes.

The biggest—the leader—paraded forward, his mouth open to show the sharp edges of fanged teeth and hunger glazing his eyes. They weren't after the horse in the stable. They'd wanted her.

Chilling fear snaked down her spine. They couldn't somehow get into the cabin, could they? They'd never tried this before, but then they could have scented the danger of an armed man on the premises. Now that powerful male presence was gone.

Fine. She could handle a few nasty predators. She could tell the lead wolf didn't think she was a threat to him. He brazenly stared back at her, as if he were well aware she had opened the window, perhaps, in his view, giving him an opening.

She wound the gun into her nightgown so the click was muffled as she thumbed back the hammer, something she'd seen Ham do countless times. The wolf's ears lifted, as if he'd heard the sound but was wondering about it. He froze but didn't retreat.

Okay, Claire, you can do this. She hadn't fired a gun before, but how hard could it be? She had to be steady. She had to make this count.

The wolf dismissed the faint click and padded forward another few paces. The two friends stalked nearer to join forces with him. The air tensed, as if waiting for them to attack.

They were huge animals up close. Much bigger than she would have guessed. Her forefinger slid into place around the trigger.

Just point and pull the trigger. That's all she had to do. As she raised her arm, bringing the gun up to the crack in the window, the lead wolf sprang.

Enormous paws clawed at the two-inch gap in the window. Horror rushed through her as she realized the window was opening. A black nose and white teeth flashed as one paw hung onto the sill and the wolf's head butted the widow frame until the glass cracked. Saliva dripped onto the floor.

Shoot! It was as if an outside force had steadied the revolver and squeezed around her finger. The .45 fired with a flash of light and smoke and the wolf tumbled away in silence, leaving a wet, dark smear on the fractured glass.

Blood? Before she could think about that, a dark force hurled against the window.

One of the panes shattered, spraying shards over her nightgown as a snout penetrated and fangs snapped open. Lethal hatred flashed in those soulless eyes before she pulled back the hammer and squeezed again.

And again.

Until there was nothing but smoke and silence.

Alone in the kitchen, her breathing rasped fast and shallow and seemed to echo in the open beams overhead. Adrenaline kicked like seven cups of coffee in her blood. She stared dully at the open window, where trees sat frosted and still. A glimpse of the sky showed her the last of the stars had been swallowed up by clouds, leaving it too dark to see anything more than the faint humps of three wolves outside.

Were they dead? Or would they spring back to life, injured and enraged by pain? Whatever she did, she'd better figure out how to cover the window, because she remembered the distant answering howl from earlier. These were not the only wolves in the area.

Something snapped in the wooded grove just beyond the house. That was her answer. More were coming. And she had only two bullets left. There were boxes of ammunition by the front door, but it was several paces away, too far to go to leave the window undefended.

Well, she'd stop as many wolves as she could and then she'd worry about it, because there was a faint shadow rearing up out of the trees. Adrenaline surged through her, making her arms jerky so she nestled the .45's nose on the wooden sill and lined up the siting notch with the center of the moving shadow.

"Claire?" Joshua's voice came as quiet as a hush, but welcome.

So incredibly welcome. The revolver slid from her grip and tumbled to the floor. "You. What are you— You're not supposed to be out here."

"Guilty. It didn't quite sit right with me to leave you out here all by your lonesome. But maybe you don't need anyone watching out for you after all." He halted near the window, where the lifeless wolves lay. "Impressive shot."

"Th-thank you." Every part of her trembled. "Joshua.

It's not safe out there. I heard other wolves." Her mind was spinning. Of course Joshua knew about the dangers.

"Hold on. I'll be in to fix that window. You'll unbolt the door?"

She nodded. Nausea gripped her stomach as she plucked the Colt from the floor and nudged the weapon onto the table. Joshua was gone. He'd merged with the darkness. The night seemed to be only a thousand shades of black.

After unbolting the front door, she listened for Joshua's footsteps as she knelt with the broom and dustpan to do something about the broken glass. Keeping her hands busy kept her from thinking about what could have happened.

By the time the door swung open, she had the floor swept clean and the broom and dustpan back in place in the pantry. She'd managed to calm her frayed nerves as well. Joshua didn't look at her but went straight to the window and right to work.

She brought a lamp from the front room and set it, lit, on the table for him to see by. He didn't seem to notice as he tapped thin nails into the wooden frame and sill until the thick square of board, a scrap he must have found in the barn, neatly covered the gaping hole.

"That ought to keep the wolves out. As long as you don't go opening any more windows." Joshua set the old hammer from the barn next to her Colt on the table and hauled out a chair. The backs of his knuckles were bruised and swollen. One had a cut that looked as if it was trying to heal over. She'd seen wounds like that before.

She blinked, aware she was staring. She could feel

his gaze, curious, on her. He'd caught her noticing. She licked her dry lips and realized her tongue was dry, too. "Do you want me to heat some tea water? Or coffee?"

"I don't have time and you don't need the bother."

"Me? What about you? You bothered to come all this way when you should be warm and safe in your bed. I could have shot you tonight, Joshua. I never could have lived with myself if anything like that had happened. I..."

Dismay flowed through her. She heard the raw, unmasked emotion in her voice as she covered her face with her hands. She'd had no intention of caring about Joshua Gable so very much. "What I meant to say is that I couldn't live with shooting anyone, and you've done so much for me."

"Sure." He nodded, as if she'd said the sensible thing. "Then I figure you know how I gotta feel. Being told you didn't want me around when you need protection, Claire. The Hamiltons are out of jail—the sheriff let them go—and to tell you the truth, unless you pick a man to marry and get him to move in here with guns enough to protect you, the Hamiltons aren't going to rest."

Her hopes sank. "Especially after this morning in town and finding out the family drained the bank accounts. Thad supposedly had documents with Ham's signature, but Ham was too protective of his money. He wouldn't have trusted Thad to have paperwork like that."

Joshua's hard face showed no hint of surprise at the news. "What did my cousin say?"

"That I was right. Thad and his wife were trying to take the land. Your cousin was very helpful, but the truth is, I have nothing but debts and there will be a legal fight about the land. He won't know until he puzzles the mess out. And for your information, I have no intention of marrying again."

"It's what widows your age do." He watched Claire's creamy complexion turn pink, and he'd lived with enough women over the years to recognize the spark of temper that flashed in her eyes and bracketed her mouth. "Now don't go getting het up."

"I'm not upset."

"I only meant that most widows wind up remarried. It's the sensible solution. Most have children or debts or land to take care of, and it's hard for a woman to learn to be a rancher overnight. Of course, some are like my stubborn sister and sell off their land and move to town and start a business…never mind."

He tamped down anger that had nothing to do with Claire and everything to do with the sister he'd been doing his best to protect. Not that she'd made it easy for him. And neither had Claire, come to think of it. "I only meant you're a sensible woman, Claire."

"Sensible?"

Uh-oh. Judging by the tilt of her slim brow, she didn't like that word. "Tell you what. You don't get mad at me for stickin' my foot in my mouth, and I'll give you the good news."

She merely quirked her raised brow higher. He hadn't expected that. He'd pretty much pegged Claire as a delicate rose. But this was not the first time he'd seen her steel, her fire. And it launched him in the direction of the door faster than if she'd outright proposed to him.

But first, there was one more thing. He unbuttoned

his coat and dipped into his shirt pocket. He handed her a thick fold of cash. The brush of his fingertip against hers held the wallop of a mustang's kick.

She rocked back on her heels, aware suddenly that she was alone with him, and that her skin beneath her flannel nightgown and long johns tingled into goose bumps.

Why did this man affect her? She looked longingly at the strong plane of his chest and remembered well how remarkable it felt to rest there.

"The cash from the cattle. Didn't get top dollar, but James did a hell of a sweet talk to get what he did. This time of season, with a winter ahead to hay feed, prices are at their lowest."

Claire felt too dazed to think of anything mundane. She glanced at the repaired windowpane and at the man who looked fierce as those wolves had been, and became *aware*.

Aware of being female, of the weight of her unbound breasts. And with the way Joshua was gazing at her with eyes as dark as the lead wolf. And, she wondered, as hungry?

He ripped away from her before she could guess the answer to that question, leaving her for the door. He walked away with his calm steady gait, his back straight, and his logger's shoulders squared. "Be sure and lock up after me. And don't tell me not to help you again, Claire."

What did that mean? Her body was tingling, crawling with awareness for him, an awakening she didn't want even as she craved to reach out and draw him back. To hold on to the long, muscled length of him and find out if he was real.

"This is over six hundred dollars, Joshua."

"Like I said, I wish it could have been more."

"N-no. This is a fortune." It wasn't the money that was doing this to her, although she stared down at it as if it was. Emotion clogged her throat. Her eyes burned so the folded greenbacks in her hand blurred. "Did you take out the money I owe you?"

His footsteps halted. Then knelled, coming closer to her. His voice sounded oddly tender in the crisp, frigid air. "What do you owe me?"

He said it as if he couldn't possibly imagine. As if he rescued women and ran off villains and rode in to save the day and it was nothing extraordinary.

He couldn't know she had less than fifty dollars to her name. That Thad's lien against the property might turn out to be legitimate once her lawyer got to the truth of the matter. That she had no notion how she was going to find and hold down a job when the closest town was fifteen miles away.

He couldn't know that she'd been sure of nothing all day, and that any number of men she'd come across in her life would have kept this money for themselves, or a good chunk of it.

It wasn't the money that mattered. It was the decency of the man before her. It astounded her. He was a tall, dark hunk of granite, staring down at her motionless, as if he wasn't sure how to deal with her and the tears trickling down her face. One brow arched in a question over his dark eyes, the hard stone cut of his face softened as he covered her hand with his, the fold of money digging into her palm.

"Claire, you don't owe me a thing."

"You're wrong. I owe you everything." Couldn't he see what he was? What he'd done for her? He was a man, real and flawed like the rest of them, but he was cut from a far better quality of cloth. But that didn't mean she could believe. "I counted up the winter supplies you brought out. It was nearly two hundred dollars."

"Keep your money."

"But that would be charity, and I don't need it. I can make my own way."

"I don't doubt that one bit." The center of his chest gave a big whack. He'd make sure the Hamiltons left her alone, no matter what it cost him. It was the right thing to do, sure, but he couldn't fool himself anymore.

This wasn't about what was right or what was responsibility. He wanted good things for her, this woman with a place in his soul. She tore her hand away and counted out two of the six hundred dollars. To his surprise she stuffed the folded wad into his shirt pocket. Neat. Easy.

And then she came up on tiptoes, so close every hair on his body stood up on end and his skin buzzed as she pressed a silken kiss to his cheek.

His heart went thump again, and began to fall as she sank her white even teeth into her lush rosebud-soft bottom lip, as if she were in deep thought. As if she were debating telling him one more time to butt out of her life.

No way, lady. It was emotion that drove him, a fierce need that drove him forward as his fingers cradled her delicate chin and he breathed in her sweet rose scent.

He could read the surprise on her face as he slanted

his mouth over hers. Time to find out if her lips were as satin soft as he hoped. As luxurious as he dreamed. As tempting as he feared.

At the first brush of his mouth to hers, he felt her satin warmth and tasted her fire.

Yes. She was beyond dreams, beyond temptation. He wanted more of her, even as he broke their kiss and turned away, blood racing and desire strumming in his groin.

Hell, he was hard with blinding need and his sensible, practical defenses would shatter into pieces if he kissed her again. If he didn't walk out that door and into the wintry, lonely night and never, ever, give in to an urge like this again.

It didn't hit him until he'd slammed the door shut behind him and he was safely outside in the dark, that she hadn't pushed him away. She'd kissed him, too. And that a mere thin board wall at his back stood between him and the worst mistake he could ever make.

He stalked away in time to notice more wolves had arrived. He checked his Winchester, fired enough shots to keep them at bay. He'd clean up the mess, make sure the cabin and the stable were secure, and then he'd head home.

If there were men hanging around, the wolves were shy by nature and smart. They knew they were no match for a man with a rifle. So their presence tonight told him Claire was safe from the Hamiltons come to scare her out of her house or, worse, blame her for their brother's death.

And he was glad for that. Because he needed to get the hell away from here. He had to get Claire out of his system. The woman's silhouette fell against the closed front-room curtains, where she sat with her head in her hands, as if in defeat.

It was how he felt, too.

Chapter Twelve

Joshua's kiss. It was all she could think about over the next few weeks and on that sunny afternoon as she guided Stormy through Bluebonnet's busy streets. Was she thinking about the bad drivers and pushy teamsters? Oh, no, she wasn't attending to anything sensible—just Joshua's kiss.

It wasn't as if she didn't have enough troubles to distract her. No, the Hamiltons were keeping her attorney busy, and four men she barely recognized had each stopped by, interrupting her work, to ask her for a sleigh ride. Honestly! Did they think she couldn't see what they wanted? Two were widowers with small children—men looking for a woman to raise their children. Another had recently lost his land—a common enough fate around the county since the last two summers' weather had destroyed most wheat crops. Another in the process of buying up land from failing farmers—those men only saw one thing. Her land.

Men seemed to be as plentiful as gophers in a field,

and she sent them all back where they came from and good riddance.

As she reined the horse to a halt in front of the town's dress shop, she couldn't think of one reason she needed a man in her life. Not one reason.

Except for that kiss.

Kisses, technically. For something she hadn't wanted, she sure spent a lot of time unwillingly re-membering. The crush of his fingertips as he held her chin upward—not brutal, not harsh, just…possessive. And not possessive in a bad way, as if he owned her. But in a heart-stopping, breath-stealing way that had made her heart tingle…and still did.

Stop thinking about Joshua's kiss. Annoyed with her-self, she tethered Stormy well to the hitching post and returned to the sled. Ever since Joshua had slanted his mouth over hers, she would forget her head if it wasn't attached at the neck. She sorted through the blankets on the seat until she found her reticule on the floorboard. It had fallen into a crate of Ham's things. Things she would drop off at the attorney's. Opal and Ham's broth-ers deserved to have Ham's personal effects, some of which were family heirlooms. There had been no more trouble with the Hamiltons. Strangely, everything had been silent. She had to wonder if those bruises and cuts on Joshua's knuckles, obviously from a fight, were the reason.

Not that she endorsed violence, so why did emotions inside her chest swell like a soap bubble? Because she could no longer blame the awareness she felt for Joshua on simple gratitude. *I'm not in love with him, either,* she consoled herself as she clomped up the wooden steps to the raised boardwalk.

I do not want to ever be in love with any man ever again, she vowed as she knocked the snow from her boots. With her common sense firmly in place, she pushed through the etched-glass door and into the dress shop.

A woman with thick hair coiled up stylishly on her head and ringlet curls tumbling around her friendly face looked up from a button display. "Claire, why you're looking well. It's so good to see you. How are you?"

Betsy Gable Hunter, Joshua's sister, was by far the friendliest person that Claire had ever met. It was impossible not to like her. "I've come to shop, so I'm doing very well. And you?"

"Oh, shopping, too. There's nothing better…wait, there is one thing better." Betsy's rosy cheeks turned rosier.

Mrs. Jance, the store's owner, breezed into sight carrying a loaded tea tray. "Why, hello, Claire. Never mind this one." She nodded toward Betsy as she lowered the tray to the display counter. "She's about to become a bride. And someone didn't wait until after the ceremony."

Didn't wait for what? Claire wondered as she accepted the steaming cup of sweet tea Mrs. Jance handed to her. Betsy's blush seemed to grow, and then Claire realized. They were talking about marital relations. If there was a polite word for that. Horror washed through her, remembering her wedding night.

No, surely that wasn't what the two women were joking about. Mrs. Jance was chuckling and Betsy's twinkling eyes were bright as stars. Certainly no woman would be speaking about that in such a merry way.

"Claire, do you mind waiting just a bit?" Mrs. Jance, polite and professional as always, picked up her tray. "I need to deliver the rest of these, and then get Betsy's items. Then I'll be right with you."

"I wanted to look around first." Claire took another sip of the bracing tea. The heat trickled down to her stomach and seemed to warm her right up. It had been a sunny but chilly ride to town. "Betsy, I owe you for the last laundry delivery. You were kind enough to leave the bundle without payment, and I stopped by your house on my last trip to town, but you weren't in—"

"Forget it," Betsy interrupted with a wave of her hand. "Granny told me what happened. I'm sorry, Claire. I'll miss stopping by to visit, of course, but I figured you wouldn't be needing my services."

They both knew what Betsy was kind enough not to mention. The only reason she'd hired Betsy out of her butter money was because of her pregnancy. Now there was no reason for her not to be lifting heavy tubs of water. As for forgetting about paying for her laundry, how could she possibly conscience that? Her pride prickled. "No, that's far too kind—"

"I have the best idea," Betsy said, and clanked her teacup into its frail saucer. "I have been looking for someone to take over my business. Now, you might not be interested and I'd understand—"

Me, take over her laundry business? Claire took a step back, hearing Betsy's words, but they wouldn't quite register in her brain. Why, she had to find work eventually, but she'd never considered her own enterprise.

"—but when I was widowed, the last thing I wanted

was handouts and when Mariah, who started the service, married, I jumped at the opportunity. Washing other people's underdrawers isn't a glamorous way to make a living, but it's good steady income and I have been quite happy. Claire, are you interested?"

"Why, I haven't thought of it. I need to find work." How to find work was a problem she hadn't felt like mentioning to Betsy. All she knew how to do was cook and clean, which left work here in town at the diners and hotels, but jobs were scarce. She'd checked. And how could she keep a job in town when she lived so far away? She had so much to consider. But this. This could work. It wouldn't matter, because she could work at home and the delivery route would be quite long—

There was no feasible way she could afford it, and she choked on the excitement building in her midsection. She'd managed her money carefully, but surely to buy a business cost more than she had. Probably much more. "It sounds like a good opportunity, but Betsy, I couldn't do it."

"Of course, you could. You could come along with me for a few weeks. I'd teach you everything you need to know. You'd be perfect for it. I don't know how I didn't think of it before."

Betsy didn't understand. How could she? There she was looking at expensive mother-of-pearl buttons, when Claire had never owned anything of real mother-of-pearl. Betsy looked like an illustration out of *Godey's* come to life with her store-bought lace fichu pinned at the throat of her tailored velveteen dress that was probably made special-order by Mrs. Jance.

Betsy looked lovely and she had lovely things. She was from one of the most respected and wealthiest families in the county. She couldn't understand. She shot a glance at the town ladies seated around the fashion books at the sunny table in the corner. They all looked up with interest.

Feeling plain and out of place in her homemade clothes, Claire notched her chin a little higher. It wouldn't hurt to ask how much Betsy wanted for her business. It was out of her reach, that was for sure. A business had to cost a lot of money.

She had a horse to buy since she couldn't borrow Joshua's mare forever. And after taxes at year's end, she would be needing to watch every penny until she found work. But maybe… Her hopes rose, she couldn't help it. Only to be disappointed, she knew, but she asked anyway. "How much would you want?"

Betsy blinked. "For what?"

"For your business."

"Oh, goodness, I don't think it's worth a wooden penny." Betsy leaned in conspiratorially, realizing the other ladies were listening.

"That can't be true."

"I took over when Mariah married, and I can't tell you what a boon it was. It's hard work, but it's provided me with a decent living. I'm getting married next month, and I've been in a quandary. How do I leave my clients who've been so good to me over the years? No, it's best I find someone to take over. How about it?"

"You shouldn't turn this into me doing you a favor,

Betsy. Surely you paid something for the business to start with?"

"Not a thing. And you would be doing me a huge favor. I need someone reliable, and my clients would love you. You're nice and my brother sure thinks the world of you."

"Joshua?" She tried to think past the turmoil his name brought. Confusion and awe and lip-tingling kisses. "He thinks the world of me?"

"I know, it's hard to tell. He's always so frowny and gruff. He's very serious about his responsibilities, and that's a good thing. He just works far too hard. What he needs…" Betsy trailed off. Her cheeks turned rosier again. "You do know that you're invited to my wedding, right?"

"Uh…your wedding?"

"You know, the holy-vows-that-a-man-and-woman-take-in-front-of-witnesses event?"

"I've heard of it." Claire tried not to be suspicious of Betsy's sudden change of subject and a happy twinkle making her eyes shine with what could only be hope. Betsy was caught up in the excitement of her engagement. Of course, she would want her older brother to be equally happy. It was hard to fault warmhearted Betsy for her very see-through matchmaking efforts.

Betsy charged right on without waiting for a response. "C'mon, say yes. This is a special day for me, and I want all my friends there."

"Me? I…"

"We are friends, you know. So come celebrate with me and my family."

"Don't you mean with Joshua, too?"

"Oh, no!" Betsy could feign innocence beautifully. "Granny adores you, and she doesn't like many people, and family events haven't been the same since our father died. Please, say you'll come. Oh, and Mama and Granny and I are sorely outnumbered when it comes to dining with the boys." Betsy set aside her teacup. "You would be doing us a favor."

What about Joshua? How could she possibly attend a wedding, surrounded by his family no less, and his mother, and not relive his kiss? She'd never known a man's kiss could be like that. Could be so everything. Passionate and fiery and tender and beautiful all at once. A kiss like that could muddle a girl's common sense. A kiss like Joshua's could make her believe in what she knew wasn't true. What was impossible.

"Now that we've got that settled," Betsy continued, "we'll discuss what day suits you best for coming along to learn the business."

A whole new life. It stretched out before her like a dream. It wasn't the same one she'd had as a naive bride in her wedding dress, hoping for happiness and love and a family. No, with her miscarriage all chances of that had died, too.

But she had this chance to make something good with what remained. Wasn't that a rare gift? A chance like this didn't come along often, and she'd been too hurt for too long not to grab on tight with both hands.

She'd forget Joshua Gable's toe-curling kiss, because that path led nowhere.

This road did. She had more than a job, she had a

business. With her attorney's help, she could keep her cabin and land and make a real home for herself. She'd be alone, but she'd be safe. And after what she'd endured, loneliness didn't seem so bad.

It was wise to keep as much distance from him as she could. She'd made a vow to herself. No more thoughts about Joshua. Not one. Not of his kiss, or the one they almost shared. Not of the man he was, how kind he was, how he'd helped her. If her lips remembered the thrill of his kiss, then eventually, that memory would fade.

That settled it. How could she say no to Betsy, who was offering her a chance at her own business? "I'd be happy to come."

"Perfect. I'll tell Mama's maid to expect one more for the dinner after." Betsy clasped her hands, radiating more happiness now that she was imagining, no doubt, and matchmaking for her brother.

Let her try, Claire decided, the ghost of Joshua's kiss still on her lips. It's simply not meant to be.

Mrs. Jance bustled into sight, carrying over her arm the loveliest dress Claire had ever seen. That had to be real silk, for no imitation could carry the luster of a precious stone. The fair, pale yellow fabric shone with a pearl's luster, and the matching lace had to be real French lace. Nothing Claire had ever seen equaled the intricate elegance of those dainty stitches.

The rich liquid rustle of the silk came as sweet as a melody once Betsy reached for the dress and gasped with delight. "It's done! You told me you weren't finished with it! Oh, this is more than I imagined. Oh, thank you. I'm...almost speechless! Me!"

The dressmaker's smile was reserved, but there was no mistaking that she was pleased with Betsy's response. "I wanted to surprise you. I promised you that I would have this done in plenty of time for the wedding. And I have a little surprise, too. An early wedding gift for your trousseau."

Mrs. Jance laid a package wrapped in dainty white paper on the counter next to Betsy's tea. She then turned her kind eyes to Claire. "I have saved up a whole box of my nicest remnants for you. Come into my office and take as long as you like to go through it. How are you feeling?"

She doesn't know about the miscarriage. Grief lifted in a fresh wave, but she managed to answer almost normally. "I was hoping to look at your remnants, thank you."

Betsy surprised her by reaching out and squeezing her hand. An unexpected touch of comfort, something a friend would do. Claire's throat ached. Unable to find her voice, she had to let silence answer, but the steady empathy in Betsy's eyes spoke of understanding.

As she followed the shopkeeper through the busy store, she felt hope wrap around her like a wool blanket. Hope that the future ahead of her would not always be bleak and lonely.

Joshua gritted his teeth, knuckled down his hat and nosed General straight into the cutting wind. It came from the east, gaining speed as it sailed across the high prairie plateau. A mean wind, and it was making his cracked ankle complain something fierce. He'd give just about anything to be inside right now soaking up the heat from a snapping fire.

But bad weather was on its way and he wanted the last of the livestock rotated into the pastureland close to home. Rustling wasn't big this time of year, but he'd lost a few animals to predators and they'd be safer off the open grazing lands.

Not that the steers understood that. The sheep had been easy—get the leader going in the right direction and the entire herd would follow placidly along. But cows, hell. They had twice the smarts of a sheep unless they were stampeding, and you couldn't keep the bunch of them together.

"Stop lollygaggin', Jordan!" he hollered, in no mood for the youngest brother's inattention. "Bring that red steer in toward the others. Hell!"

Too damn late. The young steer took off for the open prairie and Jordan after him, leaving the entire right flank open. A few other steers took notice and headed off that way, too.

"He's not a cattleman." James shook his head in disappointment. "Or much of a sheep man, either. You want to ride up and close the gap?"

"I'll take it." James had a patient eye and was good riding the tail and keeping the herd paced. As for Jordan, well, hell, he didn't know what in blazes to do about his youngest brother. The wind seemed to hurl at him faster, damn near freezing the blood in his veins. And that had been a hell of a hard thing to do once he'd kissed Claire Hamilton. His temperature had seemed well above normal ever since.

Maybe that's why he was working hard. He told everyone who'd listen that he'd fallen behind keeping an eye out for the widow, but in truth, working hard kept his mind off her. Because any thought he had seemed to center on that kiss and roll on from there. And what good could come from that?

Not one bit of good.

He convinced a few strays to mosey on back to the herd and then he set out for Jordan, who'd been distracted over one single steer. "Get your ass over here, little brother, and—"

The prairie rolled downward, giving him a sudden view of the iced-over creek bed below. And horse tracks. Shod draft horses. He got a tickle deep in his gut. Looking around, he tried to figure out whose land bordered the road to town. Not the Hamiltons'. And Deputy Logan's land was farther south.

But if they cut across this quarter section, it just might come out on Logan's land. Logan. The image of him astride Claire's sturdy Clydesdale made his stomach burn. It was a long shot, and those tracks were fresh. "Jordan, get back to the herd. I'll bring this one in."

"Uh…sure."

It was simple enough to convince the tenacious steer with a few light whacks of the lariat to head on back. Joshua met up with James, sitting his saddle as easily as if it were temperate weather. James was a tough one. "You've been keepin' watch on the deputy's place?"

"Every other night after midnight, just to see. Not a sign of the Clydesdales Miz Hamilton lost."

"You think he'd corral 'em up on someone else's land?"

"This time of year, why not? Most ranchers have their livestock close in."

"Are you up to a midnight ride tonight?"

"You mean, you want company?" James gave him a knowing wink and pulled his muffler up over his face as if he were hiding a grin. "All this effort for a pretty widow. Some might think you had some reason to be sitting on her hilltop making sure she could sleep safe and sound."

Joshua's conscience gave a kick. No one, not even James, knew he'd shot Ham that night. Maybe not the bullet that killed him, but he'd played a role in that night. And judging by the way James was laughing, he'd already drawn his own conclusion. "I'm not sweet on the widow," Joshua said.

"Sure, you're not. We do this for every new widow."

"Glad you think it's so funny." He didn't have time for this. Didn't his brothers know him better than that? He was immune to love. Or more accurately, immune to the effect of a woman's wiles, because that's what love was. A man giving in to his need for sex, that simple. He was smart because he'd figured this out long before other men his age. Maybe because he had so much responsibility, he'd been too busy to fall when his school buddies had. They were tied down, dominated, and their very happiness every single hour of the day depended on how happy their wives were. That was a man's lot.

But not his.

"Say, how's the little wife of yours, James?" He waited until he heard James groan. "Has she thawed out from being pissed at you for going down to the Great Falls auction? Or are you back to sleeping in your warm bed?"

"Be careful, Brother." James yanked down his muffler to speak, but he was grinning as if he found something tremendously amusing. "You just might be singing a different tune. You never know."

"What's that supposed to mean?"

Liam hauled back as the river of cattle kept moving forward. "I think he means that you just might have a woman controlling you before the end of the year."

"I say by Christmas," Jordan hollered over the herd.

What the devil? Were his little brothers taking bets about when he'd get married? He'd never heard of such a fool notion. "Get back to work. All of you."

"A hundred bucks for right after Betsy's wedding." James sounded…as if he were trying not to choke on his laughter.

Damn it. "This isn't one bit funny. Liam, there's a calf heading off—"

"I see it, don't get your drawers in a twist." He waved one gloved hand as if he was dismissing the house servant. "I'll match your hundred."

"I think I can come up with that much!" Jordan chortled from the sidelines. "Oh, ho! Big brother married. We all knew this day would come."

"And then I won't be the only sorry cuss with a wife to appease." James seemed to think this was hilarious.

Everyone laughed as if it were the best joke.

When it wasn't one bit funny. "All right, I can take a joke. Let's get back to work. And keep your money in your billfolds."

"It's a free country. A man can bet if he wants." Liam drew up his mare. "I say we give the whole pot to Granny and let her be in charge of it. Sorry, big brother. This is what you get for taking a spark to a pretty woman. A *very* pretty woman. It happens to every good man eventually. Sure, you think no one can see the way you're feeling, when it's about as subtle as a bonfire at midnight."

"More like a prairie wildfire," James added. "Joshua has gone a long time without a woman. He was bound to fall hard."

There was nothing amusing in this at all. They'd gone too far, and it was about all he could take. "I haven't fallen hard, and damn it, Jordan, I'd better take over."

Joshua was glad for the chance to retreat. It wasn't every day his brothers got the best of him. They were mistaken, but it was a logical assumption. He supposed he'd take more ribbing before this was over.

And it almost was. This consoled him as he took over point. He and his brothers had handled the Hamilton brothers—no big deal. It had taken five minutes out of an evening, and now he was a step closer to returning her horses to her. She was safe, her cattle were sold and this last piece would be the end of it.

The absolute end of it. No more widow, no more infatuation, no more physical intimacy. Hell, it had been only a kiss. It wasn't any big deal. Not at all. Just two lips touching. That's all.

It didn't mean he wanted to throw away every last bit of his good sense and propose.

It didn't mean that he even wanted to kiss the woman again.

It certainly didn't mean his brothers were right, because they weren't. He never had to see Claire Hamilton again, plain and simple. And he wouldn't.

Well, as soon as he'd returned her horses to her, of course. One accidental impulsive kiss was a mistake.

But giving in to temptation and giving himself a second opportunity to do that again—why, that would be a calamity. He was too careful a man to come close to that kind of woman-made disaster.

So, why couldn't he stop the feeling that he was riding to keep ahead of a storm? Behind him the horizon was clear and the Rockies speared up like giants from the prairie floor. Their glacier peaks shimmered. The sun was shining, and not a snow cloud in sight. It wasn't that kind of storm.

It tailed him all the way home.

Chapter Thirteen

The next few frosty days blurred by. Working along-side Betsy had proven exhausting, but Claire didn't mind hard work. What she minded were her sore mus-cles unused to scrubbing vigorously at a washboard for hours on end.

She winced at the muscle pain in her arms as she tacked the curtain into place. The pretty light pink cal-ico pearled in the lamplight. Claire backed off the chair and, when her feet were firmly on the floor again, she admired her work. She loved the delicate pattern of green leaves and pink rosebuds.

Mrs. Jance always had the prettiest fabric. And she suspected Betsy had informed the shopkeeper of the miscarriage, since the seamstress had bustled into the back room with more boxes of remnants.

Some losses never heal, she thought as she took the chair back to the kitchen table. Certainly her losses re-mained as palpable as the shadows surrounding her. The rustle of her skirt and the pad of her shoes echoed as she put the kettle to boil for tea water, and those movements clinked and stirred the silence.

Maybe she wouldn't always be alone, but for now it suited her fine. She snapped open the canister. The crisp aromatic scent of tea was like a comfort. Just right for a dark November evening like this one. The wind howled like a wolf outside the window, and the tiny hairs on her arms stood straight up, as if remembering the wolves that had actually been outside. She'd spotted a few prints in the morning snows off and on, but nothing as aggressive as that first night.

Still, instinct had her turning down the lamp so the flame glowed a dying orange on the wick and peeked through the edge of the curtains into the lucid darkness. Nothing stirred, and yet she sensed something.

Joshua. That's what she felt. That odd, tingling awareness she experienced in his presence. She let the curtain fall into place. That is over and done with. Why did it feel as if a part of her was holding on to him? And for what reason?

She didn't want separate lives, separate paths, separate everything. There was great goodness in his heart. She'd seen it. Felt it. Admired the man he was. But he was a man, and no matter how charming or wonderful a man seemed, there was another side to balance it.

Let him go, Claire. She'd made a hero of him in her mind, and her hungry heart had simply wanted to love. It was as if through the long years of her marriage, that part of her had been waiting, like a seed in the cold earth waiting for winter to end. Waiting to grow and bloom.

But men don't want a woman's love, she knew from

hard experience as she remembered her wedding night. Yes, a very harsh lesson that was.

She filled the steeping ball and plunked it into the bottom of the teapot. Now that Joshua's cousin had kept the Hamiltons from maneuvering her out of her home and thanks to Betsy's upcoming wedding, Claire had a new job and a real home. This cabin wasn't much, but it kept the cold winter snows out and she'd managed to create a comfortable space. Perhaps, in time, she could find a child in need of a home and of love. Heaven knows there were a lot of children who had no one.

Hope. It rose within her like a tender new sprout. The shadows in her heart seemed less barren. Yes, a little girl, she thought, imagining how that would feel. Like the brightest light, the sweetest warmth. She pictured a little tea party in progress and a dolly's things in the corner.

After crossing the living room, she knelt to fit more wood into the fire, but the tentacles of the past slipped away. As she broke apart the flaming skeletons of wood, the embers glowed bright orange, feeding on air. Like her life, she thought, as she emptied the wood bin and wedged the cut lengths on top of the old. She was satisfied when the flames licked around the moss and bark, snapped and popped. Flames roared higher.

A bang rocked the door. The poker tumbled from her hand as she startled. The clang as the iron poker hit the stone hearth rang discordant and foreboding. This time of year, it was too late for visitors to come so far to call, and she wasn't expecting anyone.

Aside from Betsy, whom did she know to come by?

During her marriage, it had taken all her energy to keep Ham as calm as possible, and that had left no time for friendships. The knock came again, and the odd tingling with it. The one that skittered like a pond's current through her soul whenever Joshua was near.

"Claire?" His baritone rumbled with the power of spring's first chinook. "Claire, are you in there?"

Joshua. Her heart sang his name and, without being aware of it, her hand was on the knob. She'd loosened the latch and there he was, his sight a relief as if she'd been thirsting for it. Tall and dark and protectively powerful.

Affection rippled through her soul. She had to fight it. She had to hold it back. She had to keep from caring. But how did she hold back her heart?

"I didn't mean to scare you." He swept off his Stetson, snow tumbling from the brim. The lamplight from inside glinted on the snowflakes clinging to his long dark hair and the wide expanse of his broad shoulders. "It's coming down so hard out here I didn't think you'd hear the horse. Hope you don't mind me droppin' by like this, but I need a favor."

Anything, her heart answered. And she feared that answer appeared on her face too fast for common sense to rear up.

Joshua went right on. "I found your workhorses."

"Thor and Loki?" That wasn't what she had expected him to say—she wasn't sure why he was here, but her horses! "You have them?" Were they safe and sound? She peered around him into the darkness, but the snowfall and night blocked all view of the barn.

"No, but I know where they are." Sheepish, he gave her a one-sided grin.

Why did that simple crook of his mouth make her senses spin? Because he'd kissed her with that mouth. Because she wanted him to again.

It was a good thing reason prevailed as she stepped aside. "Come in out of that wind. I've got some tea water heating."

"I'd sure appreciate that, Claire."

When he said her name, his voice dipped in note and resonated with warmth. Or was it her imagination? Either way, she didn't want to stay to find out. She left him and the open door and shivered into the kitchen where the cookstove's heat chased away the chill. She snatched the rumbling kettle just in time. The whistle began and died in the same moment.

She refused to observe him as the sequence of sounds identified what he was doing. The click of the door, the thud of his shoes as he removed them, the tinkle of icy snow on the floor as he slipped off his wraps.

Then there was no sound. Only feeling. No pad of footsteps, only the tingling awareness of his approach like a lover's whisper. It moved through her, like some fable out of her beloved novels, and she fought to corral it. To section off the foolish whimsy of her romantic wishes.

Not dead after all, but alive and as vibrant as the man.

Why on earth had he come? Her dazed mind fumbled for reality. Oh, yes, the horses. Her dear horses. How had she forgotten? She filled the teapot, unhappy with herself. She'd never felt like this about Hamilton, ever. Not even when he'd courted her, when he'd been so charming. Falsely charming, as it had turned out.

"This heat sure feels good." He cracked his thick knuckles and held his hands to the stove's heat. The scent of bitter ice and winter wind lifted from him.

The kettle hit the trivet with a clink and she backed away, taking the teapot with her. The boiling water turned the ceramic to an almost unbearable heat and she quickly slid the pot onto the edge of the table. But not fast enough. She felt Joshua's curious gaze like a weight on the back of her neck and then he was behind her.

"You have a piece of moss in your hair." His wide hand curved to fit the round of her shoulder and his touch seared more than fire. Rocked her more than a punch. He spoke and his low pitch fanned the bare skin of her nape. "There. I got it. You want to know something?"

Her soul sighed. *No. I want to know how I can breathe when I'm near you.*

"My brothers and me, we've been watching this piece of property. More wilderness, really. It backs into the Big Paw Range, but it's fenced. Seems yours are there in a small herd. There's one problem."

Only one? She could think of a thousand problems right here, right now. Being unable to speak was one of them. Being unable to move was another.

"We can't get to the horses because it's too close to a few hired guns. We can't risk going in to get your horses, but I was hoping you would sneak up to the fence line with me. Maybe bring along some grain. Would the geldings come up if they saw you?"

"Ah…are they…safe?"

"They've lost weight, but they're all right. Does that mean you'll help?"

She nodded, looking up at him with those wide, jeweled eyes. He saw only sweetness and innocence and a sparkling, tempered joy. "I would be so grateful to have them again. But does that mean there's some danger? If you steal them back, isn't that still horse stealing?"

"I'll keep you safe, pretty lady." The hollow in his chest ached in the worst way, and he felt savage with the need to safeguard her. Those raw feelings were a worse danger to his life than facing a couple of horse thieves. "When you look at it, we aren't really doing anything wrong. Two wrong deeds make a right one. Is that tea ready yet?"

She nodded, skirting away from him, and the hollow in his chest dug deeper. There was no denying some things. A smart man would have sent someone else. He should have sent Liam, the remote, sensible brother. He would have been the perfect man for the job.

But Joshua couldn't stand the notion of Liam knocking on her door. Of Liam making her shine from the inside out with that rare light when he'd rescued her horses. No, he couldn't stand that notion at all.

The truth was, he wanted to be here, knowing beyond a doubt he was already falling. Already making a wrong choice. But it didn't stop him from thanking her for a bracing, steaming cup of tea. Or for noticing how the lamplight caressed the creamy curve of her face.

And being jealous of that light.

It was an arduous ride. Claire silently thanked Joshua for insisting she dig a pair of Ham's trousers from the remaining crates in the barn. Riding astride the mare was difficult enough when she wasn't used to it. But in a skirt, she would have been as frozen as the unforgiving earth.

They climbed in elevation, the wind's frigid daggers slicing ever more deeply. With the thick snowfall, she was reminded of the afternoon when Ham was buried, when she'd become lost in the blizzard. When Joshua Gable had appeared out of the storm like an avenging hero come to rescue her.

He was still that avenging hero. He perched soundlessly at her side on his dark horse, as if part of the shadows, and yet substantial where the night was not. Conquering even as he forged ahead. The path narrowed and he easily led the way through the silent trees and thick branches. Moving without sound, leaving little evidence of his presence. He seemed confident as he halted to draw his rifle from its holster and the revolver from his hip belt.

"It's just ahead. We'll dismount and walk from here." He swung down without touching the saddle or the reins. His sleek well-trained gelding stood patiently. "It's steep. Will you be all right?"

A man like Joshua was probably used to a different kind of female. Although she'd never seen his family home, she did know Betsy. Betsy's modest house in town held beautiful furnishings, the nicest Claire had ever seen other than in the furniture store's display window.

Everyone knew the Gables were not a poor family. They had money and the largest spread in this corner of Montana Territory. He probably courted genteel ladies who were raised gently, whose hands were not rough from harsh lye soap.

"I'm a country girl" was her only answer as she dismounted. She sank into the snow up past her knees.

"Silence from here on out." With the rifle propped in the crook of his arm, he unstrapped a pair of snowshoes from behind his saddle. "Here, strap these on. Do you know how to use 'em?"

He sounded so doubtful she managed only to nod. She reached to take them, but she was only reaching for air. He knelt down before her, a great figure flecked with snow, and gently lifted her right foot.

What a good man. Her whole being stilled as he patiently knocked the clumped snow from her leg and shoe, fitted the flat paddle beneath her boots and tied the leather bindings snug. Like a rock skipping over a pond, the ringed ripples radiated outward and through her soul.

A tide of affection and admiration and awe that she could not stop. Any more than a pond's current could be halted. Inevitably, she felt a wave of tenderness splash against her heart. Her eyes ached. Her entire chest panged with a sweet pain.

I cannot come to love him. Agony tore through her. She did not love him. She refused to love him. And yet, how could she hold back the truth? How could anyone not love this man of might and goodness?

When he finished with her other shoe, he straightened, rising to his full height, seeming as noble and great as the ancient cedars around them, as majestic as the mountains shrouded in the opalescent clouds.

"It's pretty deep. Take my hand."

Her palm settled against his. A perfect fit.

What she ought to tell him was that she didn't need any help. She was strong. She was able. She'd managed for most of her life doing ranch and barn work in deep snow. And yet, if she told him that, then perhaps he'd remove his hand.

Perhaps he'd move away instead of keeping her close to his side, his free hand settling on the small of her back as he helped her over tough spots in the ever-steepening trail. If she pushed him away, then he'd withdraw his tenderness. He was simply helping a woman. That he treated his sister with the same regard, she was sure of it; he wasn't interested in her romantically.

She knew there was no possibility of him coming courting. So what did it hurt to allow this moment of closeness?

Nothing. Or at least that's what she told herself. The strong shield of his chest protected her from the bite of the wind. He kept her balanced when the snow beneath her gave way. He held her close as if she were the only thing in the whole world that mattered to him. His attention, his protection, his concern. He was simply being a gentleman, doing nothing more for her than he probably did for the women in his family.

But to her, it meant everything. Never had anyone ever treated her with real care. It would be so simple to lean against his chest, close her eyes and hope his arms would hold her sheltered there forever. To listen to his heartbeat and hear an echo of it in her own.

You read too many dime novels, Claire. Love—and

men—weren't like that. But she didn't care. He held an icy cedar branch to keep it from slapping her in the face.

Her pulse was racing, her hope an eager curl of a sprout trying to grow up out of the frozen earth—it could not survive. She knew that. And still she held tightly to Joshua's hand, and it was as if his blood rushed through her veins.

I want him so much. Her heart broke with it the same moment his hand left hers. She'd been so focused inward she hadn't realized they were at the crest of the slope. He moved away and she felt a yank in her very essence, as if more than a wish tethered her heart to his. And it was no thin thread but a tie more substantial and helpless. *It's only a wish you're feeling, Claire. This isn't real.*

Even if she wanted it to be. Which she didn't, right?

To her amazement the ground shadows moved. There, stretched out in the dense darkness beneath the lowest branches emerged a shade of a man. Barely visible, as was the rifle he held as he came up on his elbows to whisper with Joshua. Liam. She recognized the harsh, unforgiving cut of his iron face, the same profile as Joshua's. The two men disappeared before her eyes, blending into the shadows, a part of the darkness.

Then Joshua's low baritone, a tone lower than the night wind, spoke near her ear. "Come stretch out on your stomach and see."

"On the snow?"

"Trust me." His grip settled on her elbow, drawing her down, drawing her forward, and she was surprised when she knelt onto not snow but something else. A tarp? No, an oiled tarp, she judged by the slight rustling. She was careful not to knock askew her snowshoes.

Trust him? She should never trust any man, especially not one that made common sense fly right out of her head. And yet, all she could do was feel as he stayed at her side. They shuffled beneath the heavy thick boughs of the old cedars until the rise of the earth gave way to night sky and the faint purple-black glow of snow everywhere falling. From the inky roll of the sky to the upraised arms of a mountainside of trees to the small valley tucked below.

"They got a lookout down there in the cabin." Joshua's words brushed her temple. "In case of predators."

Her vision had become accustomed to the dark and she could make out lines of the snow-covered soddy where a single stovepipe rose up to puff smoke. And a window, reflecting the night snow, gleamed darkly. She shivered, knowing an armed man was behind those panes of glass. "Where are the horses?"

"Jordan's lured them up just under the ridge," Liam answered, his low voice like steel. "He's got the rails loose and ready, and James is covering the cabin. He'll give us a sign."

Joshua stretched out prone beside her, his bulk pressing against her entire side. Although he was absorbed in studying the valley below and conferring with his brother, the memory of their closeness lingered within her. Her blood tingled in her veins.

When she should have felt half-frozen, she felt alive and invigorated. And why? The way he'd held her, the way her soul had seemed to sigh, had been a moment in time. Not real. Not lasting.

Joshua cupped his hands over his mouth and lifted his face to the downfall. He sent the eerie call of a coyote into the night. His shoulder pressed into hers, or did she imagine the increase of pressure? Thousands of snowflakes tapped on the outstretched cedar branches and on the earth, on the cabin below where the windowpanes remained midnight-black.

Time passed as neither man beside her moved. The snow made a sort of peaceful music in the night; the patter and fall of melody and harmony and finally an answering call wailed through the night.

"James's signal," Joshua explained as he slid his rifle to the crest of the hill and sited the cabin below. "Jordan's at the fence. Can you crawl up there, do you see him?"

She squinted into the darkness where the cedar grove crowded through the fence lines and filed downhill. Although she knew the youngest Gable brother was there, she couldn't distinguish him in the darkness. She trusted Joshua to nudge her in the right direction. In the inky darkness she could just make out the steady reassurance of his gaze. She could feel what he did not say. Feel the words of reassurance. *Trust me.* She did, heaven help her. *Don't think about the men down there in that cabin with their guns.* Or how angry horse thieves would be to discover they were victims of the same crime they favored. She knew Joshua and his brothers could handle the repercussions. She ignored the sting of snow crumbling inside the lining of her boots as she inched through the darkness.

The lattice of limbs, needles and snow framed a wedge of the valley below and she saw them. The small herd of horses huddled together for warmth in the lee of the grove. Thor! That had to be his wide dark back, standing as he always did with his hind leg cocked, taking the brunt of the winter's wind for his smaller brother. Loki's haunches looked bony.

"We can get 'em to come closer. Watch." Jordan's words were followed by the rustle of a burlap sack and the sweet molasses scent of expensive grain lifted into the air.

The wind did the work, wafting the aroma of the sweet food to the horses. Thor's nose came up and his nostrils flared. The snow glossed on his coat, making it seem as if he were both fiction and fantasy as the silver-mantled creature appeared to fly up the hill.

Beside her, Jordan hefted apart the rails. He must have sawed through them early and bound them with wire, she guessed, for the sturdy wood gave way silently. "They'll come to your voice?"

"Yes." With the knowledge that the Gable brothers were keeping careful watch, their guns loaded and ready, she leaned through the icy cedar limbs and whispered her horses' names.

Chapter Fourteen

Why did Claire's every move affect him like water over rapids? Joshua's focus didn't stray from the possible danger of Logan's gang noticing they were down two horses. The rifle he held was steady and sure, and he had no problem taking the horses.

What he hated was that she was exposed, as hidden as she was in the thicket. He couldn't hear her voice, but he could feel the music of her words, the low timbre of expectation as she let the wind snatch away her whisper. They waited as the big gelding forged past the grain Jordan had flung into the corral.

An owl's *who? who?* sifted upward from the rim of the fence line below. James's call. There was movement in the cabin. Joshua's senses went on alert. The rifle he held cocked and aimed on the void eyes of the windows did not waver. His vision, well adjusted to the night, sought out any shift of shadow within the soddy. James had been watching since sundown. Rick Hamilton had been hunkered down to a nap in the back for a good hour.

Maybe the horses' movements had alerted him, or maybe they'd just gotten damned lucky and the cuss was up to take a leak. Since it was too cold to tromp outside to use the outhouse, Joshua was betting they were safe.

But with Claire here, he wasn't taking any chances. He bellied up a little farther on the ridge so he had first shot if there was trouble.

Sure enough, the horses came to her just like he figured. The big one first, snuffling past the grain to approach his mistress. Jordan snapped a lead on the gelding's halter, pulled him aside with a snap of branches and the raining down of snow from the limbs. Joshua's attention was focused solely on the cabin. That snap of wood was muffled, but enough that if Rick wanted to investigate, Joshua would be ready.

It was a hell of a disappointment that no one challenged them. Joshua would have derived a hell of a lot of satisfaction to have a good reason to shoot that bastard. Although he'd had no further trouble directly with either of the Hamilton brothers, that didn't mean there would be peace between them. Or between them and Claire. Especially since they thought he had killed Ham.

"Got 'em." Liam's terse tone held a surprising note of amusement. "It may be best if you ride home with the widow."

Did Liam expect him to jump at the chance? Already his brothers had the wrong idea. It wasn't like him not to argue about it. He wanted to say this wasn't the time or place to set Liam straight, but the truth was that he'd be lying. He wasn't about to trust anyone to accompany Claire home.

Not only did he not trust his brothers—and yet who else did he trust more?—but a glaze of red streaked across his eyes as he thought of any man—even his brothers—alone with his woman.

That's how he thought of her as she came into his arms. He didn't know how it happened, he was simply crawling down from the crest and straightening to his full height in the shadows and there she was, a welcome woman's press of heat and fragrance against his side, her arms snaking around his ribs and squeezing tight.

"Oh, thank you! Thank you so much."

She pulled her muffler down, exposing her creamy skin to the harsh cold and her mouth discovered his, inexorably, the way the snow found the earth, the way the wind encountered the air. And there was no frigid night or danger just down the ridge as the world, and his brothers along with it, faded away into the night.

There was only Claire in his arms, only the spiced heat of her velvety kiss, only the thrill of his pulse cannoning through his veins. Common sense fled right along with it, leaving only feeling.

He had absolute certainty that he would do anything for this woman. Anything. Die for her. Kill to protect her. Sacrifice everything for her happiness. Pure feeling—not one thing was rational about that—but it was as certain and steadfast as the mountains he stood on.

As long as she didn't know how he felt, maybe that would save him. Or so a man could hope. It was with a ripping sensation that she broke away from his side, and he had to look down to make sure everything was the same. That he was the same. He felt the tug like a rope noosed around his innermost heart, drawing tighter with each step she took.

He stood on the deputy sheriff's land, one of three law officers in the whole of Bluebonnet County, so this was no safe plan. But Joshua didn't feel a lick of fear as he moved away. No, he refused to be afraid of men like Logan and the Hamilton brothers. Determined, calm, he caught the lead ropes Jordan had supplied and instructed Claire to start moving.

Careful but quick, because there was no telling, despite Liam's and James's sharp eagle eyes, that they wouldn't be surprised in these dense woods by the Hamilton band. In these obscure lands horses weren't the only rustled animals.

Now he knew why Ham had taken to terrorizing the sheep on the grassland Joshua leased from the government. Because the swatch of land lay between Ham's southernmost property line, Logan's high-country spread and the livestock trail that wound south to Great Falls and the auction. A route few folks would ever use. And the western edge of the Gable family land—the original homestead Gran had claimed with her husband—nestled close to that trail, the old road south through the rugged Bear Paw Range. And that meant...

He didn't know what that meant. His thoughts stopped like a runaway train derailing and crashed into a thousand pieces. His mind no longer worked.

He could long stare at the silhouette Claire made in the thicket below, where the saddle horses waited patiently. He was suddenly beside her, although he couldn't remember stealthing down the trail and kneeling down to offer her his upturned palms.

With the way her muffler hid her face, he didn't see her smile, but he felt the beauty of it shiver through him like a dream.

You are in so much trouble, man. There was no denying it as his heart stalled when she placed her boot on his gloves. Within the span of a blink, she was in the saddle and reaching for the Clydesdales' leads.

"I'll handle it." If there was trouble, he reasoned, there was no way she could hold them.

"They're my horses." She held out her hand, chin jutting upward through the sheath of the muffler. "At least give me one lead. There's no way you can manage two, so hand it over. You've taken enough risks on my behalf tonight."

"I'm not done yet."

He tossed her one of the leads, hauling the larger gelding with him as he swung into General's saddle. He mounted up, secured the lead and carried his rifle at the ready. He heard no sign from his brothers, so he led the way along the downward slope where snow had filled the horses' tracks and made the surrounding trees and landscape change from when they'd arrived.

It was like a whole new world, pristine and full of promise.

He could tell by the way Claire kept turning in her saddle she wanted a good look at the horses. But he kept a fast pace, knowing his brothers watched his back for as long as they could keep him in their sight. But eventually the twisting path took them behind other hill-sides so he stayed alert.

The danger of meeting one of the Hamilton's gang on the road was high enough. If there hadn't been so much snowfall, he would have forged a path through the forest. But as it was, they'd be off the lonely trail through private property soon—sooner enough before they were spotted.

He wasn't going to fool himself. This was going to cause trouble with the deputy and the Hamiltons. As for Claire…this only added a new wrinkle to a real problem. How was he going to keep her safe? Especially if she was traipsing all around the county taking over Betsy's laundry service?

And what was it with women these days and their dang-blasted independence? Next they'd be demanding the right to vote, and think of the consequences. The end of democracy, surely. He liked demure women. Quiet and reasonable and sensible. Life was never that easy, was it? Claire was quiet and demure. And she was just as stubborn and determined as any other woman he'd ever known.

He squinted through the snow on his lashes at the woman shrouded in platinum and shadows, and there went his heart again, falling, as if it had leaped right out of his chest and tumbled straight down a cliff.

What was it about her, he wondered, aside from the fact that she was strong as a willow—she bent but she didn't break. And despite the hardships in her life, she hadn't grown hard or cruel. Not that she was soft, either. He remembered how close she'd been to dying in a storm more deadly than this. She was no wilting bloom.

So why couldn't he at least fall in love with a bidda-
ble woman? Was it too much to ask? Even as he thought
it, he knew he would never want any other woman.

Just Claire.

As long as he could keep that fact to himself, he
ought to be safe enough. But more than his emotional
safety was at risk. The back of his neck began to creep
and crawl and he could sense the danger like the snow
tapping across his face.

"Go!" He slapped Stormy's flank. As the mare leaped
forward, Claire looked back at him with surprise in her
wide eyes.

We've got company. Get outta here. He willed the
thought toward her.

And as if she felt his words, she nodded, turning
away. The last he saw of her was the storm and night
stealing her away, as she leaned forward in the saddle
for an all-out gallop. He was on her heels, but not fast
enough. He caught the faint low tenor first, the words
broken apart on the wind.

The dark haze of snow separated like a curtain and
there was Reed Hamilton, riding with the deputy at his
side, not five yards from the point where the main
county road met the path.

Joshua turned General hard and prayed the web of
storm would hide him from their sight. Since he
couldn't be sure, he circled his gelding around, back-
ing her and the Clydesdale down the road as he held the
gun steady, finger trigger-itchy.

Come this way, he silently challenged them. But the
night must have hid him from their sight.

The band of men, not just two riders, but closer to half a dozen, rode with their heads bowed against the storm, and disappeared south. Maybe too drunk to notice the tracks heading out.

Joshua stayed ready and alert for a long time, long enough to be sure, before he hurried to catch up with Claire. The unseen string binding their hearts yanking him like a yo-yo until he was at her side.

When her eyes smiled at him from above her muffler, that string gave a harder jerk, a noose around his heart. Holding him captive, and he didn't mind, as he rode at her side the rest of the way to her home. At her side, one of the nicest places he'd ever been.

And he knew why a man didn't mind falling so much.

Overhead moonlight wrestled with the thinning clouds to twist and writhe between the veils of thinly falling snow. Claire wished she could feel her fingers enough to cross them for luck. The storm was breaking, as if the mountains were great giants ripping apart the thick mantle of clouds and tossing them down.

Snow bled and spurted, and then there was silence. All around her the black velvet sky peered through the dying clouds, stars as white as the snow blinking awake. This wild and rugged land was all hers. It wasn't pride that filled her; it was contentment. Peace. Knowing she was finally safe. That she was in control of her destiny.

And that she would never need to live so desperately or be hurt like that again.

As the snow evaporated, it was as if the earth sighed. The moon beamed bright through the last grasping fingers of haze to polish the reverent prairie. Snow shone like a dark opal for miles in every direction, from the long wide infinity of the plains to the rim of the horizon and up the enormous slopes of the mountains, their stone faces hidden by snow and burnished with stardust.

A whisper of an updraft, more like an angel's touch than a breeze, skipped across her like a kiss. Like a promise of good things to come.

And this man beside her? It seemed as if he were a part of those good things, too. As a friend, she decided as she led the way up the sloping hill that would take her home.

As if Joshua felt it, too, he reined his gelding a few inches closer, so that they rode side by side. His presence wasn't stifling; his closeness was companionable. Right. As if he belonged here at her side, and not in his shadow, but as his friend.

Not that what was beating to life within her was friendly at all. Romantic and desiring, yes, but she couldn't hold it back. Too powerful, too irrepressible, it rose like a bubble within her, expanding until it moved through her with a pop and seemed to keep right on going.

"You've gotta be frozen clear through." Joshua dismounted at the top of the hill. "Hand me over the horses and I'll put 'em up. You go in and get warm."

"You are always this bossy, aren't you?"

"Bossy? You stand to be corrected, pretty lady. I'm a take-charge sort of man. Nothing wrong with that."

"Sure, if you're the one giving the orders."

"It's where I prefer to be."

His grin was a charming one. What man couldn't be

charming when he put his mind to it? Framed in starlight and the rugged background of the mountains so tall, she had to tip her head back to see their capped faces.

"Go on. Wait—let me come in with you first. Stir up the coals for you. Get a fire roaring so you can thaw out. Then I'll see to the horses," Joshua said.

"The trouble is, they're my horses. This is my land." She loved watching the confusion dawn on his rugged face. On the quirk of one brow as he tried to figure out if he'd heard her correctly.

Her willfulness was fun, it was freeing. It was endlessly right as she dismounted, quickly and competently enough that he didn't have time to help her down. "Do you want to go into the house and warm up? I'll be in after a while. Make yourself at home."

"Hey, wait a minute!" He looked as if he were trying not to laugh. "Give me back the reins."

"Nope. Or are you going to head straight home instead?" she asked over her shoulder as she lifted the looped end of the lead off the saddle horn. "Come on, guys. It's so good to have you home."

"You're just gonna walk away and leave a poor fellow like me in the cold?"

"I offered you my hearth."

"There is no greater gift than when a woman gives a man her hearth."

Her laughter came like the gentle pulse of bells, silvering the beautiful sound. One he'd never heard before and his entire being turned to the sound of it, to the rise and fall of music sweeter than any he'd ever heard.

Emotion crashed through him like a flash flood,

sucking him under, taking him along with the powerful current. Helpless to stop it, he accepted the inevitable like a man. The inevitable he could not hide from.

Moonlight chose that moment to find her. To guild the curve of her face and cradle the jut of her chin as she smiled. His heart was gone, forever lost to this woman who seemed unaware of how easily she'd rendered him helpless. Rendered him in love.

"If it's my hearth you're after, you're welcome to it. Temporarily." She continued on with a conversation he could no longer remember.

Frozen in place, he tried to pretend he hadn't been dumbstruck by her. What had they been talking about? That's right, he thought, he remembered. Heart. Hearth. "Temporarily, huh? I can't have your hearth forever?"

"Nope. I've learned it's wise for a girl to keep her own hearth. Men aren't the most consistent creatures."

"You've got that right. Not faithful or decent, either. Look at me."

"Exactly my point." The laughter starred her eyes, and like a bright light burning, he could not look away from the beauty of it.

From her beauty. He was a damn fool, he saw it now, for scorning his buddies who fell, every single one of them, just like this. Joshua had always thought a man could stand strong and tough and no woman could render him defenseless.

He'd never been more wrong. Kissing her hadn't gotten her out of his blood. Steeling his will against wanting her hadn't made a whit of difference. Keeping away from her and filling his mind with other things—

ranching and family duties—hadn't derailed this steaming longing for her. His insides twisted so hard it took his breath away.

Until now, he'd never *felt*. Never knew a single emotion would bring keen, physical pain. And make the world so rich in beauty. The moonlight seared his eyes, the platinum shine seemed suddenly to brighten until his eyes teared. Until every sheen and surface, every inch of ground and tree beamed as if the thousands upon thousands of stars had fallen onto the ground at her feet.

And in the center of it was her, floating as if on light, as if this magical evening had enchanted her, too.

"Look at how bony my boys are. Why wouldn't they take care of them? I realize—" she talked while she worked "—that the Hamiltons couldn't very well drive my horses where anyone would recognize them. Logan's their friend, but stealing is stealing and it's against the law. This is horrible. They couldn't have hoped to sell them."

He tried to clear the emotion wadded in his windpipe. Failed.

"How could they have gotten full value when the horses look like this? It makes no sense." She sounded more than disgusted, more than angry.

"What doesn't make sense to you?" He dismounted in the yawning mouth of the doorway.

"That there would be any excuse for this. I know, I shouldn't be surprised. I lived with Ham. I saw how he treated his animals. I know how he treated me. He thought he was infinitely more important than anyone or anything else. And that others were only there for his benefit, his gain." She disappeared into the tack room, leaving him alone and his chest feeling as if it had been ripped wide-open by a merciless bear.

I love her. His soul wrenched, but it was sweet agony as he walked more deeply into the barn, bringing the horses with him. Stormy and Thor greeted General and Loki with snuffles and snorts and low-throated neighs.

The moment *she* appeared in the aisle, the horses swung to watch her. The moonlight pried through the cracks in the high walls to crown her with brightness. Overcome, he stumbled because it seemed as if his feet couldn't find the ground.

The air he breathed filled him with the tang of snow and stardust, the whisper of the wind clearer, like words from a loved one mumbled in the dark, secret hours after midnight. Heat pumped through his veins, not naked lust, but something stronger, greater.

He was forever changed as he bent to the task of un-saddling the horses, no longer the stoic he had always prided himself on being.

It took all his hard-earned discipline not to gawk at her as she swept close, the trousers she wore accenting the feminine curve of her hips and thighs. He needed all his willpower to force his gaze from her alluring beauty—from the beauty he wanted to touch and stroke with his hands and know by memory—and heft the saddle off General's back.

"I'll rub him down," she said, shaking out a soft and sweet-smelling towel.

So close, his skin gooseflesh. His spirit swelled with longing. Love blazed within the most secret pulse of his heart. She was the blood in his veins, the air in his lungs, and the beat of his soul. He could not control it, he could not stop it, and he knew it didn't matter that he wanted to turn his back and ride away. To stop this fast and fatal fall.

"Joshua."

He turned, the saddle on his shoulder, his heart on his sleeve.

"You said you're here helping me because it's the right thing to do." There was no mistaking the honest regard that lit her up as if from inside. "You stand pretty tall, in my view. I just wanted you to know that."

His throat ached and he was lost over what in the hell to say. If he was going down, then there was no better way to fall.

Chapter Fifteen

Sometimes a man has to do what is right, whether it's in his best interest or not.

Joshua's words had stayed with her ever since he'd said them on that night, which now seemed so long ago. Everything was different from those hopeless days. And it was all because of the man who worked silently and capably at her side. Who pumped water and measured out grain and forked crisp, sweet hay into the mangers. Who took the horses from her, rubbed and cooled, and led them with a firm hand and a soothing voice.

A voice that made her want to dream.

To believe.

When she led poor nervous Loki into his corner stall next to his brother's, the gentle giant gave a low-throated gasp, an eerily human sound. As if being bedded down in his own stall soft with thick straw and topped with a layer of hay was too good to be true.

Bones sawed against his dull coat as he ambled straight to his trough. Thor whipped his head over the top bars separating the two stalls and watched with a big brother's contentment, as if glad—finally—all was right with their world.

"General's restless." Joshua stroked the fine gelding's glossy neck. "Wolves must be nearby. Let's get this place locked up tight before we head for the house."

"My thoughts exactly." That was sort of a lie—she hadn't been thinking about wolves. She'd been thinking about him. "I'll do the hayloft."

This left him to check on the only other way into the small barn—the back doors. She hurried up the ladder with relief…and felt bereft. As if being away from him was a loss. She did her best to ignore that sensation as she verified that the thick wooden shutters in the loft were locked tight.

Everything was snug and safe. There was no possibility that a wolf could get in here…even if one managed to hop onto the sloping roof. Certain her boys were safe, she climbed back down the ladder and Joshua surprised her by cupping her elbows and swinging her down the last few steps to the ground. Her entire being buzzed as if she'd spontaneously burst into flame.

"If you're worried about what the Hamiltons are gonna do when they find out these horses are back in your stable, don't." As if completely unaware of what he'd done to her, he loped a few steps toward the front door and then stopped when he realized she wasn't beside him. He turned patiently, waiting. "My brothers and I intend to pay them all a visit. Remind 'em that just because the law can be bought in certain parts of this county doesn't mean that justice won't be served if necessary."

She felt engulfed in a blinding fire that licked through the deepest parts of her. She swallowed hard, struggling to sound normal, to focus on what mattered.

Men were violent creatures. Read between the lines of what he'd said. While she was grateful for his protection, even the noble Joshua Gable was violent. He was made to protect, to defend his own, to fight and win. The rock-solid build of him, the way his iron muscles shaped his thick layers of winter clothing, making him seem even more undefeatable, even more formidable.

She knew the tenderness of his kiss…but she did not want to know the dark side, which showed as his eyes shone, like a warrior's death promise.

Maybe it was better to send him away. "I can defend my own."

"That's why I'm here. To make sure you can and will."

Did he have to say the one thing to disarm her? She wanted to think he was a wolf in sheep's clothing. To believe he was just as capable of violence as the Hamiltons, and in the same vein of it. And yet her heart wouldn't let her take that step. Couldn't. He reached out and tucked her hand in his larger one, sheltering her from the bitter winds. He kept one hand on her arm to steady her in case she slipped. But the snow cushioned her feet and the only thing in danger of falling was her heart.

Falling more in love with him.

"The wind sure is kickin' up." He dug his shoulder against the door frame. "Would you mind if I come in and bum a few hot potatoes from you? It's gonna be a long, cruel ride home."

"It's tempting to make you suffer through it, but I guess I owe you at least a baked potato." *Stop bantering with him!* She unlocked the door and led the way into the cold, still dwelling. Frigid pewter light stained the floor and dusted the furniture with a polished glow. Claire stumbled, although she could see well enough. Joshua kept having that effect on her.

"I appreciate it." He stomped the snow off his boots before he followed her inside. He shouldered the door shut and hunkered down on the hearth, stirring the banked coals before she could finish lighting the closest lamp. Taking over as if he had the right. Just like a man.

She shook out the match and laid it carefully in the tray. Maybe it was simply the ghosted memory of Ham she saw, of how he'd hitch down before the hearth and take over the tending of the fire, criticizing her all the while. Trying to bait her into arguing with him so he could have the excuse to fight with her.

Joshua was opposite to Ham in everything. But it gave the back of her neck an odd tingle. She left him to rebuild the fire as she hurried through the shadowy kitchen and saw a reflection in the uncovered window. Black fiendish eyes stared back at her for half of a second and a gasp strangled in her throat. She didn't know if she made any sound at all, but Joshua was there, his pistol cocked and aiming at the void of glass.

The image was gone. "It was nothing. A wolf."

"Not the Hamiltons?"

"No."

"You sure? How about the sheriff?"

"No, no." She gripped the back of the closest chair.

"I know it's ridiculous. The wolves have been here every night. I don't know why they startled me tonight."

"Oh, maybe because you know there might be trouble." He lowered his weapon, lowered the hammer and holstered it. "The wolves are still prowling?"

"I can handle it." He'd done enough. More than enough. And there was no mistaking him for Ham's ghost or memory as Joshua Gable pulled out the chair, tugged her by the wrists and guided her into the cushioned seat. "You've had quite a night. I'll get you some tea for a change."

"What? Do you even know how to steep tea?"

"You've met my granny. Do you think she'd put up with useless grandsons?" He snatched the match tin and knelt to light the stove. "You did real good tonight. Most women would have never gotten their feet cold."

"Those were my horses. Joshua, I am so grateful to have them back. Those men…those boys, that's what they are, I'd like to make them pay if I could. They had no right. Animals depend on us for their care. Thor and Loki didn't deserve to go hungry. Or be out in these temperatures."

"Most women would have offered to pay to get their horses back. That's what I meant. Or, well, offer more."

"And you are mentioning that because…?"

"Don't worry, I'm not hinting I expect more than a polite word of thanks." He knelt, feeling his face heat even as ice crackled on the stove's handle. "I meant it's my experience that most women these days like to stay indoors at leisure and let the men do all the dirty, hard work."

"Leisure? That's how I spend my days. After I order about my house servant, I like to nap in the parlor."

"Some women. I guess that's one thing I like about you."

"You like me?" she blurted, as if that surprised her.

"Yeah, I like you." Liar, his conscience upbraided. him. But what good would come from telling the truth? He had his life. He had his duty to his family, and as the oldest son, he'd had to take his father's place when Pa died. And he could not walk away because he wanted. Want was too weak a word. His desire for her went beyond desire, beyond lust, beyond any bond of affection he'd known before.

Overwhelmed, he cleared the aching emotion from his throat and lit the fire. Kindling sparked and snapped with a merry brightness and cadence that belied everything he was feeling. He didn't feel cheerful. He didn't feel hopeful.

He felt that everything within him was breaking. All his defenses. All his beliefs. All his resolve. And he felt far too exposed, as if he'd taken off every strip of clothing and stood naked in the unforgiving night. Knowing he'd freeze to death and knowing there was nothing he could do.

"What's not to like about you, pretty lady?"

"I guess I never wondered how you felt about me." Because I'm too busy trying to rationalize how I feel about you. She unwound her muffler the rest of the way and hung it over the nearest chair back. "I mean, you're so busy being a knight errant, a defender of widows and a Robin Hood of horse thieves, I know you must not have the time."

"How much time does a thought take?" He hiked off

his hat and tossed it across the room. His Stetson hooked a peg on the coat tree and swung into place. "I can do two things at once. Hang up my hat. Think nice things about one of the few women I actually respect. I couldn't believe how you were tonight. As calm as a seasoned lawman. It was cold and it was uncomfortable and climbing up that hill was hard work, and you didn't complain once. You even knew how to use snowshoes."

"It's how I get to the barn to do my chores in the winter."

"Your chores?" He glanced around the cabin, clean and tidy and, now, cozy. It was a real nice little place with womanly touches to soften the rust wood walls. Did she have barn work, too?

"I took care of the animals." She said it with serenity, as if there was nothing wrong about that or unusual. "What? Why are you shaking your head?"

"Didn't Ham do the barn work? And in winter?" He yanked the damper wide a little too roughly. Hell, he couldn't help it. What kind of man left the outside work to a lady? It was hard physical labor, not to mention hotter than blazes in summer and, in winter, the temperature could freeze the mercury. That was no way for a man to treat his wife. "My mother never stepped foot inside the stable, unless it was to wait for her team, which one of us was already hitchin' up for her."

"From what I've heard about your family, your mother is a proper lady. A bank owner's wife."

"Ranching was Pa's hobby. He loved it. He inherited the bank, so he was obligated to do his best by his father. Duty. The state of the oldest son."

"You didn't want to run your family's ranch?"

"Nope. I wanted to run the bank, but Pa's little brother does that. So I have the ranch." And if he had regrets about that, what good did it do him to give them a moment of time? None. Some things were a given and no force on earth was going to change them. He was in charge of his family's extensive land and livestock holdings and he'd do his damnedest. "How about you? You're gonna be the next laundry lady in Bluebonnet County. That can't be what you always figured you'd wind up bein'."

"No one's more surprised than I am."

"Betsy's had good luck with it. She's made a decent living. It's hard work, though."

"I'm not afraid of hard work. It's what I know."

Yeah, if she was used to doing barn work. Joshua didn't know if it was rage or sympathy he felt, but it raged within him like a blizzard's leading wind. Howling through him until he felt like crushing steel with his bare hands. "You worried about driving so far alone?"

"Betsy said she's had no real problems. A bear once, she said, when she was delivering up north in the mountains, but I won't have to worry about that."

Joshua's face darkened. "No. That's the bastard she's marrying."

"Betsy mentioned you didn't like him."

"Like him? I hate him. He's marrying her to take advantage of her and she doesn't see it." True agony creased his features as he turned away. He said nothing more as he spotted the teakettle and lifted it. Water sloshed inside so he set it on the stove and crossed to the front room where the fire had devoured the kindling.

Claire unbuttoned her coat, trying to make sense of the ax blade of pain that wedged deep into her heart. It wasn't her pain. It wasn't her agony. But she hurt just as fiercely as the man kneeling at her hearth. Back straight, shoulders set, head bowed. With his reverent posture, it was strange to think of this man vulnerable and hurting. "I have worried about Betsy, too. She's making a mistake," Claire said.

"Hell, yes. Nobody seems to see it. Granny and I, we've tried to make her see. Mama's indulgent, she always lets Bets have her way. But marriage once done is until death. It's a mistake that cannot be made right. I don't want her hurt. I don't want her heart broken when she realizes this man who has no job is hoping to get his hands on her inheritance."

"I suppose your family's land is very valuable. That is one advantage to being relatively, well, poorer than most. No one will marry me for my inheritance. Although, my former in-laws are convinced you're interested in my quarter section of grazing land."

"A rancher is always looking to increase his holdings, but any man who would want your land more than you is someone who doesn't deserve you."

She twisted onto her feet because she'd forgotten to put on the potatoes, spinning toward the stove and out of his sight. But the potatoes weren't why she had retreated from his sight. She didn't want him to know how much his words had meant.

Why was it when she didn't believe she could think

more of this man, he went and did something more, something that made her love him even more? When she didn't want to love him at all?

She could hear him in the front room. The clang of the poker, the thud of wood in the bin, the stir of ashes and the creak of the armchair. It never occurred to her that a man would know anything about lost dreams. Joshua had wanted to work in the town bank?

Countless times she'd been inside the fashionable brick-and-stone building, of course. She'd never given much thought to who owned it, and she didn't know Joshua's uncle had inherited it. Nor would she have ever guessed that Joshua, a man as suited to the rugged high country as the jutting rise of the Rockies to the west, would want to work behind a desk. Managing people and money with the same stoic commitment that he ran his brothers, his ranch and handled his livestock.

Was he happy? she wondered, already knowing the answer as she tugged open the cellar door. She could feel that sadness, too, within him, as black as the void of night sky where no stars shone. He was not happy with the charted course his life had taken. As she herself had not been.

The girl she'd once been—so full of dreams and belief, so certain that love could conquer all—seemed to stand beside her in the dark cellar. This was part of being an adult, of realizing that dreams were only fancies and love an invention of poets.

His footsteps made the floorboards creak overhead, and she filled her pockets and rose out of the cloistered cellar. The rattle of the teapot greeted her. Joshua stood at her stove setting the cozy on the teapot.

"The potatoes." He grabbed the hot pad and opened the stove. "I'll put them in. The coals look hot enough. Do you want me to stay awhile, to keep an eye on things?"

"Taking care of others is a habit with you, isn't it?"

"A bad habit. One I usually only burden family members with. But for some reason I seem to be very protective of you."

The man took her breath away, towering over her, pressing close, his wide, dependable chest like a shield against the heartaches of the world. Joshua had the power to melt away the world's troubles. Her troubles. Like a knight of old, he conquered foes, righted wrongs and stood a noble man when the battle was done.

She strummed with want for him. Want for his comfort. For his tenderness. For the heat of his kiss. She knew the reality of men. Of marriage. But she longed for the dream.

As if he felt the same yearning, his fingertips grazed her chin, tipping her face toward his. A perfect angle for kissing. Her gaze fastened onto his as if a physical force pinned her there, mesmerized by how deeply she could see inside him. Past the granite features and rugged shields around his heart to the real man within.

Her soul sighed; it was as if she'd taken her very first breath, newly born as he put his mouth over hers, hovering, and his free hand fitting against her jawbone in a slow, tender slide. His caress skidded across her sensitized nerve endings, crackling like dry winter air, and she felt the snap and sting of it deep within her. A sensual and emotional jolt that intensified.

It was as if their souls met.

This is a dream. Claire didn't close her eyes as Joshua stood over her, his chiseled lips parted. Her mouth softened, remembering the velvet brush of his earlier kisses. Pleasant and thrilling and nice all at once, the way a man's kiss should be. The way she'd always wanted to be kissed.

When his lips fit to hers, she curled her fingers in the front of his jacket and held on. This time was different. She could see his eyes haze over and she wondered if he felt as if he were dreaming, too. The heated spice of his kiss, the warm caress of his lips to hers, the gentle suction became more than the chaste romantic kiss she expected.

More than anything she'd ever imagined.

His fingertips held her firm, not that she wanted to move away or do one single thing that would risk this moment in time. When they breathed the same air and their hearts beat in synchrony. When the sweet thrill of his kiss spilled like wine through her limbs.

This has to be a dream, she rationalized, because nothing real could be this wonderful. It was impossible that a man's kiss could make her buoyant, as if she were standing on a rising cloud. Higher and higher she seemed to fly, but she was not afraid. She boldly pressed against the hard male length of his body and held on tight.

It was just a kiss, and yet…joy burst inside her, spilling through every part of her being. The flare of happiness that blasted to life inside her was bright enough to dim the stars from the winter sky. Dazzling enough to make her forget—for one moment only—that she didn't believe in true love. That she'd stopped wishing.

His kiss was thrilling enough for her to see, even a small glimpse, of what happiness with him could be.

Chapter Sixteen

A loud blast ripped through the stillness. Joshua pulled his mouth from Claire's, too stupefied from the effects of her kiss to make sense of anything else.

It sounded like someone had laid a half-dozen sticks of dynamite against the outside wall of the front room and lit them. The blast rolled through the cabin like a crashing wave, shaking the walls and window glass, vibrating through the floorboards. Crystal lamps clattered and the hanging pots in the kitchen bonged as they rocked.

"What in hell blazes is that?" If it was a blast caused by those damn Hamiltons, he'd make them pay and to hell with spending a few nights in jail for assault, because he'd just been forced away from the best kiss of his life. She'd left him the consistency of melted butter on a red-hot stove. He had a hard time making his muscles obey him, and all because of a kiss.

Because of Claire's amazing kiss. He shook his head. He had to forget about that kiss. He had to shove aside the fog-thick haze obscuring clear, rational thought. The blast struck again, rumbling the timbers beneath his feet.

Was it the Hamiltons? Rage seared through him as he headed to the door. He felt nothing but the certainty with which he was going to make it clear that they were to leave this woman alone. And then it struck him that it wasn't a blast, and it wasn't someone outside.

"Will you need help? I've got my forty-five loaded and ready."

There was no mistaking the lilt of humor in her words. Joshua winced. "Nah, I'm just on edge. Better to be safe than sorry."

Good thing he was facing away from her so she couldn't see his face heat. Hell, was he really on the way to wrestle down a wind gust? Sure, it was a damned hard wind, but, jeez, what in hellfire was wrong with him?

"The wind comes down from the Rockies and gains speed as it blows down the slopes. By the time it hits here, it can hit like a speeding train. This isn't bad."

"How often does this happen? I've been out here plenty of times, and in a blizzard. I've never felt this. Are you sure it's the wind?"

"Positive. It's a windstorm. If we're lucky, it won't get much worse. Let me put the potatoes in…the potatoes that are still in my pocket." She dug into her pockets and there they were, two brown egg-shaped lumps, which she shoved into the hot coals. "I'll lend you a warming iron, too. I'm going to worry about you all night now."

"You'd worry about me?"

"Someone has to." She stayed where she was, bathed

in the orange glow of the fire. "At least I won't worry about the Hamiltons tonight. They probably won't come out in this cold."

"You like silver linings, don't you?"

"I've noticed you're not the optimistic type."

"I'm a practical man. I don't have the luxury to be anything else."

"You don't kiss like a practical man."

You kiss like a fantasy. How did a man go on from knowing that? He couldn't. As much as he wanted the fantasy, he knew it wasn't real. So he forced a retreat into the kitchen, where he poured a cup of tea for her. He didn't bother to do one for him, as cold as he still was. He had to get out of there before he did something they would both regret. He wanted more than a kiss.

He wanted everything.

Some things a man couldn't have no matter how much he longed for them. No matter what he would give to be able to lose himself in her and just *be*.

As if she were intending to make the agony worse, she padded after him, the whisper-soft brush of her gait on the floorboards behind him. He swore he could feel the slightest vibration of her step with the same force as the winds. It was her voice that curled around his soul and hung on.

"I'm sorry. I never should have said that about your kiss. You don't have to run off. I'm not expecting…anything."

"If I don't leave now, you will be."

"What does that mean…" And she fell silent as realization struck.

He poured her tea with quick jerky movements and

wished. He wished everything was different. Longing filled him with a blinding wave, a breath-stealing cascade of a riptide that dragged him under.

What kind of sense did that make? He didn't trust women and he didn't believe in love. He knew marriage was a miserable trap most men bemoaned the rest of their livelong days.

And yet to have the chance to love this woman, who gazed at him with a pure, guileless understanding in her eyes, whose soul felt wedged, in part, inside his. He broke away before he was completely, utterly lost.

"I've got to go." There was nothing else to do but swerve past her in the narrow space between the table and the archway. It took only a second to grab his hat and haul his gloves from his jacket pockets.

"So, I was right." She watched him with her arms folded beneath the soft rounds of her perfect breasts as if to attempt to shield her heart. "You can't just kiss me like that—"

"Like what?"

Her face crumpled. "Like a fiction becoming real. I've read too many dime novels, I know, but the way you made me feel. It's not right to do that so casually. Maybe you aren't aware—"

"Oh, I'm aware." This was what he wanted to avoid. This tangle of emotions and affections and starting something that could not be stopped. Now was the sticking point, the stopping place. And he would go no further. His heart cracked, and his voice with it. "You weren't alone in those feelings. Is that what you want to know?"

"I…" She sputtered, as if that wasn't at all what she expected him to say. "Really? I just assumed…" She swallowed hard. "That kissing is such an easy thing for a man to do. And, well, more physical things. I hadn't realized…"

"That I had feelings for you, too? Believe me, there's nothing simple about this. Not for me."

Not for me, either. Claire didn't know if she was relieved or more upset. Somehow knowing this tug on her heartstrings wasn't one-sided, that Joshua was experiencing it, too, made her next step more consequential. Feelings were one thing; decisions and actions were another. Those were the things that affected a person's life.

She had no intention of acting in any means or manner on these emotions, which felt so raw and new and intense. Love was a fairy tale. She'd believed in the power of it once to her own folly. And yet she'd never wanted to believe more. Never felt that there was a man so unerringly good and worthy to believe in. Joshua Gable was, on the outside, everything a man ought to be—everything that made the woman she was stretch tight with a deep, instinctive longing.

It felt as if she were ripping apart a piece of her soul as she struggled to sound unaffected. And failed miserably. "This is very simple for me."

"How's that?"

"Because I know what marriage is."

"Yep, me, too." He looked anguished. He crushed his hat in his hand until the brim looked ready to blow apart. A muscle ticked in his jaw. "Hell, I don't know what to tell you."

"I know this powerful feeling, this…affection." It was a small word for what she experienced, for what tripped within her soul whenever he was near, but she could not admit it was more. "This is a fleeting thing. It doesn't last. I *know* this."

"As do I. I take care of my grandmother and my ma. Which I'm bound by duty to do until they pass from this earth. I run the family holdings and make damn sure to do it well, so my brothers and their children will have something of our father's. Something that lasts."

"I understand." She felt his despair, his wrenching heart, because it was as if it were hers, too. "You have duty and family. Those things matter. And I have my life here, one I don't want to put at risk."

"What if the Hamiltons wind up with your land? It's none of my business, but they sure seem determined, having Clise go head-to-head with my cousin. I suppose a woman in your position wouldn't mind having a man feeling the way I do on a string. Just in case."

"Is that what you think of me?"

It would be so much easier to walk through this door if I did. Joshua winced, but he'd come this far and he wasn't going to chicken out instead of simply saying the truth, so he said it. "I see that you're a woman working hard to make her own way. I don't doubt you could be married within a month, if you were inclined to take on a husband to pay the bills. I'm not saying anything in judgment of you either way. I'm only saying that man won't be me. Can't be."

"I never thought otherwise. That's why this decision is so clear." She lifted her chin, not at a haughty angle, but one that denoted determination and inner strength. "How many times have I tried to say goodbye to you for good?"

"I don't seem to leave you alone, is that it?"

"That's it. Don't mistake my gratitude. You've made an enormous difference in my life. You changed everything for me that night you rode up here."

"I was damn furious at your husband. And when I saw how he treated you… Claire, no man should ever treat a woman that way. I'm glad I came that night. I'm honored to have helped you. We've always known this, whatever this is between us, has to end. Right?"

"Right." She granted him a small grin.

One that lit her up from the inside; one that made his soul brighten with a blinding white heat. *It's time to end this, and end this right.* Joshua released his death grip on his hat and worked the battered brim back into shape. He wished this didn't hurt so damn much, but to stay, to give in to this momentary need to be with her, to cradle her in his arms and to make her his woman…

Leave now, Gable. There was no sense in that. No good possible outcome. She said it herself. She didn't want the consequences any more than he did. Love doesn't last…if it even exists. As for these needs, urges, well, as much as he wanted to give in to them, they were momentary. And they would not change the inevitable.

All he could do was to tip his hat to her, leaving just the way his gut instincts were hollering at him to do. "If you ever need anything, anything at all, you know where to find me."

She moved once, a single nod, hardly a movement at all. Was her soul wrenching, too, as if it were being torn asunder? He had to end this now. No good could come from all these feelings wrenching a person apart. "Goodbye, pretty lady."

She didn't blink. She didn't appear to breathe. With quiet dignity she watched him go, her heart in her eyes, and he knew as he yanked the door shut against the vicious wind that she did indeed feel this, too. He was no coward, but he wasn't a fool, either.

I did the right thing, he assured himself as he bowed his head against the wind and gave himself up to the night. He was numb clear through by the time he reached the stable. The problem was that the knifing cold deadened everything.

Everything but his soul.

Claire let out her pent-up breath. Was he gone? She circled around the corner of the table and pulled back the edge of the ruffled curtain. Moonlight shimmered like a halo, casting a magical luster across the silent night. There, moving against the pearled landscape was Joshua, astride his great strong gelding and riding away from her as fast as his horse could go.

And taking her heart with him.

It was strange how she thought it had been frozen over, but she'd been wrong. The tiny blossom of love was new and tender, yet fierce. Like those delicate snowdrop flowers that pushed through the ice of late winter to bloom and greet the spring.

There was no spring. Not in her life. There would be no man—even Joshua—stepping into her life to be what Ham was not. *Men. Whenever one comes courting, he's the best man on earth. Once he gets a ring on your finger, then it's a different matter.* Her mother's words ripped through her like a nightmare into a dream.

Mama, I don't want you to be right this time. With her hopes sinking, Claire pivoted to keep Joshua in her sight. He wasn't taking the road, but the horse path that cut through the property. Gilded in platinum, graced by stardust, he was naught but a silhouette, a rider on his proud horse; but she knew his characteristics so well.

Love swelled within her, making it hard to breathe and harder to see, and his hat and his granite profile blurred, becoming sharp pinpoints of light as wetness streaked down her face.

Just let him go. Her fingernails dug into the sill as he rose over the crest of the hill and disappeared from her sight. He took with him all the brief images of what it would be like to be held in his arms all the cold night through. She remained at the window, as if waiting, even though she knew he was gone.

Forever.

An owl's lonely *who? who?* echoed across the night. Joshua pulled his hands out of his pockets, yanked off his gloves and swore. He didn't regret leaving Claire's house when he did, but he sure could have used a baked potato in each pocket right now. He wouldn't be fumbling to send back the answering call—the all-clear signal.

Liam kept to the shadows. "We got visitors. It's the deputy this time and he's pissed."

"How many ridin' with him?"

"Just the Hamiltons. Figure on taking the back trails

through this time. Cut through the hills, in case we're watching for them. It's good cover. James is keepin' watch on them now. He'll signal when they're heading toward the widow's stable."

"I was halfway hoping those bastards wouldn't come after the horses. They ought to let this be. Then I could be at home with my feet up in front of the fire."

"Dreamin' of the pretty widow?"

Joshua hated that his brother was right. Claire had stayed in his heart ever since he'd escaped her kitchen. "I have my reasons for makin' sure she's safe. Not because of the reason you think."

Liam arched a brow and wisely said nothing. James's coyote call skidded across the rolls and draws of the prairie, and several distant coyotes answered with their high-pitched howls.

"Time to move." Joshua yanked on his glove, guiding General with the touch of his heel. "Let's get this over with."

He kept to the draw of the hillside, staying just out of sight so they wouldn't be spotted over the ridge. The scraggly stands of cedar and pine hid their progress just enough so that they even surprised Jordan just beneath the top of the ridge that led directly to Claire's barn.

No words were necessary and it was too damn cold to bother talking. Joshua nosed General into the line, and they waited with the wind tossing around cedar limbs and hundred-year-old pines. It was as if the very earth was avenging the wrongs done to the woman safe and warm in her little house.

Joshua didn't dare break his concentration to look

over his shoulder, but he knew what he would find. Her lights would still be on; maybe she'd already changed into her nightgown and housecoat. With the wind moaning like a tortured soul, he could still feel the connection in his soul that bound them. Her sadness hit him like a ruthless gust. There wasn't much he could do to mend her sadness. But as he heard James's signal sail loud and clear overhead, he steadied his rifle and led his brothers over the ridge and into the path of the men who'd come to do harm.

"Hello, boys." Joshua squeezed off a shot, and Reed Hamilton's revolver flew from his hand and hit the ground with a heavy thunk. "Deputy, if you draw that, I'll stop you."

Logan looked fit to kill. "You got a reason to be drawing on me, Gable? I'm the law in these parts."

"Not on this land. You are trespassing." Joshua nodded to Liam, who was circling around the deputy to disarm him. "You know the law better than any of us. I'm within my rights to hang a horse thief I catch in the act."

"Horse thieves? You're mistaken, Gable. We're just passing through." Logan's one-sided smile was a slow curve of arrogance and cunning. He looked like a man who thought he could get away with anything. That he was above the law he enforced. "What are *you* doing on the widow's land? I'm helpin' the boys here to keep their sister-in-law safe. Put down your weapons and—"

"I know how you're gonna lie about this come morning," Joshua said, not caring if he got in trouble with the town sheriff. What he cared about was leaving Claire undefended and vulnerable to the greedy men hovering around the rocky land, eager to possess it.

And now Joshua knew why. Like Logan's land, Claire's property was along an old path north and into Canada. Rustled livestock could be herded, without crossing off Hamilton land, until they hit the border. And after that, money could be made at the Wickshaw auction.

I'll keep you safeguarded, Claire. And he'd make sure these so-called men understood. There would be no more harassing of the gentle lady, whom he could still see clearly in his mind's eye and how pale she went at her confession.

"I don't suppose the sheriff is gonna believe his best deputy is in on a rustling ring," Joshua said.

"Watch what you say, Gable." Logan's eyes narrowed with an unmistakable warning. "The sheriff ain't likely to take kindly to a man like you threatening and harassing a lawman."

"And the rightful owners of this-here land," Rick Hamilton spoke up. "That makes you boys the trespassers."

Joshua considered the way James was emptying all the bullets from Rick's Winchester. "You may be right about the land. We won't know until the attorneys are done arguing it out. But for now, the land is Claire's and I'm here to make sure it stays that way. James, did you get all the weapons?"

"Almost done, big brother."

"Then listen up, boys." Joshua paused while James divested Reed of his knives. "If you steal back those horses or do anything to harm that nice lady down there, we'll come hunting you down."

"You can't threaten a deputy."

"It's a free country, and I protect what's mine." It was too late to take back those words, and in truth, he meant them. It was his job to protect Claire Hamilton. If not him and his brothers, then who? "Turn around and get off this land."

"It's not your land," Reed spit. "Not unless she's got your ring on her finger and even then, the joke is on you, Gable. This land belongs to my family."

"If and when it does, then you can come back. But until then, if I see you on this land again, we'll shoot first and not even bother with this polite warning."

"Yep, next time we'll be burying you right here," Liam commented as he closed in and they stood together as brothers in an unyielding line. "No one'll miss you. They won't even know where to find your bodies."

Joshua nodded toward Logan. "Stay away from the woman. We mean it."

As the furious men spun their horses around on the path, Joshua stayed stoic and vigilant. He kept his rage under control, but it was hard knowing what those men stood for. How they behaved. Ham had been one of them, and it made Joshua sick to think about how Claire had been treated.

Joshua had always looked at marriage from the same perspective: his own. He didn't want a woman as domineering as his mother, as free-spirited and willful as his sister or as cantankerous and used to getting her own way as his gran. He had just about enough of those traits in women as he could tolerate. He provided for the women in his life and he didn't begrudge his duty, but Lord knows those women weren't easy on a man.

He'd never taken much time to consider how hard some men were on their women. Claire's haunted look of pain and sorrow remained with him, shaming him, as he made sure Logan and the Hamilton brothers were well off the property.

Even late that night, warm, finally, in his bed in his upstairs room in his mother's house, Claire's sadness stayed with him. A heavy weight in his soul.

Chapter Seventeen

Claire let the door of the church close behind her with a hollow thud. Hollow, like places in her heart would always be. There was no repairing some things. No way to go back and piece together a failed pregnancy.

At least now the pretty nightgowns and baby blankets and shirts she'd made for her little one would help keep another baby warm. The pastor's wife had been sure she could find a family needing new baby things.

And I can try to forget. She'd been clearing out the cabin of memories, for no memories associated in that house could be good, and she'd saved the baby clothes for last. Folding away the little things into a crate had been too painful, and even now the bleakness of it tightened like a band around her chest.

That's done. I never have to do that again. She didn't know why that made her feel more lost as she avoided the patches of ice on the shady steps and crunched through the snow. Only one more thing to do. Just one.

And then she could close the door and turn the lock

on the past. On the destruction that love—or rather, believing in love—had brought her.

Thor nickered a friendly greeting as if he sensed she could use a friend. And he was a friend she was grateful for. She loosened the knot and unwound the tether from the hitching post, allowing herself the comfort of burying her face in the warm heat of his neck.

His rough mane scratched pleasantly on her face, and the crushed velvet of his coat was a luxury as he nickered again, curving his neck to lay his head against her back. A horse hug. She held on tight.

"I missed you, my friend. I am so glad you're back with me again."

With the wisdom of a good horse, Thor nodded sagely as she stepped away and climbed beneath the furs on the narrow board seat. As they headed down the quiet lane, she couldn't stand how his coat was still rough in patches and he was far too thin, but he'd weathered neglect better than his brother had. Loki was still too nervous and sickly to drive.

Thank heavens for Joshua. She'd never be able to remove the image of him riding tall through the night. Or how he'd steeped tea for her in her kitchen. How he looked as torn apart as she felt.

Whatever this connection was between them, she wanted it severed. She wanted it gone. Even now, the place in her heart where he seemed to be throbbed like a deep, untreatable wound. She wanted to let him go. But how did she cut him out of her soul?

"Claire."

She jumped. She'd been so lost in thought she was surprised to see the blue-gray shadows on the dull snow and the bare tree limbs reaching like skeletal arms overhead.

Joshua? No, it couldn't be him. She blinked and the man on the horse in the street before her came into focus.

Deputy Anson Cooper Logan leaned on his saddle horn, as if to emphasize the holstered repeating rifle within easy reach. There was no mistaking his dislike. "You've just saved me a trip out to visit you."

"What are you doing in town? I thought you spent most of your time at the trading post on the other side of the county."

"Don't take that tone with me. Not when I've come in as a deputy and not as your husband's best friend."

Foreboding twisted deep in her midsection. Claire tried to calm Thor, who was sidestepping in his traces as if he wanted to get as far away from Logan as possible. So she had her hands full and she nearly missed the gleam of triumph in the deputy's cold eyes.

He knew about Thor. Her stomach wrung tighter. Whatever he had to say was not going to be good news.

"I've been over to the sheriff's office. We've had a long discussion about you."

Her grip tightened protectively on the reins, as if that could keep him from Thor. "What on earth would you have to discuss about me with the sheriff?"

"The fact that Ham's murderer still hasn't been caught. We've got a couple of suspects, you know. Not enough evidence, but let me tell you this. A woman cheating on her husband may be motive enough for murder."

"What?"

"You were there on the property the night he was shot. In fact, there was just you and Hamilton there. And Joshua Gable came along, pulled a gun and shot your husband dead. Isn't that what happened?"

"No!" Horror coursed through her like black fear. She watched his attention slide again to Thor, a pure-bred Clydesdale worth more than Logan earned as a deputy in two years.

This was retribution, she knew that. And what he was accusing Joshua of—while heaven knew it could be true—he had no proof. None. Or he would have pulled this much earlier.

Just stay calm. Fortunately staying calm was a skill she'd learned in her marriage, and it was useful now. "Logan. What is wrong with you? Have you been drinking?"

"The question is, what is wrong with you, Claire? Cheating on your husband. Shame on you." Logan's manner grew harsher, a tough lawman scolding a criminal.

Except she was no criminal. And she was not as easily bowed. He'd only seen her as Ham's wife, placating him, working to keep the man from losing his temper. It hadn't been her choice, but it had been the consequence of her decision to marry. And there was no way on earth she was going to bow down to another man. To let any man, even an armed lawman, talk to her that way.

"Deputy, that is enough. You know good and well I was true to my husband—"

"How long have you and Gable been together?"

"Ham barely let me leave the house alone. I had no chance to have a liaison with anyone."

"How long, Claire? How long did you want your husband dead?"

His face burned red with rage, but it was a sly and calculated one as well. Thanks to Hamilton, she had learned the difference. "This is a public street. You either take me to the sheriff's office or leave me be. You're out to make trouble and I know why."

"I'm a law-abiding deputy. I don't make trouble." With a cool grin, Logan eased back in his saddle, his purpose apparently fulfilled. "You best consider coming with me to the sheriff's office."

"We both know I did not kill my husband."

"We both know that if you didn't, I have evidence to arrest someone else."

Her stomach turned at the darkness that seemed to drift off him like a foul odor. "You have no evidence and no witness."

"I can pay for one."

Her mouth hung open in shock.

"Here's the sheriff now. I know you figure Gable and his brothers will be riding to your rescue, but this is one thing he can't blame me for. You're the one who killed your husband." His eyes were laughing at her. "Not even your highfalutin lawyer will be able to get you out of this. You should have let the Hamiltons have the land, Claire. And let me have your horses. A humble deputy has to make what money he can."

Her mind was spinning. None of this made sense. Logan was a good liar, but the sheriff, surely he could see through the truth. Logan was mad, that was all, and her attorney could sort this out. There was no need to panic. No need to worry. Liars didn't always win. She was innocent.

But Joshua… The blood iced in her veins. Joshua was not.

Coop Logan leered down at her, his malice palpable. He knew the position she was in. The stifling feeling pressed in on her as if from every direction. She was helpless. Trapped.

Just as she'd been as Ham's wife.

Joshua clamped his jaw tight in frustration. The women in his family were going to be the death of him. If it wasn't his grandmother getting into arguments in town or his mother with her list of ways to improve his life, his sleep, the right woman to marry, it was his sister, as bright as the sun in the flawless sky.

He was worried sick about her. She was so happy. If this marriage didn't turn out to be all she hoped it would, then it was a long, long way to fall. He didn't want to see disappointment and heartbreak hurt his Bets.

"This is the last trunk, I promise." She snapped the latch and bounced up, shining.

Hell, she was beaming happiness.

"Joshua, you're frowning. Stop!" She laughed like a lark's trill and kissed his cheek. "I'm happy. Trust me for a change. You're not the only one who can make a good decision."

"That man is not good enough for you. We both know it."

"You're right. He's far too good for the likes of me. I'm just lucky he wants me to be his wife." She swirled away in a cloud of yellow calico.

"This is too much happy for me."

He hated how bright the sunshine was streaming through the window, as if to mock him while he knelt to heft the enormous trunk onto his shoulder. He'd protested, done everything he could to stop this relationship and, still, Betsy was determined. If he pushed her any harder to abandon her wedding plans, then he knew he would lose her.

"You didn't like me working as a laundry lady, and that worked out wonderfully." Betsy led the way down the stairs, clearing away Jordan, who'd collapsed on a step to eat a cookie he'd stolen from her kitchen. "I met my Duncan on my laundry route."

"See why it was such a bad idea?"

"You're glum because you were wrong about my business and my fiancé." She held the door.

He shouldered through with the impossibly heavy trunk. "What did you put in this thing, anyway?"

"Go ahead and try to change the subject, but you are wrong every once in a while, my dearest brother." She huddled on the front step in the cold wind. "I saw Claire today."

Claire. All thoughts flew out of his head. His toe jammed into the steel belt of the wagon wheel and pain jolted through his foot as the trunk tumbled from his shoulder.

The crash as it hit the wagon's tailgate said it all.

Betsy had mentioned the one thing that could rattle him. And she'd done it on purpose.

"Go inside. You don't have a coat." He scowled, hoping he looked mad enough to send her inside so the subject of Claire wouldn't be debated and henpecked to death. "Go on. Git going."

"I'm used to your bark, big brother." When she should have scurried inside, she calmly swooped down the stairs, her gentle love for him undeniable. "What happened? Claire came by to leave off a wedding gift and your mare. I gathered from what she didn't say that you aren't courting her any longer."

"I never was courting her."

"Fine. Then, uh, calling on her."

He gave the trunk a shove so it wedged up tight against the porch chairs he'd stacked in earlier. "I wasn't calling on her, either."

"But I thought—"

"Everyone just assumed. I was helping Claire out, that was all. I had my reasons, but that's all it was." He was lying to her. He was lying to himself. But damn it, it was easier than admitting the truth. Betsy was in love. She'd lost all rational sense. She'd never see his view of things.

It didn't matter anyway, because Claire understood. They just had to wait out whatever this attraction was. It would eventually fade. All things changed. All things ended. She had her life. He had his responsibilities. That was a lot to toss away on the chance a marriage might be a happy one.

He didn't have that much trust in anyone.

Different lives, different outcomes, different choices. They would never be. It was that simple.

"Claire told me that you boys stole her horses back for her." That was Betsy, tenacious without end. She followed him up the steps and back into her house. "You wouldn't have risked so much unless she meant a great deal to you."

"She does mean a great deal to me." His confession startled him, mostly because he'd vowed never to admit it. Especially to himself. And because in saying it, he made it real, and in making it real, it hurt that much more.

"Oh, Joshua." Betsy squeezed his hand, a comfort as always.

He was a man; he didn't need comfort. "I'll grab Jordan by the ear and haul him upstairs with me. We can fit that bureau on the back of the wagon."

"Good news." Betsy sighed, holding on to his hand as if she didn't want to let go. As if she could sense the deep well of sadness he didn't want to admit to having. "The road to my Duncan's house goes awfully close to Claire's home. You could stop on the way back and see her. Maybe you should see her, Joshua. Talk to her. I had so hoped you might find someone to love."

"I don't need love. I need another hand around to help me out with the ranch." It wasn't true; they both knew it. But it was easier to let the lie be than to erase it with the truth—that he needed Claire more than he could ever say, ever measure, ever believe.

And that's why he intended to send Jordan with the wagon. And stay behind to do the evening chores.

The less temptation, the better.

* * *

"Let's go over your story once more to make sure I have it right." The sheriff hunkered down on the chair across the small scarred table. "You were coming home from town. The mare lost her footing on the hill."

"There was an ice storm. It was slick."

"The horse fell, the wagon wrecked and you were hurt."

Images racked through her. She'd been pregnant. She'd been afraid for her baby. Joshua had come out of that storm like a mythical hero come to life. How could she mention his presence that night? How could she ever harm him?

She couldn't. She could not tell the truth since that would condemn him. There was no mistaking the Hamilton brothers, who were seated just beyond the metal bars at the sheriff's paper-strewn desk. If she mentioned Joshua was there that night, then they would hear. And they would leap to all kinds of wrong conclusions. Ones that could only hurt Joshua.

"I was pinned to the ground for a while." Claire remembered every detail of how Joshua had stood up to Ham and defeated him. How Ham had fallen to the ground, bleeding, trying to shoot Joshua...and how he'd failed.

One thing she would never forget was the gentle regard Joshua, a stranger, had paid her that night. Helping her up. Carrying her to the cabin. Rushing for the doctor.

Making sure Ham wouldn't hurt anyone again. But that didn't make him a murderer. If Joshua had killed him, then it had been self-defense. Not that she trusted the sheriff to believe that. Not with the Hamiltons sneering in the back room.

The sheriff didn't seem interested as he asked, "Who helped you up from the wreckage?"

"I helped myself. I learned to do that a lot after I'd married Ham. He wasn't a good husband."

A thud came from the next room. Reed was on his feet, his drunken howl so nearly identical to Ham's that it sent shivers creeping down her nape.

"Ham was a better man than the likes of her deserved!"

His temper seemed nearly the same, too.

"Sit down, Reed!" Logan snarled somewhere out of sight. His voice dropped into a whisper and she couldn't hear what he was saying. But she could feel it. Feel the malice in the dank, musty air. Feel the glee at their victory so close…and it did look as if they would win. The sheriff was on their side. She hadn't realized that until she'd walked into the jail and spotted the Hamiltons lying in wait.

"I went straight to bed and there I stayed until morning."

"Alone?"

She remembered how Logan had hinted that she'd been unfaithful, so she was very firm in her answer. "Alone. Don't believe everything you hear, Sheriff. Some men have no decency, so telling a lie is nothing to them."

"And it's the same for some women." The sheriff pushed back his chair and stood, unfolding to his full height, but he wasn't as tall or as impressive as Joshua.

Joshua. Even here in the cool must of the town jail,

she thought of him. Her soul yearned for him, like a summer wildflower watching and waiting for the dawn.

The sheriff caught hold of the open cell door. "I'm charging you, Claire Hamilton, in the shooting death of your husband."

Everything within her stilled. No, it couldn't be true. She'd done nothing wrong. At night anyone could have shot Ham. She was in the house, wounded and afraid she was losing the baby, which she had been. The doc had arrived, the rest of the night was foggy and vague. She'd awoken the next morning exhausted and hurting in more ways than she could count, and Ham was simply not there.

And if you say this, then those men will keep looking. They'll logically decide to question him next. And what if they find out the inconsistencies?

What if they discovered she'd lied to keep Joshua out of this mess? She loved him. How could she say the words that would ruin his life?

"Hey! Woman!" Reed lurched onto his feet, his hands fisting and his temper as hot as fresh coals. He crowded into the narrow space between the desks and the cells. "I'm gonna make sure you hurt. That was my brother you killed so you could play the bitch to high-and-mighty Gable."

"Out of my way." She lifted her chin, preparing for whatever came next. She wasn't afraid of being hit. She wasn't afraid of anything. Not anymore. She couldn't explain it as she shoved past Reed to take her place inside the empty cell.

The door clicked closed with a metallic snap, and the echo of it resounded off the stone walls and floors.

"You can't talk to me like that! Hey, Sheriff, she can't talk to me like that—"

Reed's words faded away. Claire felt her knees giving out and so she dropped onto the only piece of furniture, a cot—not comfortable at all—and listened to the final clicking turn of the key, locking her in like a criminal.

This can't be happening. She couldn't believe she was free one moment and jailed the next.

On the other side of the bars, the sheriff snapped his key ring onto his belt. "I expect you're using the Gable family's lawyer? Do you want me to send for him?"

Yes. She was scared inside. Joshua's cousin was an excellent attorney. He'd know what to do. He'd help her. He could get her out of here and prove that she'd had nothing to do with Ham's death.

And yet, would that only force Logan and the Hamiltons to accuse Joshua? What if he was here right now instead of her? He had the largest ranch in the county to run. He had his family to take care of and care for. Everyone in the Gable family depended on Joshua.

"I won't be needing my lawyer, thank you."

"All right, then. I'd feel sorry for you, a woman locked up in a cell. But the truth is a man's dead because of you. Ham was a friend of mine, too. Believe me when I say I'm gonna make sure you get exactly what you deserve."

Getting what those men thought she deserved…that's what she was afraid of.

Chapter Eighteen

Joshua's back was killing him. Did his sister have to have such heavy furniture? He would have been grumbling about it, since he was so damned miserable anyway, but the arrival of Betsy's fiancé became a greater torment. Betsy was downstairs right now with the mountain man who was probably only interested in sweet Bets for her inheritance.

Red hazed his vision as he tamped down a dynamite rage. He heaved the feather mattress off the bed. It hit the floor with a boom that echoed in the rafters above.

Boots pounded up the stairs. Too fast of a gait for Jordan. Too powerful for quieter brother James. Joshua wasn't surprised to see Liam march into the room with his typical dour determination. "Got that headboard ready? No. What's wrong? I thought you'd have the whole house moved into those mountains by now."

"I'm in no hurry to pack Betsy off to her new husband."

"That Duncan isn't such a bad sort." Liam caught the end of the headboard. "I got to talkin' to him downstairs.

He's not as lazy as you think. He's a woodworker. He sells furniture to several of the furniture stores in the county."

"He's a mountain man."

Joshua didn't want to like the man and he wouldn't. Nothing was going to change his mind. Too much was at risk for him to be swayed now. Claire Hamilton's misery at the hands of her husband had convinced him he was right.

Betsy might not listen to him—she might marry the man anyway—but Joshua was going to make damn sure that no man hurt his little sister. No matter what. That Liam had been taken in by this mountain man irked him even more. He wrenched on the braces and yanked the headboard from the frame.

"Whoa, brother. What did the bed to do you?"

He didn't answer.

"Oh, I know." Liam shook his head and grabbed the footboard before it could tumble to the floor, leaving the fact that this was to be his sister's marriage bed unspoken between them. "Are you going to be able to give her away at the wedding? Or am I gonna have to get all dressed up in a coat and tie?"

"If it were up to me, I'd fly her up to the moon and banish her there."

"But how do you know there aren't a bunch of mountain men who live on the back side of the moon? The minute you'd leave her there, if you could get her there, one of them would be bound to charm her into loving him."

"I want her safe. I want her happy. I'd think, as her brother, that you'd want the same."

"Sure I do. I want her happy. But we both know there's no such thing as safe. Not in this life. Living is a risk. Loving is a risk. That's why I'm not a courting man. Some risks are best to avoid. Others, well, you just can't."

"It's always a wise decision to avoid women, romance and marriage." Bitterness curdled on his tongue as he hefted the headboard toward the doorway.

"So that's what's got you in this foul mood." Liam followed down the stairwell with the footboard. "What happened with Claire?"

"None of your damn business."

"Well, then, I guess Ma won the bet."

Joshua skidded to a halt. "Ma? Our mother does not gamble."

"You'd be surprised. She bet that you would never marry Claire. She said that you won't marry anyone. Too stubborn. Too set in your ways. That you couldn't hand over that much control."

"She didn't say that." Although like a lock clicking into place, he knew the truth when he heard it. She'd hit the nail on the head, all right. That was why he'd walked away from Claire that night. Why he'd protect her, defend her, take care of her and befriend her, but why he'd never trust her enough for more. The notion terrified him. He was in control of his life. And he liked it that way.

So why did it only make him feel more desolate?

"If it's any consolation," Liam continued as they pushed out onto the front porch, "Gran predicted you'd get Claire in a family way and have to marry her."

Gran knew the look of a man who was falling hard,

Joshua realized. He hadn't fooled anyone—not one member of his family. He'd only tricked himself into believing he wasn't in love with Claire. And that it hadn't changed him. Of course, he wouldn't admit this to anyone, least of all his brothers. He was the head of the family; it wasn't by choice but by duty, and he'd gotten used to it. He had to shrug off this weakness, because the stronger he was, the better decisions he made for his family.

Except now that wasn't enough. There was nothing on this earth that could begin to patch up the hole Claire had left in his heart. And in his life.

He slid the bottom edge of the headboard onto the tailgate of Duncan's wagon and climbed up into the bed. From this height, he had a perfect view through the dining room window, where Betsy stood in her fiancé's embrace, gazing up into his face with all her loving heart.

What defeated him was the way the mountain man— the man he thought so disreputable and bad for Betsy— was gazing down at the woman in his arms. Strong. Protective. Deeply tender.

It was surely an illusion, a trick of the light. Joshua stubbornly refused to believe anything else. His own father had been miserable every day that Joshua could remember. Every day. Heaven knows he loved his mother, but she was a domineering woman who had pushed and henpecked and prodded Pa into outright misery.

Look at James. He couldn't even come help today because his wife had other plans for him. The same excuse she'd used for nearly every holiday and family gathering since their wedding day.

Joshua was in love with Claire. He couldn't deny it and wasn't going to pretend otherwise. He'd fallen, and he'd fallen so hard he could feel the beat of her heart within his own.

But he was making the right decision, to stay strong. He didn't need love. He didn't need her.

He didn't need anyone.

Claire huddled in her coat. Her breath rose in foggy clouds in front of her. How long had she been trapped with the walls creeping in? She had no notion. The sheriff was still at his desk, sipping steaming coffee. The scratch of his ink pen on paper filled the unending silence. What had seemed like infinity sitting here in the damp and dark could only have been a few hours at most.

What would it be like to live like this for days, weeks, months on end? Her stomach fisted. She was going to find out. Not that she liked that notion at all. What about Thor? He was left tied to the hitching post outside. She could hear the wind buffeting the thick stone walls and smell the plumes of smoke driven down the stovepipe from the harsh gusts. The temperature had to be falling. Was Thor cold? Thirsty? Afraid?

And what would become of Loki at home? She needed to send someone out to feed him. And her business…she didn't want to think of the duffels and bags of laundry she had yet to deliver today. And the dirties she'd intended to pick up.

She was an entrepreneur. She had responsibilities. Betsy had wanted to find someone dependable for her loyal customers. And now Claire felt sick with the realization she'd let Betsy down.

Worse, she realized she'd never see Joshua again. Not even from a distance. Not to bump into him on the street. Nothing.

Why did love hurt so much, as if a noose had lassoed tightly about her heart and was dragging her behind a horse? Every inch of her stung. More than injury. More than heartache. More than grief could ever do alone.

What kind of love was this? She wanted this to be over. She wanted this to end. Why couldn't she will these feelings away? Even locked away from the world, she still felt the loss of him within every fiber of her being.

The whoosh of the wind and the rattle of the potbellied stove's door told her someone had arrived. The Hamiltons again? They'd warned that they would be back.

Only one pair of boots tromped on the plank floor. A fleeting hope flashed through her. Awareness skidded over her chilled skin like a summer breeze.

Joshua. She could feel his presence like a voice in her soul. She straightened beneath the blanket she'd swaddled around her like a shawl, overwhelmed by the snap of awareness telegraphing down her spine.

The sheriff's pen continued to scratch, the fire to roar in the belly of the red-hot stove, but to her everything changed. She waited for him in the gray stone room beyond the cell, her spirit turning toward him like the earth to the moon in search of its light.

He's very near. She felt the twisting recognition in the deep, private places of her soul. And she knew it was

Joshua before the sound of footsteps halted just outside the sheriff's office.

It's him. Deep down, she celebrated the sight of him as he burst into the office, all fierce male energy, not violent, not frightening, no. It was a different kind of fierce. A different kind of fear. He stalked to the sheriff's desk like a soldier home from a victory, charging the room with his dazzling presence.

Well, Claire realized, maybe she was the only one dazzled.

"Gable. I didn't hear you come in." The lawman looked annoyed that his work was being interrupted, his quill held midway between the inkwell and the paper. "Are you havin' more trouble with your sheep?"

"Not since Ham passed away. Funny thing, don't you think? I came to see why Claire's horse is tied up outside." Joshua glanced around the small serviceable room. There was no sign of a woman—or of another person—in this place.

Panic began beating a quick rhythm in his chest. Was there a problem? Should he have dealt more harshly with the Hamiltons last night? It's just that he'd been sure the boys would back down. The last thing they could afford was to spend more time in jail calming down—

Something caught his attention. There in the dusky corner of one of the two cells. A shape too small to be a man, too fine boned to be an adolescent. If he squinted just right, he could see her familiar, delicate profile sitting on a battered cot on the far side of the cell, huddled beneath a shapeless blanket, her lustrous hair tumbling everywhere.

Claire. All the misery fled from his heart. All the darkness from his core. His entire being pulsed with life, as if he'd awakened after a long slumber.

He could still feel the space she'd claimed in his soul. How unlikely was that? He'd done everything he could to rip her from his very spirit and nothing, not one thing, could diminish the brightness she'd put in his heart.

"What are you doing in there?" Fury roiled as he put the pieces together. Logan and the Hamiltons had gone against him, discounting his threats. How could she be arrested for the theft of her own horse? "Sheriff, there's a problem here. Get your keys."

"Sorry, Gable. There's no mistake."

"Bull. Claire doesn't belong there." Joshua turned to her, his manner reassuring and kind. "Don't worry, baby, I'll get you out of this." He seemed unaware of the endearment as he stormed over to the sheriff's desk and pounded his fist on the wood surface.

The pen flew from the lawman's grip. "Whoa, there, Gable. Don't you go blamin' me for this."

"She's innocent, and you damn well know it." Joshua seemed to rear up like a furious grizzly; he was taller, stronger, and so fierce the stone walls vibrated with his raw fury. *"Give me the keys."*

"Watch it, Gable."

The sheriff's warning bounced off him like hail—he wasn't scared of the lawman. He was too enraged at the sight of the woman he loved—no, the woman he didn't want to love—locked in a cage like a rabbit in a trap. He seized the ring from the lawman's belt, yanked and fumbled through the keys on the way to the cell.

The sheriff was shouting something, but Joshua didn't care. He only knew he had to get to her. He'd failed to protect and defend her. By God, he would not fail her now.

The key turned, the door opened and he tossed the ring back at the sheriff. The lawman's mouth moved, but Joshua couldn't hear anything above the roar of fury in his ears and the thrum of urgency in his heartbeat. He was barely aware of the cold biting his skin and stinging his eyes as he dropped onto his knees before her.

"Claire." Emotion choked him. For a man who didn't have feelings, they were spewing up as if from a newly dug well, rising higher and higher until he was swimming in them. The raw, dark pain he'd been living with died the instant he took her small hand in his. So cold, so vulnerable, so dear. He pressed his lips to her knuckles and lost hold of his heart. Uncontrollable affection left him drowning.

And like a man swept into a flooding river, there was no firm ground to stand on, no way to swim to shore, no chance in hell to stop the force of the current that had seized him. He was a drowning man lost as he laid his face in her lap, so grateful just to be near her. Just to know she was going to be all right. He'd make sure of it.

"You can't be here." Her fingers squeezed his tightly, holding on as if she were drowning, too. "It's not good for you."

"Me? You're the one in here." It was killing him seeing her, so good and gentle in spirit, punished like this. "I will not let you be condemned. Don't you worry. I'm here now."

"That's the problem. You can't be here. Logan knows somehow that you were at my place the night that Ham was shot. I guess I never thought about it. Of course he was shot. That's how he died."

"Haskins is the only doctor in the county, Claire. His brother is the undertaker." Joshua pitched his voice low, so the sheriff couldn't hear, but the lawman had marched out of sight, probably to bring in reinforcements. "They made sure the cause of death was blamed on a fall, not a bullet. Ham was shot in the back. I'm sure it was self-defense, Claire. The doc, hell, even the undertaker knows that. Anyone with eyes could see how Ham treated you."

"What? Me? I don't understand. Surely you're not trying to blame me? Not when you—" No, that wasn't right. Joshua would never betray her like that. The moment she thought it, she discarded it. Ham would have gladly blamed her for a murder and sent her in his stead to jail, but not Joshua. Not noble, honest, decent Joshua. "I thought you—"

He only stared at her, his eyes great dark pools. "I'm going to get you out on bail. It's late, but I'll fetch Callan from his house and we'll be back. You won't stay in this godforsaken cell a moment longer than necessary. I swear it. I'll get you out of this."

"It's not your responsibility." And if Joshua hadn't shot Ham, in self-defense as she'd imagined, or for any reason at all, then someone else had. Someone who had a lot to lose.

She knew how cruel people could be—she'd seen far too much of it in her life. And it didn't matter if she was married to a brutal man or not, the world was full of such men.

And if anything happened to Joshua, if he were discovered in a field with a bullet in his back as Ham had been, well, then the loss would be staggering. Not only to her heart, but also to all the people who loved him. He had family. He had a good life. She saw all that could happen to him in a flash—*if* the lawmen decided he was guilty of murder.

I would never want that for you. Falsely accused, wrongly imprisoned. The punishment for murder in this territory was hanging. *That's no way for a good man to die.* For she had no more doubts, not one, that Joshua was a good man. When he reared up in a temper like a vengeful bear, it was for rightness' sake and not for his own.

So much stood between them, he'd lost faith somewhere along the way. So had she. Maybe, if they'd met before Joshua had become embittered and before she'd met and married Ham, *maybe* this great love they shared would have had a chance.

But now…the unforgiving walls and bars of steel crept in ever closer as if to whisper, *There's no escape.*

"Not my responsibility?" he choked out, as if he couldn't believe she'd told him that. As if he couldn't see they'd made their choices, and those choices had taken them further apart. Different lives. Different directions. "I gave my word to you. I promised you that I'd keep you safe."

"That is not yours to promise. They think we are lovers, Joshua. And you know that's not true. They think we were seeing each other before Ham was killed."

"Those things are easy enough to prove. We have the truth on your side." He stroked his hand along the curve of her jaw, cradling her face. A tender gesture.

I don't want to feel this way for him. She tried to rein in her emotions, but they went right on. Although she remained motionless, ignoring him as if he weren't in the room, she was aware of him with every inch of her body. Goose bumps covered her skin. Her blood rushed warm and tingly through her limbs. Her heart's center flooded with feeling and she felt the tug and pull of him, as if he were right there in the very center of her soul. *I love him so much. I don't want to love him so much.*

But she did. More than her life. More than anything. There was no use in denying it. Not now. Not when everything in her life was lost.

There was a crash in the entrance and the hammering of several pairs of footsteps in the hallway. The sheriff broke into the room, face red with fury, a small army of men marching in behind him.

"Your time's up, Gable. You don't own this town, as much as you'd like to think you do. Get outta that cell. I'd be more than happy to lock you up, too."

Joshua rose slowly, deliberately, as if he wasn't bothered at all by the armed men surrounding the cell. "Did you think I came in here to break her out? How dumb are you, Sheriff? Dumb enough to lock up an innocent woman, that's what."

Reed Hamilton shoved into sight, his stone-cold gaze glittering. "There ain't nothin' innocent about that woman. You oughta know. The two of you murdered my brother."

"You're just angry I won't let you bully her into handing over the land and the horses." Joshua moved so he stood in front of Claire, protecting her from the men and their drawn guns. "I know you're a gambler, Reed. A gambler who's always on the losing end. And this time you're wrong, as usual. Claire didn't have anything to do with your brother's death. That's the plain truth."

"How do you know that?"

"Because she wasn't there when he was killed. I was." Joshua held up his hands, approaching the open doorway to shield Claire from what was to happen next. "I shot Ham."

Chapter Nineteen

Claire watched in horror as Reed's fist flew. Joshua raised his arm to block the blow, only to receive Rick's left hook square in the jaw. His knees buckled.

"Joshua!" She sprang from the cot as he fell. Time stretched out in long, tormenting ticks. She hit the floor, her hands already reaching, but not fast enough.

The back of his skull cracked against the stone floor.

She caught him as his head bounced upward, recoiling from the impact. As she cradled his head in her lap, she ignored the commotion outside the cell, and stroked her hand along Joshua's face. "Can you hear me?"

His forehead furrowed as he groaned, fighting even as unconsciousness dragged him back down.

She pressed a kiss to his cheek. "Joshua? Please wake up. You have to—"

Strong hands banded her arms and yanked her upward. "No!" She couldn't leave Joshua. The Hamiltons' hatred hung in the air, tainting it like a smoldering fire's smoke. "Joshua!"

He moaned, his head twisting out of her hold as she was wrenched away. His skull smacked against the floor again. No! He was defenseless. He was outnumbered. He was alone. She wouldn't leave him. She twisted and fought even as Logan and Rick hauled her from the cell.

"No, let go!" She dug her heels into the floor to try to stop them. She jerked against their hold on her, feeling her skin burn as she twisted and kicked. "Let me go!"

"That's the idea." Logan gave her a shove out the door. The men released her at the same time, swinging her hard. Her shoulder slammed against a post. The air slammed out of her lungs as she skidded to a stop on the boardwalk. Dusk had fallen; ice crisped the boards as she crawled onto her knees and stood. She had to get back to Joshua. She had to save him. "Wait! Rick!"

The big brute, as beefy and hard as Ham had been, turned in an eerily similar way, the light from the hallway shading him in darkness. "We're no longer family. Get lost."

"You have to stop this. Joshua didn't shoot Ham. You know he didn't. You know it, if you'd just stop to think—"

"You know what I think?" His sneer was slow and evil. "Ham was too soft on you. He never taught you your place, not good enough. Or you wouldn't be crawling onto your feet wearing a blue dress. Blue, not black. That was my brother your lover killed."

Claire wasn't fooled. There was no real conviction in his manner—only triumph. "What do you want? What will it take for you to leave Joshua alone?"

"Oh, so now you're willing to bargain. Logan, go

back inside. The little lady and I have some business."
Rick's beefy hand caught her around the back of the
neck and squeezed.

She felt the impact of his silent warning. The tiny
hairs on her nape prickled. Every instinct shrieked at her
to run.

Run? No. She'd never give in to that possibility. I will
no longer be afraid, she vowed as she fastened her gaze
on his. She refused to live in fear. She was through
being bullied and controlled. She braced her feet, ready
to pay whatever cost. Right here and right now. "You
want the land?"

He crooked his left brow. "What? Are you going to
sign it over to me?"

"What I want is for you to go in there, stop Logan and your brother from harming Joshua, drop the
charges and call a truce between me, your family and the
Gables. And I'll give you everything I have. The land. The
cabin. What remains in my savings. Just spare Joshua."

"You're willing to sign whatever our family attorney
puts in front of you?"

"Yes." There was no debate. There never could be. No
matter what it cost, she wouldn't let Joshua sacrifice his
life for hers. It wasn't every day a woman found herself
an ordinary, everyday hero. Not the kind made of legend, but the flesh-and-blood man who stood for what was
right, who walked tall, whose nobility never wavered.

Rick's leer traveled over her from bosom to hip like
a filthy touch. "The land won't be the only thing I'll be
wanting. You understand?"

She swallowed, feeling the last wisp of dreams fade.

Revulsion wrenched her midsection and she covered her mouth with both hands to keep her stomach contents where they belonged. Bile soured her mouth.

She couldn't speak, only nod. For Joshua, she thought. For him, she could endure anything.

There was a terrible thundering sound. *Ka-boom. Ka-boom.* The noise ricocheted through his foggy, shocked head.

Joshua registered pain next, arcing like the snap of a bullwhip through his skull, between his eyes, hammering in his jaw and lashing downward. A worse pain burned in the middle of his back, and it felt as if a cannonball had burned a hole through his ribs and was sitting against his lungs. Every breath was an effort.

At least I'm not dead. I hurt too damn much. He didn't know if he just couldn't see or if he was alone in the dark. Silence echoed around him except for the blast of his pulse in his ears. He tried to move; pain struck like a lightning bolt of searing white light.

Hell, he hurt. His guts clenched. Sick with pain, he concentrated on breathing slow and steady. What in hellfire had happened to him? Where was he?

Ka-boom, ka-boom. His brain hurt right along with his skull. Thought wasn't possible. He shivered from pain and shock and cold. Frigid wind skidded across his bloody face. Hell, he was outside somewhere.

But where? Near the mountains? Falling ice turned to slush on his skin. His guts cramped as he saw the looming giant of a cottonwood towering above him like an enemy, great black limbs lashing in the wind.

They'd dumped him in the middle of nowhere. They'd left him here to die. He realized now he had a bullet wound. They'd shot him in the back.

Just like his father.

He was dying. He was alone. And a coyote howled nearby. Maybe a hundred yards to his north. The eerie yowling resounded through the night, one predator calling his pack. Joshua wondered how long he had before the other dogs came and encircled him.

Weak, he couldn't fight them off. Blood rolled out of him like ice from the sky and he knew without bothering to search that his weapons had been taken from him. He was defenseless. And, damn it, being taken out by a coyote wasn't the way he'd prefer to exit this life.

Claire. Fear for her welled up, when he hadn't been afraid for himself. Not even now. He blinked the ice from his lashes, and forced the fog of pain that had filled his skull. He had to think. He had to remember. They'd been in the town jail. The details were fuzzy, but that wasn't surprising considering the hellish headache that felt like someone was slamming a sledgehammer against the side of his head.

Think, man. Think. All he knew was that Claire had been behind him in the jail when the Hamiltons ganged up on him. Was she still in that cell? Or had his confession freed her?

Or was she lying like this, injured and dying? The thought of her in pain and afraid tore a roar of agony from his throat. The coyote called again, this time closer.

Come to me, you bastard. If Claire is out here, stay away from her. Or I will hunt you down, I swear it. His hand scrabbled along the snowy ground until he found a fallen branch slick with freezing ice. At least he had a weapon. He wasn't done fighting. Not by a long shot.

He managed to wrangle his body into sitting up. Longer still before he could use the trunk of the cottonwood to lean on as he struggled to stand. Hell, his cracked ankle beat with pain. The pounding surged in his head as he sagged against the tree, slick with his own sweat and with the icing rain.

So far, so good. Clutching the broken limb like a weapon, he staggered forward. Nausea gripped his guts. Blood oozed down his chest, freezing on the front of his shirt. He slumped back against the tree, trying to figure out what to do. He couldn't keep going with blood rolling out of him. Finally he ripped his shirt, stuffed fabric into the wound and used his belt to hold it tight in place.

He had to get to Claire. A rising sense of panic drove him forward. If the Hamilton brothers had taken her, who knew how they were treating her. It was almost too much to hope that the sheriff had released her, that she might be tucked away in her warm and cozy home, safe from the cruelty men were capable of. Men like the Hamiltons. Like Logan.

Joshua would find her, even if it was the last thing he ever did, and no matter the cost.

All he cared about, well beyond his own life, was hers.

As he took a second step, the hairs on the back of his neck straightened.

The coyote had arrived, and he wasn't alone.

Claire did her best not to let her anger show at the tracks of melting ice on her polished floor. It was a small thing, considering what she'd once had to endure.

And might well have to withstand again.

Rick grabbed the dime novel from where it rested and tossed it. The small paper volume slapped against the corner wall and slid to the floor.

She tried not to picture the bent and maybe even torn pages, but failed. Temper beat within her like the first pellets of ice against the window.

"It's gettin' nasty out there." Rick kicked out a chair and knocked off her ruffled chair cushion. "The boys'll be needin' hot coffee and vittles when they come in. You don't look like you're workin' hard to me."

"What do you know about hard work?"

A muscle in his jaw ticked. "Ham hasn't been long in the ground and look how fast the manners go. You went and got yourself some gumption. Well, that'll be easy to get rid of. Get me a drink, woman."

Oh, what I'd like to give you. She gritted her teeth to keep her anger inside and fisted her hands to keep from tossing things at him.

She whipped open the cabinet and grabbed a tin cup to serve his whiskey in. Next to the tinware, there was a small unmarked canister of cascara bark, Joshua's grandmother's secret home remedy for deserving men.

Wasn't it thoughtful of Adelaide to leave a good supply? Claire took the tin and canister with her into the pantry, where she intended to sprinkle a scant portion of the small flakes into the whiskey bottle she'd kept for medicinal purposes.

But what if Rick noticed the little pieces of ground bark in his cup? The Hamilton men were serious about their alcohol. She might be better putting it into something else. Like the cinnamon rolls sitting on the shelf, already iced and topped with ground cinnamon. The cascara flecks blended in perfectly.

"I thought you might be hungry," she explained as she set the plate of rolls down next to the bottle and cup. "You don't have to sit in here and guard me. I'm not going anywhere. You keep your word about Joshua and I'll keep my promise to you."

"I'll let him live." Rick uncapped the bottle and splashed a generous portion of whiskey into the mug. "But I tell you this. If I ever see Gable on this property, I'll shoot first and ask questions later."

Rick's words made her shudder. How could a man be so repulsive? It sickened her to look at him, because all she could see was his fist flying into Joshua's jaw. She felt no remorse at all for the cascara. "Would you bring in some coal for the stove?"

"I don't take orders from a woman. Get it yourself."

She could have predicted that one. She left Rick to his liquor and carried the coal hod to the back door. Night came early this time of year on the high northern mountains, and the driving ice tinkling and cracking over the landscape reminded her of the first night Joshua had made his way here.

She melted from the inside out, remembering. He'd come out of the darkness, as if a part of it, astride his fine horse, his shoulders wide, his dark hat tipped just right to shade his eyes. What an impressive silhouette he made against the gray shroud of ice and flinty sky. His rugged face, his uncompromising jaw, the wide, strong promise of his chest—just like a hero, Claire breathlessly thought.

Her hero. Without him, she would have never known that good men existed. Joshua had given up his freedom for her sake. She hadn't wanted to trust him, and she'd done everything in her power not to all along, sure he was not what he'd seemed. But she'd finally caught a glimpse of the real Joshua Gable, beneath the protective male shield he wore, beneath the capable mask he so carefully presented to her and to everyone. The real Joshua Gable was selfless and true. She loved him all the more for his genuine heart. She loved him now, when being with him was impossible.

Wherever you are, Joshua, please be all right.

She'd never had the chance to go back inside the jail and see if he needed her help or care. *Even a moment of comfort.* He'd hit his head so hard. Worry drummed wildly in her chest as she draped the old shawl over her shoulders and pushed out the back door.

Ice fell with a tinkling cadence and made it seem as if the vast night were singing. As she knelt to scoop coal into the hod, she tried not to think of the man who'd made sure she had winter fuel and winter staples. Impossible.

It was as if he were nearby, for the way her pulse skipped a few beats. But she had to be imagining it, she thought as she let the lid bang shut on the bin and hefted the heavy hod with both hands.

Feeling the cresting wave of affection moving through her, she turned to squint into the dark and storm. Ice stung her face and clung to her shawl as she searched the shadows and hollows and the cedar grove.

Nothing. She only imagined she'd sensed him.

Wishful thinking, that was all. For her heart would always be wishing for and wanting Joshua.

Always.

Her heart was a cold dark place as she hefted the heavy hod of coal into the crook of one arm and shoved open the door with the heel of her free hand. Her feet slipped and slid, her shoulder hit the door frame hard enough to rattle her.

"You got any butter?" Rick hollered from inside the house.

Reminding her of the price she'd paid for Joshua's freedom.

Claire. She was alive. The sight of her dropped him to his knees. He could blame it on his wounds. He had hobbled across the wintry prairie until he liberated a pony from its pasture and had found his way here, to Claire's property.

He hadn't been aware of how terrified he was to find her cabin dark and her gone, disappeared, maybe dead—until this moment. Until he saw her shadow cross the front room curtain. She was safe enough to walk. She was home. She wasn't moving as if she'd been injured. *Thank God.* His guts were a tangled knot of fear, a knot that didn't relent as he hunkered down beneath the wide, protective limbs of an ancient cedar and swiped blood and ice from his face. It felt as if he'd been to hell tonight and crawled his way back to the world.

He coughed. Blood sputtered into his bare hand. The metallic scent of it told him he didn't have much time.

Every time he moved his torso, blood oozed from his bullet wound. He could feel weakness taking hold.

Whether he lived or died didn't much matter to him at this point. He'd never been so miserable. Never been with so little hope.

His family would be all right without him. He could see that now. Liam was a great horseman; he'd been helping manage the vast ranch holdings for years. James was mighty good, too, and Jordan was going to settle down and fit right in, in time. Betsy was to be married. And with all her sons around her—well, all but him should he die—Ma ought to be happy. And Granny was entirely capable of taking care of herself. She could probably run the ranch single-handedly better than he ever could.

Claire's shadow passed in front of the curtained window again—a sight that hurt worse than the bullet in his back. She would be all right without him. She had the laundry business to make her way, and his brothers would look out for her. Betsy had befriended her. She wouldn't be alone.

He'd been smart, staying a bachelor, working hard instead of wasting time courting. Even when he'd finally succumbed to a woman and fallen hard in love with her, he hadn't let himself need her, really need her. His life had stayed the same. He had stayed the same.

Smart. That's what he was. And not sad for all that had passed him by. The lamp in the front room glowed against the pink calico curtain, casting a pearled light on the shimmering curtain of falling ice pellets.

He'd never before missed being with a woman. Never thought he'd regret not being in a front room with her while the fire crackled, he read his ranching journals and she knit with the lamplight, contentment between them. On a wintry night like this, how snug it would have been. Homey.

He'd never thought he could thirst for a woman like this. For the chance to lie beside her at night, to love her body and soul. To wake up with her tucked against his chest, her long lustrous hair tickling his chin and bare chest. To love her until she grew round with their child…

Joshua willed his thoughts to stop right there before the regrets seeped out of him along with the rest of his blood. He'd never let anyone into those vulnerable places within him.

Claire had changed him, after all.

He coughed again and tasted the blood. Scented it. Saw the dark stain of it across his hand and his shirt. On the snow in front of him. He didn't have much time. Now that he knew she was at home safe and sound, there was one more duty to see done before he passed from this earth.

With the same determination as he'd clubbed off the coyotes, he crept onto his feet.

He didn't have to go far to find Logan. There was a soft slosh of a boot on icy snow and then the click of a revolver's hammer.

It seemed Logan had found him—unarmed.

Chapter Twenty

"You killed my father."

"Gable. I can't believe my eyes. You're alive, damn it, but barely, judging by the look of you." Coop Logan braced his feet apart, the rifle he held aimed in the dead center of Josh's chest. "What does it take to kill you? Apparently, one more bullet than it took to kill your old man."

Red hazed Josh's vision. The bastard was saying it so blandly, as if it were nothing, as if a good man's life lost was nothing. "He discovered your rustling route through the mountains, didn't he? The one that passes by our land."

"I gotta give you credit, Gable. I didn't think you were sharp enough to figure that one out, else I woulda shot you before this."

I'd give anything for a gun right now. A knife. Even a rock. But the freezing rain coated the snow layered on the ground in an impenetrable sheet. There wasn't a single thing nearby he could use as a weapon. He wanted Logan brought to justice, so bad he could taste it.

On a good day, and without being shot and bleeding, he could take the deputy in a fistfight, no problem. But today? Well, he'd just have to see about that. He was bleeding and weak, but he felt like steel. Will and determination held him up. He hadn't come this far to fail now.

Another shadow came out of the storm and Reed Hamilton halted at Logan's side. "I don't believe it. See? I shoulda pumped another bullet into him."

"He killed Ham." The deputy's lie sounded like victory. The storm surged around him, hail plunging like daggers. "You want to do the honors, Reed?"

"You know I do." Like a starving man salivating over a big meal, Reed licked his chops at the idea and drew his revolver.

This isn't good. "Hey, Reed. I didn't shoot your brother in the back."

"You were here that night. I saw you!" Reed aimed and cocked.

"Then you saw me carry Claire to the house and leave to fetch the doc. Right?"

"You came back with the doc!"

"I didn't see Ham again. Someone else did. Who was with you that night? You weren't alone, right? It was Logan. Think about it."

"I don't have to think about it. You killed my brother."

Joshua counted the seconds as Reed began to shake and his gun tremble. He began to realize. "Reed, were Logan and Ham arguing?"

"Hell, don't listen to him!" Logan turned to his so-called friend, his gun swinging away from Joshua and toward Reed. "You know Ham and I argued about money all the time. It was nothin'."

"You wanted a bigger cut of the cattle sales. And you killed him for it? Why, you bas—" A gun fired, and Reed looked surprised as he clutched his chest, gaping for air that did not seem to come.

Then he slid to the ground, already dead.

Damn. Joshua couldn't believe his eyes. Logan had killed a lifelong friend, just like that. Over keeping his crimes secret.

"You're next, Gable. On your knees."

Joshua didn't move. He wasn't sure if he could. "You wanted to frame Claire for Ham's murder. That would have been easy. Everyone would have believed she did it."

"You had to go and confess. I'm gonna have a hell of a time trying to convince the sheriff you and Claire were in cahoots. Having an affair. Killing Ham. And how you broke out and attacked poor Reed here. I had to shoot you."

It was all making sense. And that meant Claire wasn't safe, after all. She would be in even greater danger once Logan pulled that trigger.

"And Claire, poor Claire," Logan chortled, a low, mean sound as lifeless as the falling ice. "She's got to be a good time. Ham wasn't cold in his grave before you lifted her skirts. I've always wanted to get my hands on her pretty little body—"

Rage beat through Josh's veins like a speeding locomotive. With a war cry, he lunged, full speed and full strength, filling up with blinding savagery. Claire was his woman. And protect her he would with his dying breath.

He heard the thunder of Logan's rifle and saw the flash of powder igniting, but it became distant as seconds began to slow and stretch and his feet left the ground.

Deep primal anger overtook him as he felt the bullet pound into his chest. He tasted blood even as he knocked the rifle aside when it fired again, and he landed with his hands around Logan's neck.

Then they were falling, rolling together over the slick sheet of ice, until Joshua slammed into a fence post. Pain exploded across his back and he felt something give inside him. A fresh, warm wash of blood streamed down his spine.

"You and your woman are gonna pay for this!" Logan scrambled to his feet and pulled a knife from his boot.

"Sounds like Logan's signal. You got that stew hot?" Rick pushed away from the table, licking his fingers. "I want more of them cinnamon rolls and more coffee."

How long did it take before Adelaide's secret weapon would take effect? Claire placed the last of her dishes in a crate before moving over to snatch the coffeepot from the stove. She didn't trust a Hamilton. She knew the kind of cloth they were made from. But if this could save Joshua from them, then she had to try.

She grabbed the coffeepot and kept the length of the table between them as she poured. "I signed over the deed to you. That means I'm leaving tonight as soon as the storm lets up."

"Maybe we'll ride back to town with you. Just to make sure you get there safe." Rick had the same smile

Ham had when he was up to something. "After all, a woman alone has to be careful."

She knew what his leer meant, too. Would she ever make it to town, or did the brothers have something else planned for her? She shuddered with revulsion and turned away just in time to avoid his hand reaching out to grab hold of her fanny.

Disgusting. She was wasting time here. She had to incapacitate Rick before the others came. While she still had a chance to escape. Joshua, wherever he was, needed her. The place he held in her soul was oddly silent.

She plunked the coffeepot back on the trivet with an angry clatter and considered adding more of the cascara bark to Rick's food, when she heard it.

The rumble of his guts, like fast-moving thunder. He bolted from his chair and his feet hit the floor already running. He jerked open the door and disappeared into the bitter storm.

Thank you, Adelaide. Finally alone, she rushed to her bedroom. The room was dark and chilly and the tap of ice against the window seemed to whisper *hurry, hurry!* as she dug the revolver from her top dresser drawer.

A peek out the back door told her that the outhouse was occupied. Rick's tortured groan of agony echoed along the hillside.

Maybe I used a little too much. It was hard to feel guilty about that. She yanked her wraps from the hook and darted outside, sliding on the icy sheet that had adhered to the hard-packed layer of snow.

There was no way she could ride hard in this. Getting back to town and making sure Joshua was all right—if she could convince the deputy on duty to let her into the jail—was going to take half the night.

Another cry of anguish rose like a death knell above the drum of ice and howl of wind. Claire turned toward the horrific sound, but it wasn't coming from the Hamilton brothers. There, at the bottom of the hill, were two figures, groping and fighting. A flash of steel oddly glinted in the shadows, catching the light from the window. She saw a sharp blade, a man lunge.

And a man fall, his strangled gurgle lost as the storm surged, ice hailing down as if from the leading edge of a twister. The man with the knife stood the victor. Slowly, his gaze found her on the crest of the hill.

Joshua? Even before he stepped into the swatch of light, her spirit knew him and she started running, slipping and sliding. Joshua. He was here! He was all right. *Thank God.* Heart filling, sobs ripping through her, she ran, slipping and sliding down the hillside. Relief beat through her, and then she was in his arms, her huge grizzly of a man, wet and bloody and sweaty. The man she loved more than her life. More than anything.

"Claire." His voice came strangled and strange. The knife in his hand clattered to the ground.

Something was wrong. This was her Joshua, but she didn't recognize this huge grizzly of a man, hair dripping, face ruddy with a primal savagery. Two lifeless bodies lay at his feet and he was coated with blood.

It was everywhere, smeared on his face, staining his shirt, streaming down his left leg to mix with the ice and snow sluicing off him. But it was her man, her Joshua. So injured. His eyes seemed dazed, his skin translucent and ashen. Blood sputtered across his bottom lip when he exhaled.

She skidded to a stop before him. *Oh, Joshua.* She hurt in sympathy. He looked as if he'd gone through hell and worse to come to her.

What a man. She splayed her palm against the bruised cut of his jaw. His day's growth rasped against her skin, his sweat and blood and the melting ice from the storm wet her hand. It felt so good to touch him, to feel this blinding connection with him again. "Believe it or not, handsome man, you are a sight for sore eyes."

"Me? You don't know how deep I had to dig to find the strength to make it here. Sheer will, Claire. That's what you mean to me." He gasped for breath and squeezed his eyes shut, in obvious horrible pain. "But it was worth it. To see you one more time. They didn't hurt you? You're not harmed? Hell, I couldn't stand it if anything happened to you."

"That's the way I feel about you." Love fierce and overwhelming surged through her, warming all the cold places within, drowning all doubts. Some men were honest and mighty and righteous. Good of heart, strong of soul. This man standing before her was one of them. And the chance to be with him was worth any cost. "I signed away my land so they wouldn't hurt you. It's the only thing I could do to try to save you."

"You gave them your land?"

"For you. Can you believe it?"

"No. No, I can't." Joshua couldn't make his mind accept her incredible words. Her land. The home she'd fought so hard for, worked so hard to keep. She'd given it up for him.

He'd never heard of such a selfless act from anyone, from any woman. She stared up at him with the clearest eyes he'd ever seen. "Those men left me to die. Baby, you didn't get your money's worth."

"Oh…" Her face crumpled as she studied his chest and his face. Hell, he had to look like a monster; he didn't feel half human. But the way she looked at him, with absolute concern, he'd never seen the like. Never before in his life.

He needed and loved her beyond measure. He felt the certainty of it land in his soul as she pressed her lips against the bruise on his jaw. Then next to the gash on his cheekbone. On the swelling lump of his left eyebrow. Healing, comforting.

Giving.

Her lips brushing the sensitive spot in front of his ear. "Having you right here is worth anything. Everything."

He could see all the way through her, into her heart and past her soul to the truth beneath. A truth there was no denying. Not anymore.

Don't pass out yet, man. His knees sank to the ground. He wasn't done talking with her. He had to tell her the things that mattered now. Because his life was draining out of him with each beat of his heart. But his life didn't matter. Only hers did. Only hers.

"Joshua? Oh, we have to get you into the house. I have to tend these wounds—" The concern soft on her lovely face changed as her gaze focused behind him. She tensed with what could only be terror.

Was it the other Hamilton brother? Joshua cast around for one of the fallen guns, but they were too far away. He had to defend her. He had to save her. He had to—

Claire pulled a .45 from her skirt pocket, thumbed back the hammer and fired off two bullets with the ease of a gunslinger. He heard the thud of two bodies hitting the ground. He twisted around, groaning in agony, and saw a pair of wolves motionless on the snow.

What a woman. Fierce hot love welled up, overtaking him. A longing in the dark center of his being pounded to life with the same strident, mind-numbing demand as if he'd been cut off from air. The virulent need to breathe drove him, but it wasn't air he sought or his instincts fought for.

It was the right to love her. To take her as his wife. To spend his life at her side. To trust her with all he was, with everything he had. But there was no time. There was no way for them to be together, not now. He was dying. There was no getting around that. He doubted even Gran could work her healing magic on him and save him.

Nothing could save him. Not even the love he felt for the woman before him, with silent tears rolling down her cheeks.

He held out his hand, palm up, for her.

The instant her gloved fingertips settled lightly on his, a lightning bolt of certainty ravaged his chest. His love for her blazed so true nothing could ever snuff it out. Not even death. "If I could, I would make you my wife."

Her eyes darkened with realization. She swallowed hard, and her chin came up, all strength and steel and soft, beautiful woman. God, he loved her.

She knelt before him, as if they were in a church sanctuary and not the wild Montana Rockies in the middle of an ice storm. "Do you mean you'd marry me?"

"I am so in love with you." He choked on the truth; words could not describe or measure the love he felt for her.

"What a coincidence. I love you, too. Honestly love you. I can see the man you are, Joshua Gable. Are you sure you would want to marry a simple country widow like me?"

"More than anything."

"Then I'm not about to let you use death as an excuse to leave me. You proposed, I'm going to make sure you keep your word."

"I'm d-dying."

"Then I intend to save you." She felt the power of her promise, a vow meant to be kept for all time. And as if the night agreed, the storm broke, leaving only silence and the soft sheen of moonlight peering through flinty clouds.

There was hope, after all.

Epilogue

Rain tinkled against the glass panes, a happy sound that rustled the budding trees. Claire looked over the top of her knitting needles in time to see a gust of wind carry a cloud of pink apple blossoms past the window like a celebration from heaven.

She counted her stitches on the little baby sweater. So many good things had come her way since she'd become Joshua's wife. A new house built on his family's land, a loving extended family, and a happy marriage that became better with every passing day.

She knew he was close even before the kitchen door whispered open. Joy filled her at the sight of her handsome husband and the quiet steady shine of love she felt flowing between them.

Joshua had recovered from his injuries, although he

still limped slightly, but that was improving day by day. With his father's murder solved, he'd been more relaxed. At peace.

"Hey, sweetheart." His low baritone rumbled through her, an intimate sound that made her tingle deep inside. "How's my lovely wife?"

"Perfect now that you're here." She put down her knitting needles, careful not to lose any of the stitches of the little baby blanket she was making. "What about the lambing?"

"I left Liam in charge of things because I needed to come home and check on my wife." His hand curved over her swollen belly. "I love you, beautiful."

"Oh? What a coincidence. I love you, too."

"I have been thinking of you all afternoon. I need you, baby." He held out his hand, still her strong and protective and tender man.

Love filled her so swiftly and deeply, she was borne away on it. She slipped her hand in his and let him help her onto her feet. Gasped as he swung her into his arms and carried her up the stairs and into their beautiful bedroom, where he laid her down in a pool of warm afternoon light.

"I'm so happy, Joshua." She kissed him so he could feel all the love she harbored. "Thank you for marrying me. For changing my life."

"It was you. You changed mine. Come, let me love you."

As the rain sang like music against the sides of the

house and the wind added a low cello's rhythm, Joshua took his wife into his arms and showed her just how much he cherished her.

* * * * *

If you enjoyed ROCKY MOUNTAIN WIDOW,
you'll love Jillian Hart's next romance,
HEAVEN'S TOUCH,
from Steeple Hill Love Inspired,
available September 2005!

If you enjoyed what you just read,
then we've got an offer you can't resist!

Take 2 bestselling love stories FREE!
Plus get a FREE surprise gift!

Clip this page and mail it to Harlequin Reader Service®

IN U.S.A.	IN CANADA
3010 Walden Ave.	P.O. Box 609
P.O. Box 1867	Fort Erie, Ontario
Buffalo, N.Y. 14240-1867	L2A 5X3

YES! Please send me 2 free Harlequin Historicals® novels and my free surprise gift. After receiving them, if I don't wish to receive anymore, I can return the shipping statement marked cancel. If I don't cancel, I will receive 6 brand-new novels every month, before they're available in stores! In the U.S.A., bill me at the bargain price of $4.69 plus 25¢ shipping and handling per book and applicable sales tax, if any*. In Canada, bill me at the bargain price of $5.24 plus 25¢ shipping and handling per book and applicable taxes**. That's the complete price and a savings of over 10% off the cover prices—what a great deal! I understand that accepting the 2 free books and gift places me under no obligation ever to buy any books. I can always return a shipment and cancel at any time. Even if I never buy another book from Harlequin, the 2 free books and gift are mine to keep forever.

246 HDN DZ7Q
349 HDN DZ7R

Name _____ (PLEASE PRINT)

Address _____ Apt.#

City _____ State/Prov. _____ Zip/Postal Code

Not valid to current Harlequin Historicals® subscribers.

Want to try two free books from another series?
Call 1-800-873-8635 or visit www.morefreebooks.com.

* Terms and prices subject to change without notice. Sales tax applicable in N.Y.
** Canadian residents will be charged applicable provincial taxes and GST.
  All orders subject to approval. Offer limited to one per household.
  ® are registered trademarks owned and used by the trademark owner and or its licensee.

HIST04R ©2004 Harlequin Enterprises Limited